NOVELS BY ROBERT BYRNE

Mannequin 1988

Skyscraper 1984

The Dam 1981

Always a Catholic 1981

The Tunnel 1977

Memories of a Non-Jewish Childhood 1970
(Reissued in 1981 as *Once a Catholic*)

MANNEQUIN

MANNEQUIN

ROBERT BYRNE

Atheneum
New York
1988

This is a work of fiction. Names, characters, places, and incidents are either the product of the author's imagination or are used fictitiously. Any resemblance to actual events or persons, living or dead, is entirely coincidental.

Atheneum
Macmillan Publishing Company
866 Third Avenue, New York, N.Y. 10022
Collier Macmillan Canada, Inc.

Library of Congress Cataloging-in-Publication Data
Byrne, Robert, 1930–
Mannequin.
I. Title.
PS3552.Y73M3 1988 813'.54 88-16627
ISBN 0-689-11836-8

10 9 8 7 6 5 4 3 2 1

Printed in the United States of America

To Cindy
For reasons beyond listing

They hang us now in Shrewsbury jail;
  The whistles blow forlorn,
And trains all night groan on the rail
  To men that die at morn.

—A. E. Housman

MANNEQUIN

CHAPTER 1

Welding sparks cascaded from a steel tank in one corner of the garage. In another a mechanic on a roller board was under a truck. At the far end light streamed through an open bay, beckoning. No more time for second thoughts, Gil Ellis told himself, for hesitating, for "on the other hand." Stealing old man Draegler's limousine and escaping without getting killed meant acting now, before he was missed. No one would expect such recklessness from him, which was why the plan might work.

He tightened his fingers on the wheel and took several deep breaths to get up the nerve to start the engine. The jacket he had taken from the chauffeur was tight on his shoulders, and the cap sat oddly high on his head. The guns were beside him on the seat. Did Trainer and Draegler really think he would just sit quietly in his office while they decided his fate? They were in for a surprise. They had underestimated and patronized him for the last time.

"Now or never," Gil whispered, and turned the key. The engine awoke and purred quietly. He released the brake. There were sunglasses on a shelf; he put them on. Slowly, very slowly, he drove toward the garage door. He had never been at the wheel of a vehicle so big; it was like being at the helm of a battleship. Everything about it was luxurious. The interior was immaculately clean and smelled of leather.

The mechanic at the truck was standing now and watching him pass. Gil could only hope that in the shadows he wouldn't look past the jacket and cap. Keeping his face hidden as much as possible behind the door post, Gil waved casually through the open window as he glided into the sunshine of the Nevada desert.

He made a wide turn to the right, getting the feel of the limo. It was easy to handle and responded to the slightest pressure on the accelerator. The problem was not a lack of power, the problem was to fight off the impulse to panic and crash through the gate like a cannonball. Gil had to ignore his shaking hands and racing heart and keep his speed down to five miles an hour. The old man hated speed and always made Carlos drive as if they were in a funeral procession.

The limo moved at a crawl past the Draegler Chemical Corporation parking lot, where a guard was posted at Gil's Mazda sedan. Gil sat stiffly and stared straight ahead.

He turned slowly and grandly to the left and stopped at the main exit. The guard there jumped to his feet and rolled the chain-link gate aside. Gil didn't drive through the moment there was room enough; he waited until the gate was open all the way, as if he had all the time in the world, then eased the limo forward, tapping the horn lightly in acknowledgment, the way Carlos always did. The tinted windows made it impossible for the gatekeeper to see that the company president wasn't a passenger, but he peered at the driver from a distance of a few feet. As he passed, Gil turned his head away and down as if fussing with his seat belt.

There were shouts in the distance behind him. Looking back, Gil could see figures emerging from the administration building, waving their arms and running toward the gate.

"Hold it a second, Carlos," the guard called, "looks like something's up."

Gil closed the power window and gradually increased his speed. "Wait," he heard the guard shout. "Hey!"

Gil could also hear the sound of engines starting. He floored the accelerator and felt the limo surge forward powerfully. Ahead were six miles of two-lane road that followed the twisting rim of Sentinel Canyon to the junction with Nevada Highway 445. If he could make it that far before being overtaken, he would probably be safe. It was June 27, and there was a lot of tourist traffic on 445, which connected Reno and Sparks with Pyramid Lake; Draegler's guards wouldn't try anything there.

What he needed was about a ten-minute head start. With that much lead time he could make it to the gas station on the north edge of Sparks, where there was a phone. His first call, he had already decided, would be to Karen. They hadn't lived together for three months and she had filed for divorce, but she was the one person in the world he knew he could trust completely. His job would be to make her believe his story, which wouldn't be easy because he could hardly believe it himself. He had also decided to phone her at her music studio and hoped that she was there with a piano or clarinet student. Trainer might have her home phone bugged.

The road leading away from the plant was straight enough for the first half mile to give Gil a view of the main gate in the rearview mirror. Before a curve cut off his line of sight, he saw several cars careen out of the parking lot and take up the chase. The speedometer arrow crept higher with agonizing slowness: forty, forty-five, fifty. "Come on, baby," he said under his breath, "now's your chance to show your stuff. . . ." He kept the gas pedal floored, something he guessed Carlos had never been allowed to do. After a minute of steadily increasing speed he had to lift his foot to make sure he could negotiate a series of sharp bends. Ahead was a narrow section of the canyon where the road angled down the side of a cliff with almost vertical drop-offs on the right side. With CAUTION and SLOW signs instead of guard rails, it wasn't the kind of road he would have chosen to take at high speed in an unfamiliar vehicle.

His heart was pounding like a hammer, and there was so much sweat pouring down his face he had to keep blinking his eyes.

The limousine had a low center of gravity and took the curves well, but in the short straight stretches it didn't give Gil the explosive acceleration he needed to keep ahead of his pursuers. It seemed ponderous and heavy, and it occurred to him that it might be bulletproof. He tightened his lips. Maybe steel panels would turn out to be worth more than lively response.

Bad news in the mirror: a black Mercedes was in the distance and gaining. On the next curve Gil nearly lost control. His stomach rose to his throat when the limo hit a patch of gravel and skidded onto the shoulder, coming within inches of the canyon edge before straightening out. He accelerated again into the next curve and was going so fast he had to use the brake to stay on the pavement. To the right a rocky slope pitched steeply downward into a boulder-strewn dry wash a hundred yards below. To the rear, no more than a dozen car lengths away now, was the Mercedes; farther back he could see two more.

Gil tromped on the gas pedal and leaned into the steering wheel, trying to urge the limo to its top speed. Two sharp thumps made him think the Mercedes was bumping him from behind, but a glance in the mirror showed it was still thirty or forty feet back. As he watched, his rear window took a hit and was instantly transformed into a web of radial cracks. The sons of bitches were shooting at him! If they were trying for his tires, they were lousy marksmen. So much for the possibility that they only wanted to overtake him and pull him over. They seemed to be aiming at his head.

With only his left hand on the wheel, Gil found the .38 on the seat beside him. He had never fired a handgun before in his life; this would have to be the first time. He turned and aimed it through the rear window, stopping himself before squeezing the trigger. If the window was bulletproof, it was protecting him from behind. A shot at such close range might shatter it and leave him exposed. He touched a button and lowered his left window. At the next curve to the left, he let up on the gas and thrust his head and right arm outside. Bracing himself against the rush of wind, he sent six quick shots at the Mercedes, which was now so close it had to slow down to avoid plowing into his back bumper. Every shot missed but one, which pierced the windshield on the driver's side and sent the car into a sideways skid. The second Mercedes couldn't stop in time, and the resulting collision flipped the first one onto its roof and sent them both careening into the rock wall on the left side of the road. With a shower of sparks and the shriek and roar of metal against asphalt, they rebounded, spinning as a unit onto the pavement, and came to rest in the center of the road. Gil kept his eyes on the spectacle so long he almost lost control of his own vehicle, suddenly having to throw the wheel violently to the left and right to keep from going into a skid himself.

In the mirror he saw that he hadn't gained much. Two more cars had found their way around the wreckage and were coming so fast that they would be on him in less than a minute. This time one of their bullets might find his tires . . . or his head. As for his own marksmanship, he couldn't count on getting lucky a second time; he didn't even know if there were any bullets left in the gun. Another chilling possibility occurred to him: Trainer or somebody at the plant had almost certainly radioed ahead. When Gil emerged from the canyon into the flats two miles farther on, he might find himself facing a roadblock. What would he do then, try to get away on foot? The barren, rocky slopes didn't look as if they would offer many hiding places.

It was then he saw the telephone.

A cellular telephone! He could phone Karen right now! He snatched it from its dashboard holder and while steadying the wheel with his forearms he punched the numbers. Please, God, let her be there! Let her be teaching or practicing! What time was it . . . three o'clock? She often had students then. The clicks, buzzes, and pauses seemed to take forever . . . then the ringing signal: once, twice, three times. "Please be there," he murmured. "Please, Karen, pick it up. . . ." In the mirror he saw that his pursuers had closed to within a couple of hundred feet. Another black Mercedes. Somebody had his head and shoulders out of the passenger's window and was aiming a rifle.

The fourth ring was cut off by a click and a faint rushing noise. "Oh, God, no," Gil said, shaking his head from side to side and almost bursting into tears, "not the *answering machine*!"

"Hello," he heard himself say on the tape in a bland, relaxed tone of voice, "this is Gil Ellis." To avoid presenting herself as a woman living alone, Karen hadn't changed the tape Gil had once made for her studio machine. "Neither Karen nor I can take your call right now. If you'd like to leave a message, you can do so at the sound of the beep. Thanks!"

Pause. Beep.

"Aw, shit, Karen," Gil said, not knowing where to start, "they're going to kill me. . . . I've stolen Draegler's limousine and I'm headed down the canyon. . . . I don't think I'll make it to town. . . . You've got to believe me and not what they tell you. . . ."

The words rushed out in bursts mixed with sobs and curses, and as he talked Gil had a horrible feeling that he was making no sense, that if his garbled plea got through at all Karen wouldn't know what to make of it. Even if she recognized his voice, she might think he was drunk again and erase his words from the tape as she was already erasing him from her life. He had mentioned his suspicions to her several times in recent weeks when they had met to discuss the divorce, but only in a veiled way. Maybe she would remember and take him seriously now that he had proof.

"Three silver tank cars," he shouted into the mouthpiece as he struggled to steer with one hand, "don't let them leave the plant, don't let Trainer lie to you about—"

He saw the truck too late—an Alhambra bottled-water truck laboring up the slope and straddling the double yellow line. Gil dropped the phone, slammed on the brakes, and cut the wheel hard to the right; when the limousine went into a skid he released the brakes and threw the wheel to the left. The driver of the truck—Gil could see him screaming—veered into a drainage ditch at the base of the cliff just in time to avoid a head-on collision. The truck hit a rock outcropping and stopped so suddenly that an avalanche of blue water bottles surged over the top of the cab. Gil missed the truck by inches, but was now out of control, sliding at a forty-five-degree angle toward the opposite side of the road and the empty depths of Sentinel Canyon.

Marking the edge of the precipice were blocks of quarried granite spaced ten feet apart. The right rear wheel struck one squarely, causing the limo to flip into the air and over the edge as if had been launched from a catapult.

Gil hadn't bothered to fasten his seat belt, not that it would have saved him. He clutched the steering wheel with all his might and closed his eyes as the limo rolled in the air and dropped straight down. It struck the slope a glancing blow and plunged toward the canyon floor, spinning violently. His hands were ripped from the wheel and he could feel himself being thrown around like a stone inside a concrete mixer. The limo's heavy construction stood up to the punishment without collapsing until it crashed against the boulders at the bottom with a final, stunning explosion of noise. The silence that followed was broken only by echoes from the rock walls and by the rocks and pebbles that rained lightly on the wreckage.

Gil was flattened between layers of mangled steel, as immobilized as if he had been immersed in the Mannequin gas. He saw through glazed eyes the sole of a shoe inches above his head; there was a foot in it, which was attached to an ankle, which was attached to a leg. He wondered if the rifleman had gone over the edge, too, and was now trapped in the debris above him. I still have the gun, he thought. When the guards come to get me, I'll jump up and open fire. For the moment I'll pretend to be unconscious.

He wondered about bleeding. There was a glistening band of red on a piece of metal close to his face. Blood might attract ants. Or scorpions. He hated ants and scorpions and hoped he wouldn't get bitten. At least he didn't have to worry about Ordman's poisonous jellyfish and clams from the Indian Ocean. There were no sea creatures in the desert, he thought, trying to think logically. Everything in his field of vision turned ultraviolet, the way it was in the company aquarium the day Ordman showed him the source of Mannequin. He felt as though he was underwater, wading through a bed of clams, listening to the clicking of shells as his feet pushed them aside.

No, Gil corrected himself, clearing his mind, he was trapped in a wrecked car. He was probably dying. Holy mother of God, how had this happened to him? How could he have let himself get into such a predicament? It was the monkey, yes, the monkey was to blame. A long-tailed macaque it was, a baby just a few months old, and watching it die had been more than he could stand. His emotions had taken over from his reason. That was almost always the source of life's problems, in his humble opinion. The monkey's face danced before him. Cuteness was the monkey's name. A female baby macaque. Her facial muscles were locked in position by the gas like the rest of her body, but her eyes were darting back and forth in terror, the same terror he began to feel himself when he realized that the thin red stream was his life draining away and there was nothing he could do to stop it.

CHAPTER 2

Two weeks before Gilbert Ellis's first and last ride in a Mercedes limousine, two weeks before he left a message on his wife's answering machine that would change her life forever, Karen Ellis was spending a day in San Francisco feeling better about the future than she had in a long time. After three job interviews in the morning, she met a friend for lunch downtown. She hadn't seen Jessica Fullerton since they were students together at Juilliard ten years earlier, but they had kept in touch with annual Christmas letters. Jessie had given up music as a profession, taken a job in the mortgage banking business—the nature of which she tried unsuccessfully to explain—and found a husband, apparently a good one.

"Maybe I'm not cut out for marriage," Karen said between bites of salad at Circolo's in the Galleria on Post Street.

"Oh, everybody going through a divorce feels that way. What you really mean is that you don't know a man at the moment you want to marry. I got lucky and so can you. With your looks? Men love tall Swedes."

"Tall, yes, fat, no," Karen said, pushing a basket of warm French bread to Jessie's side of the table. "Fortunately for you, they also love short, voluptuous brunettes."

"What made you pick Gil Ellis in the first place?"

"The usual reasons. He loved me, he had a good job, he was smart, he was nice-looking, and we laughed at the same jokes. I thought I loved him. I *did* love him . . . and still do in a way. I knew he drank too much, but I thought that would change. I can't believe I thought that! Well, we had one pretty good year together. Then came the gas leak in Boston I wrote you about, where the people got killed. He blamed himself and the drinking got really bad. And the cheating . . . that's one thing I wouldn't stand for."

"I wouldn't, either. How did you find out? Did you catch him in bed with somebody, or what?"

"Nothing that gross. He started coming home late from work smelling of soap. I guessed he was taking showers to wash off the smell of something else, and I was right. When I confronted him, he admitted it, and there were tears and apologies and promises and so on, all of which I'm sure were sincere at the time. He's a decent guy in a lot of ways. I wish I could have helped him more. I tried my best, but finally got to the end of my rope."

"Don't *you* start feeling guilty now! It takes two to get married and two to get divorced. It's over, that's all. Doesn't help to talk about guilt, or blame, or who's at fault."

"I know, but it's sad all the same."

"Be thankful it isn't like the old days, when people had to stay married until it killed them." Jessica lifted her wineglass. "To the future! To women who deserve to be happy and soon will be! I guarantee it!"

"What a friend you are! I feel better already. Let's talk

about something cheerful. Your marriage, for instance. John sounds wonderful, even if he is a lawyer."

"He proves not all men are swine."

Karen laughed. "Can I quote you on that?"

"We're DINKS, too, which helps. Double Income, No Kids. The only way to go. Spoil yourself rotten."

"DINKS? Looks like I'm going to be an OINK. One Income, No Kids."

They were laughing so much by the end of the meal that the other diners were happy to see them leave. They embraced and said good-bye on the Bank of America plaza beside an enormous black rock that Jessica insisted was a work of art placed there deliberately by people generally thought to be sane. Karen promised that on her next trip she would stay with the Fullertons and not at a hotel.

"We'd love to have you," Jessica said. "Would you mind sleeping on a futon?"

"Not if he doesn't snore. I have nothing against Southeast Asians."

One thing was certain, Karen thought later as she drove around town savoring the sights, if she was going to be an OINK, San Francisco was the place she wanted to be an OINK in.

What a city! Block after block of charming, beautifully restored Victorian houses, streets steep enough for mountain climbers, and around almost every corner on Nob Hill, Russian Hill, and Pacific Heights startling views of the Bay, the towers of the financial district, and the two great suspension bridges. Several times Karen was struck by views of such splendor that she stopped the car and gaped . . . until the horns of cars behind her reminded her that she wasn't Alice in Wonderland.

She tried to imagine how it would feel to call this city home. There was a chance she would find out fairly soon, based on what she had been told at Dominican College in San Rafael, College of Marin in Kentfield, and the San

Francisco Conservatory of Music. Everyone she talked to was impressed by her educational background and her experience as a chamber music player in the Northeast. None of the schools had staff openings at the moment, but it looked like enough private clarinet and piano students could be steered her way to keep her going until a salaried job did open up. On her next trip she would call on Mills College in Oakland, the University of California in Berkeley, and the local opera, symphony, and ballet orchestras. She was sure she could find something eventually. If not, she would be happy just standing on the hilltops drinking in the view and inhaling the fresh, sea-laced air.

After parking her car at the Union Square garage, she found herself walking along Market Street, part of the stream of office workers headed for subways, buses, trolley cars, and ferryboats. She was a tall woman—at five eight almost as tall as her soon-to-be-ex-husband—and she walked with long, forthright strides, her blond hair bouncing on the shoulders of her charcoal jacket. Cool air caressed her face, and she felt so good she gave a dollar to a street musician who was playing Bach's "Jesus, Joy of Man's Desiring" on a battered saxophone.

Market Street was lined by sycamore trees, and the sidewalks were made of bricks laid in a repeated swirling pattern. In the center of the broad thoroughfare were tracks carrying a variety of antique streetcars festooned with banners and flags—apparently a transportation festival of some kind was under way. Even the pedestrians were fascinating to Karen; she hadn't seen sidewalks crowded with such a richly textured cross section of humanity since the last time she had been in midtown Manhattan. Reno and Sparks seemed as remote as the moon, which parts of Nevada resembled.

The buildings were a mixture of the old and the new and the tall and the short, but mostly tall and mostly new, and they faced each other across Market like spectators at a parade. A handsome old one on the south side caught her eye, twelve stories of exquisite brickwork with an ornate cornice ringing the top. Chiseled into granite above the entrance were the words MOUNTAIN PACIFIC RAILROAD COMPANY.

Seeing the name made Karen think of Gil, for MP was the railroad whose tracks ran through Reno and Sparks. When Gil was at the house the day before, he had been worried that Clem Trainer was intending to make a rail shipment of a dangerous chemical. She didn't know how seriously to take him. Gil tended to treat even ordinary concerns like Greek tragedies.

One thing about the meeting was clear in her memory: her sense of sadness at seeing him coming up the walk toward the front door. A man once a picture of health and confidence looked as if he carried the world on his shoulders. He had put on weight, and the lines of his face were soft and rounded. His shoes needed polish and his corduroy sport coat was ready for charity.

She was glad she hadn't bothered to put on makeup. Her eyelashes, eyebrows, and lips were almost as pale as her skin, and unless she added a little color her face tended to vanish completely, or so she felt. Why make herself as attractive as possible? She didn't want to tempt him or make him feel worse than he already did.

To her surprise, he kissed her on the cheek. It was their first physical contact since he had moved to the motel three months earlier.

She poured two soft drinks. They walked through the house they had shared for a year and stood at the patio windows. The house was high enough on the hillside to provide a view of the mountains to the west, darkening now in the dusk. In the mid-distance was the glow of lights from the downtown casinos and hotels; above were the crimson streaks of a Sierra sunset. Husband and wife were silent for a time, like strangers at a cocktail party who didn't know how to start a conversation. Everything had already been said, and at painful length. Karen could remember standing beside him like this with her skin tingling in anticipation of being in his arms. It was tingling again, but now it was in fear that he might attempt an embrace.

"Thanks for coming over," she said, deciding that getting down to business was the best defense. "Gil, this is awfully hard for me to say, but I've filed for divorce. You'll be getting some papers in the mail. I didn't want you to be surprised, and I didn't want to tell you on the phone."

"I wondered what was up. What's the hurry?" He tried to sound casual, but there was a hollowness in his voice. A divorce would be one more burned bridge in his life.

"We've been apart three months. I'm over the shock and I can see now that it's never going to work between us. We simply aren't right for each other anymore. I've thought and thought and thought about it, and what I've decided to do is leave Nevada. I'm going to San Francisco tomorrow to look for a job. When I find one, I'm going to move. I'm terribly sorry, Gil."

After a silence, he said, "End of an era."

"I hope the beginning of a better one for both of us."

He was looking into the distance, at the mountains. "I'll miss you, Karen. I . . . I wish it had worked out better. I hope you'll remember me with . . . well, with some affection."

"Of *course* I will, Gil! I'll worry about you too. You're still . . . troubled, and . . . oh, I don't know, I just think you don't do enough for yourself. You should at least talk about your problems with somebody. Somebody who knows how to deal with them."

"There are things I don't like to talk about," he said. "I admit that. Words—I don't know, you're just more of a talker than I am. As for my problems, I think they'll more or less take care of themselves, given enough time." His voice trailed off as if he realized the inadequacy of his defense. After a moment he added, "You haven't been happy ever since we came here. Maybe we should have stayed in New England, but leaving was the only way I could stay in the industry after what happened."

"So get out of the industry. Take up something else." She had made the suggestion before.

"I can't. Things at the plant right now are . . . very difficult. I can't tell you how difficult."

"Why not? That's one of the things I hated most, that you wouldn't talk about your job. In Boston I could visit your office, I could walk around the plant, everybody was friendly. Soon as we got here a curtain came down."

"There was a reason."

"Oh? What was it?"

Gil seemed uncertain how to continue. He thought for a long time, and when he spoke again he made an effort to choose his words carefully. "Draegler has come up with a new . . . a new gas. A kind of pesticide. It's still in the development stage. It's so powerful and has so many commercial uses that a wall of secrecy has been built around it. I had to swear when I was hired that I would never mention it to anyone, not even you."

"You went along with that?"

"Lots of companies have secrecy pledges. Lately I've been spending most of my time working with this new . . . compound. That's why I couldn't talk about what I do at work."

Karen said nothing.

"The gas is called Mannequin because of the way it locks muscles in position. . . . It's so terrible I wish it had never been discovered. It could turn out to be worse than the atom bomb."

"You must be exaggerating."

"I don't think so. You should see the people Trainer has brought in. Thugs. Tomorrow we have to run some tests on monkeys. I'm not looking forward to that."

"Oh, Gil, honestly! Why don't you just quit? Get away from the whole damned business?" Karen wondered if he was unconsciously trying to draw her back into his world, a world she wanted to escape.

"I want to find out what Trainer is up to. I think he's intending to ship the gas by railroad, even though there would be a terrible risk to the public. I want to be there to make sure it doesn't happen."

"Aren't there laws about shipping hazardous substances? Don't you need government permits or something? Mountain Pacific won't take the shipment if there's a terrible risk."

"Trainer might not tell the railroad. He might say it's just another load of fertilizer."

"So *you* tell them. If you think the stuff shouldn't go out, pick up the phone and tell the railroad why not."

"I will if I have to, and when I know what's going on and have the facts in hand. That's why I can't quit right now."

"I wish I could help you, Gil, but I don't see how I can. I'll talk about it to help you decide what to do, but it sounds like something you're going to have to work out yourself."

"Thanks, but I've said too much already. Promise me you'll never tell Trainer, or anyone, that you know anything about Mannequin. You might be asking for trouble. How much trouble, I don't know. That's one of the things I want to find out."

"Mum's the word."

"I shouldn't have told you about it, but I wanted you to know why I was so evasive about my job. It wasn't that I didn't *want* to talk to you."

"I understand, Gil." She squeezed his hand. The touch seemed to fluster him.

"Better be on my way," he said. "If there's something I'm supposed to sign, just ask."

At the front door Karen brought up the subject of dividing the furniture, the kitchenware, the artworks, and the books they had acquired together. He left it up to her. As for the house, he suggested putting it on the market and splitting the proceeds.

"You should get a lawyer," Karen told him, worried about his indifference, "to protect yourself against my lawyer."

"Maybe I will," he said with a shrug. "Not because I don't trust you, but because I don't want to think about such details right now. Good night, Karen." He surprised her with another kiss on the cheek. "Be careful."

"You too."

She watched him walk down the sidewalk to his car, more convinced than ever that he needed professional counseling. If only he would come to that realization on his own. He looked smaller than he used to, and his jacket hung from his shoulders as if the pockets were full of rocks. At least he had talked to her, that was a change. The result, though, was the same: a vague feeling of depression. Maybe more communication in their marriage would have made it worse.

Gil! What on earth would become of him? She trudged up the stairs to her bedroom wishing she didn't care.

Now, in San Francisco, Karen found herself deciding to do him a small favor. She crossed Market Street, or rather allowed herself to be guided across by the flow of pedestrians headed for the Trans-Bay Terminal at First and Mission. Inside the lobby of the Mountain Pacific building was a black woman seated at a desk. She smiled at Karen and asked if she could be of help.

"I hope so. I want to get some information on shipping hazardous materials, the regulations and procedures and so on. Is there a booklet you could give me?"

The woman knitted her eyebrows. "You mean, like, chemicals and explosives and radioactive wastes?"

"Well, chemicals."

"Hmm. I guess that would be Operations. Just a minute . . ." She talked with several people on the phone, then looked at Karen brightly.

"Take the elevator right over there to the eighth floor and go to Room 873. Ask for Mr. Eagan. Better hurry, 'cause he's on his way out. Tell him Monica at the front desk thinks you should send those chemicals by truck."

Mr. Eagan, James J. Eagan according to the nameplate on his desk, was a large man with a full head of salt-and-pepper hair and a walrus mustache so bushy and ferocious, Karen had a hard time keeping her eyes off it. He was on his way out all right, and not just for the day. His coat was off and his sleeves rolled up as he busied himself emptying the contents of his desk into two cardboard boxes.

"Mr. James? I mean, Mr. Eagan? I was told you might be able to give me some information."

"You must be the lady who wants to ship the dangerous chemicals. You don't look like a person who would do such a thing. Have a chair." He fished a glossy photograph from the rear of his center drawer and studied it with a frown.

"Last year's Operations picnic. I tried to break the world's beer-drinking record, but all I broke was my arm sliding into third. I don't want to be reminded of it. It was not a shining hour." The photo went into the wastebasket, already full to overflowing.

"I'm sorry to interrupt. Are you moving to another office?"

"You could say that, yes," he said jovially. "It's on a sailboat. I'm taking a year's leave of absence in search of adventure, maybe never to return. I deserve it. I've given the bloom of my youth to this company. Now then, what can I do for you? What kind of toxic wastes are you interested in shipping?" He laced his fingers on the desk and gave her his full attention.

"I'm not shipping any toxic wastes," she said. "They aren't my line. I'm inquiring for my . . . an associate." She stumbled over the words, almost saying "my husband." She was still married, but should she announce the fact? There was no room in her life at the moment for a man, but on the other hand there was no reason to scare one away. James J. Eagan seemed to be looking at her with more than professional interest—or was she imagining it? He wasn't wearing a wedding band, and she wondered if he noticed that she wasn't either. She smiled at herself for having such thoughts—it had been a long time since she had taken any personal interest in a man's marital status. Thinking of herself as single was going to take some getting used to.

"He works for a chemical plant," she added when she realized that Eagan was waiting for further information, "and was wondering what the railroad's policies were on accepting loads that, well, posed a risk to the public."

Eagan looked at her with a pleasant but uncomprehending expression, and she felt herself reddening. He is probably wondering, she thought, why my "associate" doesn't ask the railroad himself instead of sending a clarinet player. No, he doesn't know I play the clarinet. I wonder if he's musical? With that sonorous voice he could be a singer . . . a baritone, maybe, or even a bass.

"He's very busy," she went on quickly, "and I was just passing by and thought I'd drop in and see if you had a book of regulations or something I could pick up and give to him as a favor. I gather you're in charge of hazardous materials?"

"Not really," he laughed. "Unless you mean when I cook or do my laundry. You were sent to me because the people in public relations have left for the day and nobody else likes to take the time to deal with strays. I'm going part-time for a month or two, which means not only do I lose my office, I get the strays. No offense, but that's what we call people who walk in off the street. Railroad buffs, mainly, looking for photos of old Number Five, that sort of thing. What's your name?"

"My name? Karen."

"Karen what?"

"Just Karen." Cowardice gripped her at the thought that she had inadvertently blundered into the singles' jungle, and she shifted uneasily in her chair. She had come into the building looking for a booklet, not a personal relationship. Not that Eagan wouldn't do in a pinch. He was an impressive figure and seemed to be good-natured, and as Karen looked at him she had a vision of Santa Claus. With a pillow under his belt, a red suit, a white beard, and a bit of rouge on his nose and cheeks, he would be perfect. He already had the necessary twinkle in his eyes.

"Just Karen? Okay, I'm just Jim. Can you tell me more about the material your . . . associate . . . wants to ship? Is it animal, vegetable, or mineral? Is it bigger than a bread box?"

"I don't have any details. It's some sort of experimental pesticide, I think, and he's afraid his company might ship some by railroad, maybe secretly, which he is against. If the railroad were told, I would imagine they would be against it, too, wouldn't they? I mean, I would think that with a phone call to the railroad a person could kill the whole idea."

"Absolutely! I wouldn't accept a hazardous load if I were a railroad! Toxic wastes and explosives and experimental pesticides are exactly why Mountain Pacific should stick to the real estate business, which it's very good at, and leave running trains to people who like that sort of thing. Strays, for example." He turned and scavenged through his wastebasket. "I shouldn't joke . . . but, you see, I'll be out of a job soon and I'm idiotically happy. Let's see if I can find some printed matter for you."

"If it's too much trouble, I—"

"Tell your associate," Eagan said, his arm disappearing into the basket, "not to ship anything that poses a risk to the public without telling me. If there's a derailment, for instance, or a leak, emergency workers have to know what they're up against. Ah, here we are." He lifted a yellow booklet from the debris and handed it to her. "That's the Sierra Region timetable. There's stuff on the last few pages on hazardous materials. The car carrying it has to be placarded—explosives, poison gas, radioactive—and there are rules on where it can be in the train, so many cars away from the engine or the caboose, and so on. If the stuff is really dangerous, the railroad might require guards or technical escorts to go along with it. If you'll give me your address or the address of the shipper, I'll have more information mailed to you."

"No, this will be fine for now. I don't want to get anybody into trouble. All this is just rumor, so far. If I have any questions, I'll phone. Thanks for your help."

"It was a pleasure. You're the nicest stray I've ever been forced to deal with. Good-bye, and give my best to your associate, the lucky dog."

They stood up and shook hands. His hand was warm and engulfed hers like a bear paw. Much to her relief, for she didn't know how she would have reacted, he didn't prolong the contact longer than was strictly necessary.

Walking down the hall toward the elevators, she wondered about the handshake. When you go into an office building and ask a conglomerate for a booklet, are you normally given a warm handshake as well? It seemed odd only in retrospect; when it happened it had been natural and enjoyed by both parties. She pushed the down button and checked her reflection in the glass of a bulletin board on the wall. Her hair was not as neatly pinned back as it could be, and her face looked colorless. She quickly tended to her hair and applied some lipstick, wishing she had done it before coming into the building.

She peered at one of the messages on the bulletin board:

> HOUSEBOAT FOR RENT
> Sausalito. Commute by ferry. One BR down, one up. Deck. View of Mt. Tam. Charm! $750 per mo. Gate Five, Yellow Ferry Harbor. Owner will show weekdays after 6:30 P.M.

Karen ignored an elevator that came and went as her mind spun with visions of living on a houseboat and commuting to San Francisco every morning on a ferry-boat. She could make it happen if she wanted to! Maybe she *was* Alice in Wonderland! Pinned beneath the notice were small, hand-drawn maps of how to find the place. She snapped one off and tucked it in her purse.

"Thinking of moving?"

The voice beside her was easy to recognize.

"Hello, Mr. Eagan. No, but I have a friend who is." Now why did she say that? She would have to learn to drop her guard a little.

"You have a lot of friends and associates."

"No more than anybody else, I'm sure." She wished he could do something about the twinkle in his eye, which was very distracting.

"If you like houseboats, that's a nice one. I've been on it."

"I'll tell my friend." Karen pushed the DOWN button.

Jim Eagan started to say something, hesitated, then surprised her with an invitation. "Excuse me for being so forward, but could I interest you in a drink or dinner? I could meet you in, say, thirty minutes."

"Oh, I'm sorry," Karen said, feeling a blush coming on, "but I'm afraid it will have to be some other time. I'm going back home in the morning and I simply have too many things to do tonight." The light in the corridor was dim, but unless she was mistaken, Jim Eagan was blushing too.

"Home is where?"

"Nevada, at the moment."

He shook his head in mock amazement. "You are leaving the Bay Area for Nevada?"

"Silly, isn't it? But I'll be back."

"Could I have your phone number?"

"Well . . . no. It's going to change soon."

He scribbled something on the back of a business card and handed it to her. "Here's mine. Call me and you'll find out that there is such a thing as a free lunch. And free sails on the Bay. I have a sailboat, as I think I said already, and I'm always looking for crew."

The elevator arrived and Karen stepped inside. "I love sailing. That's a tempting offer."

Jim held the doors open for a moment longer. "I have a terrible feeling that you've never called a man first in your life and that you don't intend to start now."

"Maybe I'll surprise you." She smiled and the doors slid shut.

CHAPTER 3

While Karen was saying hello to Eagan, Gil was saying hello to a monkey. Kong was less than three feet long, not counting his tail, which he held aloft like a battlefield banner, and he weighed only fifteen pounds, but his manic energy made him as hard to handle as a jungle cat and almost as dangerous. Gil watched and winced as Stinson, the teenage animal handler, roughly pushed the monkey's cage across the floor with a broom, thereby staying out of reach of the groping arms and the sharp teeth.

Of all the things Gil hated about his job—about his life, for that matter—working with laboratory animals headed the list. It was not the sort of thing an engineer with fifteen years of experience should have to do. What choice did he have? In the Nevada desert, where it was hard to get trained professionals to work, you sometimes had to forget about job classifications. Besides, he was lucky to have a job of any sort in the chemical industry. He was trying to prove that he could handle managerial responsibilities again, and if that meant working for a company as obscure as Draegler and doing a few menial chores, fine. Protesting would only make salvaging his career harder than it already was.

The loss of a hundred insects or a dozen rats didn't bother Gil particularly, but dogs, cats, and monkeys were another matter. Monkeys, with their expressive faces and humanlike gestures, were the worst. They were smart enough to be unwilling subjects, and some of the paralysis tests they were put through left him shattered for a week.

Stinson's goal at the moment was to transfer Kong to a waist-high glass box where he would later be given a dose of the Mannequin gas; Kong's goal was to make the handler's life as miserable as possible by chattering, squealing, and jumping up and down. Already in the glass box were Queenie, a female macaque, and her two-month-old baby, Cuteness. Queenie sat hunched in a corner staring fixedly, her arms wrapped around her body like the sleeves of a straitjacket. Cuteness ignored Kong's histrionics and explored her surroundings, poking fingers at an overhead shelf on which was fastened a wire-mesh box containing two white mice and a jar of cockroaches.

The animals in the cages that lined the rear wall of the room showed varying degrees of interest. A dog barked in hopes of being allowed to join the fun. The rabbits were mostly facing away, as if deliberately ignoring the commotion, though their ears were twitching. Despite the efforts of a ventilating fan droning behind a grating, the air was heavy with the odor of a zoo.

"Soon as he saw the box," the handler said to Gil after getting the two enclosures together, "he hit the ceiling. Man, he is something, isn't he? Look at him!" Kong had taken hold of the bars and was throwing himself back and forth with such vigor that the cage was rocking and was in danger of tipping over. "I'd sure like to use the dart gun. Or a baseball bat."

"No tranquilizers," Gil said. "The feistier he is, the better for the demonstration."

"Who's it for?"

"Very hush-hush. Somebody's coming in a private plane from San Francisco." All he had been told about the observers by Clem Trainer, the plant manager, was that they were from a foreign country—a country, Gil guessed, needing a new weapon against agricultural pests. The demonstration was to be conducted under Code Nine security restrictions, which left Stinson and the rest of the handlers and technicians out; Gil would have to do the dirty work himself. Code Nine was customary where Mannequin was concerned. Patents were not yet secure, and it was important to keep companies like Dupont and Dow in the dark. Even so, Gil felt that Trainer, a former army general, was carrying security precautions to ridiculous extremes. The remote location of the plant at the end of a canyon twenty-five miles north of Reno was security enough, in Gil's opinion. Trainer acted like he was running Los Alamos.

After a struggle, Stinson managed to thread the broomstick through two adjacent handles on top of the cages and raise the sliding doors. He was strong, but not strong enough to hold the doors up with one hand while pegging them in place with the other. Gil stepped forward and inserted the door pegs, careful to avoid the macaque's clutching fingers.

"Thanks, Mr. Ellis. Did you know old Smith, the guy who had your job before you? No, I guess not. He would never have touched those pegs. He would have let me wreck myself before lifting a finger. A real perpendicular asshole, like most of the engineers around here, know what I mean?"

Gil didn't, exactly, but said nothing. Stinson was a husky youth who would have looked at home on a surfboard. That he worked all day with unhappy animals was shown by the scratches and adhesive tape that decorated his face and hands.

Stinson rummaged through a desk drawer at the side of the room. "You're different. You're a nice guy. But you know what? You should lighten up a little. You're too serious all the time, know what I mean? A job's a job and you should try to have some fun with it. That's my theory, anyway. Hey, I got a lot of fucking nerve giving you advice! Sorry!"

Gil shrugged. "You're probably right. Next time I'm in Trainer's office I'll wear a nose and glasses." He smiled, but it felt forced. A job isn't a job when it's a career, and when it's in jeopardy it's hard to find any fun in it. Yes, he probably was too serious. A few days earlier he had run across a two-year-old snapshot and had stared at it for long minutes. It had been taken at his wedding party a year before the Boston gas leak that nearly ended everything, and he looked so happy he hardly recognized himself. His curly brown hair and bushy eyebrows showed not a trace of the gray that was now descending on him like an early frost, and his face radiated a forgotten faith in the future. His title then was Chief Engineer, and his company was one of the fastest growing in New England; he had reason to be smiling. Beside him was Karen, showing those straight white teeth and those clear blue eyes. Her good looks were of the Scandinavian sort, and she looked the same now as she did then, while he had aged ten years. Stinson would be surprised to know that Gilbert Ellis was only thirty-seven years old. He wondered if he would ever smile that broadly and genuinely again. The psychiatrist told him that people who had been through a disaster sometimes suffered permanent personality changes, especially if a perception of guilt was involved, but more often than not the passage of time, together with a little luck and professional help, enabled them to recover their senses of humor and joy of life. A year had gone by and Gil Ellis was still waiting.

"No problem getting Queenie and Cuteness in," Stinson said, looking at the cages. "Just took an apple and some lettuce. Kong pretends not to be hungry. He takes a little persuading."

Gil's eyebrows rose when he saw what Stinson had taken from the desk drawer: a thin cylinder with two prongs on the end. "You're going to use a cattle prod?"

"Better than trying to reason with him or punching his lights out. Works like magic. Watch . . ."

Well beyond Kong's reach, Stinson adopted a sword fighter's stance and made several flamboyant thrusts. "Aaiiyaa! Take that, you skunk! Oh, he hates to be called a skunk."

Kong drew his arms inside the cage and gripped the bars, staring at the handler intently. He stopped chattering and formed his lips into a circle. The gray whiskers that outlined his mouth trembled and his tail slowly sagged to the floor.

Stinson moved close to the cage and displayed the prod. "Recognize this, Kong? Nothing wrong with your memory. It's your attitude that needs adjusting."

"How strong is that?" Gil asked. "You could kill him with something intended for a steer."

"Naw, we cut the voltage way down. Enough left to get his attention, though. I don't have to really use it, anyway, just show it to him. I've only had to use it once. Well, twice. Okay, Kong, are you going to get into the box or am I going to have to give you a few zingers?" He waved the prod back and forth like a magician with a wand.

As if understanding every word and gesture, Kong turned silently and glided through the two doors, moving beside the female and adopting a similar sitting position. He raised his tail aloft and resumed chattering to show that while he may have lost the battle, his spirit was far from broken. Stinson pulled the pegs and let the doors drop. "Where do you want this happy family, Mr. Ellis, in the test room?"

"Yes, by the gas canister." As he helped Stinson wrestle the box onto a wheeled dolly, Gil couldn't help saying, "I'm glad I don't have your job."

"It beats working in the casinos." Rolling the dolly through the doorway, Stinson laughed and added, "Besides, I love animals."

In the late-morning heat two men worked their way up a rocky escarpment. It was hard going; often they had to grope overhead for handholds without being able to see if they were reaching for a rattlesnake or a scorpion. One man looked lean and hard and climbed with little apparent effort; the other was thirty pounds overweight and was drenched in sweat. Both had black hair, brown eyes, and mustaches.

"God," said the heavier man, "this is the most work I've done since . . . since pushing my car to the gas station. Or painting the kitchen and falling off the stepladder."

"You should run with me and go to the gym, Alek. Get yourself in shape."

"For what, dealing blackjack? All I need is a good wrist."

"You never know for what. It pays to be strong and fit."

"Oh, I don't know, I like being fat and happy. I'm not the intense type."

"Fat and dead before your time, that's what you will be. But maybe not today. We've climbed high enough."

"You like this place?" Alek Mirkafai asked, raising his arms and looking around.

Jamal Rajavi nodded. "It is perfect."

Jamal's accent was heavy. He sounded like a man reading from a textbook, and at the end of every sentence he pursed his lips slightly as if the words left a sour taste in his mouth. Alek, the heavy man, spoke English in a natural, unaffected way, almost like a native.

Their vantage point was a chest-high rib of rock they could hide behind and yet have an unimpeded view. Towering above them was a slender column of wind-sculptured sedimentary rock that jutted into the sky like a minaret and gave the area its name: Sentinel Canyon.

Jamal rested his sinewy forearms on the rock ledge and raised binoculars to his eyes. A few turns of the knurled wheel brought the canyon floor into focus and made it seem no more than a hundred yards away. Slowly, he scanned from right to left. The asphalt airstrip was beside a dry streambed. There were no edge stripes, lights, or arrows, nothing to identify it as an airstrip except a forlorn wind sock atop a pole. A dirt path led to a gravel road, which was paralleled by power lines and a railroad track. The track wasn't well maintained, judging from the rust-colored rails and the weeds between the ties.

The chemical plant covered several acres and was outlined by a chain-link fence topped by a spiral of barbed wire. At the front gate was a guard house and a sign that could be read easily through the glasses:

DRAEGLER CHEMICAL CORPORATION
—Pesticides and Insecticides—
for Fifty Years a Supplier
of Agricultural Products
for a Growing America

RESTRICTED AREA
DANGER! NO TRESPASSING!
VIOLATORS WILL BE PROSECUTED

Behind the gate was a parking lot and about fifty cars and vans. A row of shade trees had apparently been planted at some time in the past in an effort to keep cars from turning into furnaces during summer afternoons, but they had died long ago and stood now as stark reminders of how hostile the desert was to living things larger than insects and lizards.

The plant resembled a combination of an army base and an oil refinery. In front was a three-story administration building complete with an American flag above the main entrance, and behind it was a series of long, one-story wooden buildings with small windows and low-pitched corrugated metal roofs. The rear of the site was covered with steel tanks, pressure vessels, bins, and chutes of every size connected by a maze of color-coded pipes and conveyors. Two tank cars labeled AMMONIA stood unattended on a siding. Where converging rock walls marked the end of the canyon, the plant seemed abandoned: tanks and mechanical equipment were unpainted, and brown range grass marked cracks in the concrete walkways. Only the structures nearest the front gate were freshly painted and showed signs of prosperity.

Alek wiped a sleeve across his forehead and took a swig from his canteen. "See anything?"

"Half the place looks deserted. When they lost their military contracts a few years back, they nearly went bankrupt. That's the story I get from Sara."

"What about the guard?"

"You sound nervous, Alek. We're just looking for wildflowers. Get your *Audubon Desert Guide* and magnifying glass out of your pack and put them in your shirt pocket. We are breaking no law. Relax, my friend."

They waited an hour before anything happened. In the early afternoon a silver limousine emerged from a building on the far side of the plant, moved slowly past the employee parking lot, and paused at the gate. A section of the fence rolled to one side. The uniformed guard waved at the driver as the limo rolled by. When the limo was parked by the airstrip, the driver and a large man in a white shirt and dark tie stepped out, shaded their eyes, and looked toward the mouth of the canyon a mile away where the purr of distant engines could be heard. A red-and-white twin-engine plane flashed into view, coming up the canyon high and fast. Jamal and Alek ducked to avoid being seen as the plane passed by only slightly higher than their own position. The plane rose sharply and banked to the left, disappearing as it circled behind Sentinel Spire. A minute later it was coming up the canyon again, this time much lower and with flaps down.

Jamal watched through the binoculars as the plane landed, using almost the entire length of the runway. It turned and taxied back to the limousine. The engines died. A door opened and a tall man in Western clothes dropped lightly to the ground and wedged chocks on each side of the tires. He helped a man in a business suit to the ground. There was a round of handshaking.

"See him?"

Jamal stared intently through the binoculars. "The tall

one in the hat must be the pilot. Trainer is in the white shirt. You can tell he used to be a general."

"And the guy in the suit?"

"I can't see his face—yes, I see him! It's Aref!" As his voice rose in excitement he reverted to Farsi, the language of his childhood. Jamal handed the binoculars to his companion and turned away. He lowered himself to a sitting position, letting his back slide against the rock. "Aref! It's like seeing the devil in the flesh. . . ."

"It's him, all right," Alek said, fine-focusing the glasses. "They're in the limo now. Going back to the plant." He watched until they were gone, then sat beside Jamal.

"It's amazing," Jamal said softly, shaking his head. His face was as thin as his body, and deep-set eyes gave him an ascetic look. "I had to see for myself. Now we have to find out what he's doing here, halfway around the world from the battlefield. Not to buy poison for mice, you can bet on that. I'll keep the pressure on Sara. She can get the answer."

"Don't count on it."

"Sara Schuler is my woman. She'll do what I say. When we find out what he's after, we'll decide on a course of action."

"The action part, that's what worries me. Can't we just tell somebody we saw Aref? You have contacts—let them handle it. I'm not cut out to be a spy, and I could never be a hit man."

"Killing him wouldn't help. Somebody else would be sent."

"Thank God for that."

"Not that I couldn't kill him," Jamal said distantly. "I could strangle him with a smile on my face."

"Kill somebody with your bare hands? I doubt it. I know I couldn't. Oh, maybe if he was running at me waving a knife. I don't have the stomach for it." He patted his midsection. "I've got a stomach, but not for that."

"What if he was waving a knife at your mother and father? That's how you must think of Ahmad Aref."

Alek sighed tiredly. "One of the reasons I came to this country was to get away from all that eye-for-an-eye and tooth-for-a-tooth stuff. It never ends. The sight of blood makes my balls shrink up like prunes." Alek got to his feet and shouldered his pack.

"Sometimes you disgust me," Jamal said, not moving.

"When I eat?"

"No, when you think. You joke about what a coward you are, but when the time comes you will find the courage to do what must be done."

"Think so? I wonder. We're different, Jamal, more now than we used to be. You've become a pit bull, I'm still a chicken. Come on, let's go. I've got to be to work at four. There are cards to deal and hearts to break."

CHAPTER 4

In the preparation room, Gil studied the clothing hanging in his locker. The C-suit, made of fabric impregnated with absorbent charcoal, was relatively light and cool, but he never felt sure it would keep every trace of Mannequin off his skin. Completely safe was the Army's POTMC—the initials stood for Protective Outfit, Toxicological, Microclimate Controlled—but it couldn't be put on without help and was too heavy for comfort.

He decided on a tentlike plastic coverall, removed it from its hanger, and carefully stepped into the legs. Although it was fragile and could get as hot as a sauna, it was the lightest of the three and the best for short periods. It was made in one piece, including coverings for the feet, hands, and head, and was entered through a zippered slit that ran from crotch to chin. Once inside, Gil peered at a wall mirror through the glass face panel. With gloved hands he adjusted the helmet—the most awkward part of the suit—from which breathing tubes led to a small tank on his back. He picked up a roll of adhesive tape and wondered if he should go to the trouble of double-sealing the zippers. In the mirror he saw the hallway door open and Clem Trainer come in.

"Gil, Gil, Gil," the general said, shaking his head in dismay, "do we really need all that?"

Gil opened the zipper and slipped his head out of the helmet. "Sir?"

"We're just conducting a short test," he said with a patronizing inflection, "and the suit will make it look more hazardous than it is. I thought we had agreed."

Trainer was a big, broad man with watery gray eyes and a flat, pink face. His gestures and baritone voice were those of a man used to getting his way. Gil noticed that the knot of the tie, normally perfectly snugged at the throat, was pulled to one side and that there were uncharacteristic beads of sweat on his forehead.

"I don't remember any agreement," Gil said. "We talked about it, that's all. I like to be as safe as possible."

"I know, and that's good laboratory procedure. Trouble is, today we have to do things more like they'd be done in the field."

"In the *field*? You are thinking of testing Mannequin in the *field*?"

"Dammit, Gil, there hasn't been an accident in the test room in three months, not even the tiniest leak. You said last week the suit wasn't strictly necessary, and I thought that was the end of it. All right, I'm sorry I didn't make it clear that I wanted no suit for this demo. Mea culpa. The risk in the test room is almost zero, so what's the problem?"

Gil spoke softly in reply. "Why take even the smallest risk if it isn't necessary?"

"Jesus Christ, you take bigger risks every day and think nothing of it. Walk out of the house in the morning and you might get hit by lightning or a skateboard! It so happens that the client I've got here today is very important to the success of the program. If we can sell him, we're in the clear on funding. He insists on standing next to the box. He wants to be assured that the stuff can be used without a whole slew of precautions."

"But it can't be, not safely. We don't know enough about it."

Trainer rolled his eyes and threw up his hands. "Oh, God . . ."

Gil's heart was pounding. He had never before opposed the general so directly. "Who is the client?"

Trainer tightened his fists and held his breath for several seconds before speaking. "A government official from the Middle East. Ahmad Aref is the name. Secretary of Agriculture, something like that. Wants to try Mannequin on rodents. Apparently they are up to their asses in rodents over there. Huge buggers. No suit this time, okay? I don't want to say it's an order, but I will if I have to."

Gil could feel his fingers trembling inside the plastic gloves. "Well, all right, but I still think protective clothing should be worn in the test room. And I think visitors should stay in the observation booth. I want to go on record on that."

"Fine, you're on record."

Gil was tempted to let himself get angry and say that letting Mannequin out of the laboratory, even thinking about it, was crazy—it was far too lethal and unpredictable—and that he, Gilbert Ellis, would not let it happen. Instead, he heard himself say, "Could we have a talk soon, General? I'm not . . . well, I'm not clear on what the company plans for Mannequin. I have some fairly strong feelings about it and I'd like them to be considered."

Trainer left the room waving his hand over his shoulder. "Don't worry, your views will get a full airing, believe me."

But Gil didn't believe him. His knees were trembling; to stop them he sank to a bench and pressed them together. His mind wandered to the flask of scotch he kept in his third-floor office, and he wished he had brought it with him. He could use a little calming down.

The three macaques watched Gil as he examined the tubing that connected their enclosure to the gas-metering console. He made sure Stinson had properly sealed the joints with petroleum jelly and tape. The time-lapse clock on the wall showed zero, as did all other gauges and dials. Three oxygen bottles and a coiled water hose were on a workbench within easy reach in case of an emergency. The room itself reminded him of a multiple shower stall, with concrete walls and a tiled floor that sloped to a central drain. After a Mannequin test it was routine to scour everything with a jet of hot water and detergent. The odor of disinfectant was so strong, he breathed partly through his mouth.

He bent over the glass box. The mice were alert, their tiny eyes bright and their whiskers quivering. Queenie and Cuteness, mother and daughter, embraced each other and watched Gil's every move while Kong chattered in defiance.

Gil ran a hand-held meter along the transparent hoses that led from a red steel tank labeled PERM. There were no signs of leaks, but he felt uncomfortable nevertheless not wearing a body suit while in the same room with a canister of full-strength Mannequin.

Trainer came in with two men. One was introduced as

Jack Vanneman, agricultural consultant, a tall, rangy man wearing tooled leather boots, jeans, a denim jacket, and a wide-brimmed leather hat. He gave Gil a quick, strong handshake, then went back to the story he was telling about the plane ride from San Francisco. The second man, Ahmad Aref, square-faced and unsmiling, had shiny black hair combed straight back and was wearing a heavy tweed suit, fine for Canada but a poor choice in the desert. He said nothing during the introduction, barely touching Gil's hand and not looking at him. His eyes moved around the room as if he were trying to memorize details.

"When we came over the mountains," Vanneman said, chuckling, "and could see Nevada, I said, 'There it is, Colonel, the Great Basin of North America, two hundred thousand square miles of brutal desert where rivers never reach the sea . . . they just dry up in the sun.' You know what he said, Clem?" Vanneman was having a hard time suppressing his laughter. "He said, get this, 'In my country it would be an oasis.' I split a gut and we almost went into a spin!"

Vanneman and Trainer laughed. Aref ignored them and stared at the glass animal enclosure. The macaques were agitated at the intrusion and were moving back and forth on all fours with their rear ends and tails high. Kong bared his teeth and made lunges at the new arrivals.

"You are a character," Vanneman said, giving the unmoved Aref a light slap on the back. "You live up to your advance billing as rude and unsociable! It's okay, though, because I know you are a man of your word. I am, too, as you know and your government knows. If you cut a deal today, Colonel, I know I won't be forgotten."

For the first time since entering the room, Aref spoke. In a monotone and with his lips hardly moving he said, "Not Colonel. It is Mr. Aref. My trip here has not military significance."

"Oh, yeah, right." Vanneman slapped his forehead with the heel of his hand, knocking his hat to the floor.

"All right, gentlemen," Trainer said, "shall we proceed? Are you ready, Gil? Good. See the bald gent on the other side of the double-paned window? That's Everett Ordman, our scientist in charge of research and development. He'll monitor the quality and pressure of the air inside the test room, and in case of an accident, which is hardly likely, he'll sound the alarm, change the air, turn on the sprinklers you see on the ceiling, and one thing and another." Ordman nodded to show he was ready.

"If you *don't* cut a deal here," Vanneman said quietly to Aref, "we can go back to the Pyramid Lake option."

The reference interested Trainer. "The Pyramid Lake option?"

Gil busied himself with the equipment, realizing that the conversation was not intended for his ears.

"Yes," Vanneman said, lowering his voice to a conspiratorial whisper. "Before landing I gave the colonel a look at Pyramid Lake and the big rock that's covered with bird shit. My idea is to drop a couple of loads of guano on the Ayatollah. He'd run up a white flag pretty fast then, eh? I can get a couple of C-3's that the Air Force is dumping and Boy Scouts with pooper-scoopers can load them."

Trainer looked at Vanneman in pain.

Aref said, "Do you really desiring the war ended, Mr. Vanneman? It has made you rich."

"Hey, I'm for peace! Peace through strength."

"As for planes, we have enough. What we need is spare parts very much, especially Russian spare parts."

"The Russian stuff is tough," Vanneman said. "If you were willing to work through the Israelis—"

"Jack, please!" Trainer pleaded. "Later! No more interruptions! All right. The safety features you see here won't be available in the field, but we do whatever we can in the lab. Within reason. The meter Mr. Ellis is using can pick up one part in a million, or is it ten million, Gil? Ten million. We can supply you with as many meters as you need. We make them right here at the plant."

The four men gathered around the animal box, Trainer beside Gil, the visitors facing them.

"We have electronic detectors on the test stand," Trainer went on, "and if those bells go off, you'll know it. And *how!*" Trainer took a jar with a perforated lid from the top of the enclosure. "Moths," he said. "They're extremely sensitive to the gas. If you see their wings starting to curl, walk, don't run, to the nearest exit."

Vanneman wasn't interested in the technicalities of the demonstration and drifted to the far side of the room; either that, Gil thought, or he can't stand looking into the faces of the monkeys.

Trainer pointed at a coiled rubber hose along the wall. "If gas escapes, we'll hit it with a stream of water. The sprinklers on the ceiling will also turn on, automatically if Ordman falls asleep. Water nullifies Mannequin completely. Neutralizes it just like *that.*" He tried to snap his fingers, but his hands were too sweaty. "That's why we would advocate having a few tanker trucks around in a field situation. The Russians have developed some high-powered mobile units for decontaminating equipment exposed to nerve gas. Those would be ideal. Maybe Vanneman can get you a couple. He can get anything. Right, Jack?"

Trainer and Aref looked at Vanneman, who was leaning against the wall. "I'll see what I can do," he said.

No explanation was given to Gil of why an agricultural consultant might be able to acquire Russian military equipment. He drew his own conclusions. Gil had suspected for months that Trainer was more interested in the military uses of Mannequin than the industrial, and now there was no longer any doubt about it.

"If you happen to get a whiff of the gas," Trainer said,

turning back to Aref, "grab an oxygen bottle. Extra oxygen in the bloodstream does the trick. Blocks the paralysis effect, or reverses it. Oxygen is the antidote. Funny, no matter what chemical agents anybody comes up with—tabun, sarin, soman, even the V group that is absorbed by the skin—somebody else comes up with an antidote, though they don't always work too well. Of course Mannequin isn't a chemical, exactly, being toxin-derived with a lot of genetic engineering. In a military application, which of course we aren't concerned with here, surprise is the key when using chemical agents. Hit the enemy when he doesn't know what he's being hit with. Isn't that right, Colonel?"

"Mister. Not Colonel."

"Right. Gil, suppose you explain the pressure differential system."

"It's warm in here, as you may have noticed," Gil said. Aref's baleful, unwavering gaze was unnerving, so Gil addressed his remarks to the macaques. "That's because the room is pressurized to one-point-five atmospheres. Inside the animal box the pressure is one atmosphere. If there are any leaks, the flow will be from the room to the box, not from the box to the room."

"Brilliant, eh?" Trainer said with a grin. "It pays to hire good people."

"On the red tank," Aref asked in his tight-lipped way, pointing, "what meaning is the PERM?"

"Short for Pseudo Rigor Mortis," Trainer answered. "It's what we called the gas during the early stages. Then somebody, a lab worker, I think, started calling it Mannequin because that's what a janitor looked like one morning. Died right on his feet holding a mop and staring straight ahead. It was sad, because he would have suffered no harm at all if we had found him sooner and gotten some oxygen into him. Anyway, the name just sort of stuck. As bad as I felt for the man and his family, I couldn't help thinking of an enemy fighting force rooted in its tracks like that. Mannequin someday might be seen as the greatest humanitarian weapon of war ever discovered. Freeze the aggressor, disarm him, then revive him with oxygen. Any other questions?"

Gil glanced at Aref. Minister of Agriculture? He looked and acted as much like a man of the soil as Henry Kissinger.

"Why," Aref asked, "can't the gas be manufactured as—how would you say it—two friendly aromas? The technical term is what, twins? No, binary?"

"Binary is the word," Trainer answered. "Good question. It sounds like a good idea to furnish toxic gases in two harmless parts that can be combined at the point of use, inside an artillery shell, say, on its way to a target, and as you know the United States is converting its chemical arsenal to that configuration. The hell of it is, you never can be sure how well the parts will be mixed. How can you plan an attack . . . on rats, for example . . . if you don't know how strong your poison is going to be?"

By referring to rats Trainer was continuing the charade that Aref was interested in exterminating rodents. Did he think Gil was blind and deaf as well as stupid?

"Another difficulty," Gil said, just loudly enough for the others to hear, "is that we haven't figured out *how* to separate Mannequin into parts. More research is needed on that, and on control of potency, stability, persistence, safe methods of storage and transport—"

Trainer drowned him out by saying loudly, "They don't care what our problems are on the manufacturing end, Gil, which are quickly being solved." He stepped in front of Aref and glared at Gil with an expression that showed anger close to boiling over. "Suppose we begin the demonstration. *Do you read me?*"

Fuming, Gil turned to the array of valves and dials above the tanks of PERM and oxygen. He couldn't deal with Trainer and keep his emotions under control; arguing with him, even looking at him, could lead to an outburst he might later regret. He tried to lose himself in technical details.

A quarter turn of the largest valve made a small digital display rise from 0.000 to 0.015 to 0.115 to 0.500, the right-hand numbers changing too fast to read. A pencil-thin blue line appeared on the inside of a tube and grew from the red tank toward the animal box, widening and thinning out as it went. Within fifteen seconds the several feet of tubing had changed from colorless to pale blue.

"The gas tends to cling to surfaces when it is first released," Trainer explained. "Something to do with surface tension and openings in the outer electron rings of the molecules that makes it bond with other materials. Gil here could tell you more if you're interested; he's the chemical engineer. When the film is two molecules thick, additional molecules begin migrating through the air. The blue is something we add so we can see it. In its natural state it's colorless and tasteless."

Gil advanced the dial another quarter turn. The readout blurred and settled at 0.900. In the box the macaques were moving faster, pacing, examining the corners, trying to find a way out, bumping into each other. A puff of dark blue gas rolled down the tube like cigar smoke and into the enclosure, immediately flattening against the inside surface of one wall. One after another the six walls of the box were coated. The gas didn't spread across like a growing stain; instead, after a pause of a second or two at the corners, it seemed to appear instantaneously all over the flat surface. One moment a glass pane was clear, the next it was tinged with blue, as if a film of neon had been activated by electricity. Gil turned the valve back to the starting position and watched the readout return to zero.

"Notice that the mice inside the box have stopped

moving," Trainer said. "They look like toys, don't they? The monkeys will be next. They'll get it first through the soles of their feet, then through their lungs. Look at the cockroaches—completely unaffected." With a chuckle he added, "Forget the United States and Russia. Cockroaches are the real superpowers."

The movements of the monkeys grew slower, as if they were getting tired. Within thirty seconds they appeared to be wading through chest-high water. Thirty seconds more and the work of pacing had become too great and they stood in place, slowly bending and straightening their arms and twisting back and forth at the waist as if they had been trained to do stretching exercises. Gil kept his eyes on Cuteness, the smallest of the monkeys and the one with the most humanlike features. He knew it was foolish to draw anthropocentric conclusions from a primate's gestures and facial expressions, but he couldn't help feeling that what Cuteness was trying to convey was terror, the terror a child feels in a dream when it can't run from danger. Her teeth were bared, her eyes were round and darting back and forth, and she was moving her hands in small, repeated circles from her chest outward, as if trying to fend off an invisible assailant. The assailant was not invisible; a trace of cobalt gave Mannequin the color of a clear sky, and it could not be waved away with the hands. It was percolating through the skin on her feet and palms, being drawn into her lungs by gasps of fright, being pumped through her body by her heart, attacking her muscle cells like a million tiny clamps.

Gil watched as the writhing movements of the animals slowed down and finally stopped entirely, leaving them rigidly facing in different directions like exhibits in a taxidermist's window, their faces Halloween masks of fear. Allow a gas of such obvious evil to leave the plant? Use it on human beings on a battlefield? If that was what Trainer was considering, Gil thought, he had lost his mind. Near the door, Vanneman groaned in a way that suggested that he was going to be sick.

What would Karen think of all this? Gil wondered. How could he justify this part of his job to her? There was no way he could make her understand. Tell Trainer to go jump in the lake and call the cops on him, that would be her advice. He told himself to quit wondering what Karen would think. She was out of his life and he had to learn to make decisions without her. But he had to talk to *somebody. . . .*

His train of thought was interrupted by an urgent whisper from Trainer. "Gil, take the gas out."

With a start Gil realized that the gas had to be drawn off immediately if the animals were to be revived. He quickly turned a vacuum valve and watched the faint blue vapor reverse its direction and stream through the exhaust tube. Within ten seconds the glass enclosure was clear. The hairs rose on his neck as he realized he might have acted too late.

"It attacks the extremities first," Trainer said to the visitors as if everything was under control, "and the major muscles, gradually freezing them in position. Muscles controlled by the autonomic nervous system—the heart, the glands, the lungs, and for some reason the eyes—are affected last. Look closely. See?" Trainer and Aref leaned close to the glass. Gil rested his hand on the oxygen valve and watched Cuteness, who seemed to have absorbed a greater dose of Mannequin than her parents and whose pose, with arms outstretched and bent grotesquely, made her seem to be hardly more than a caricature of a living creature.

"They can't move," Trainer said in a self-satisfied voice, "but as you can see they're still breathing, and their eyes are darting back and forth. They've been through this before, so they probably aren't as scared as they look. Before you ask, Mr. Aref, let me tell you that they'll stay locked like that for hours . . . depending on how much of the gas has gotten into the bloodstream. Too much and the involuntary muscles stop and they give up the ghost."

Aref looked at Trainer and cocked an eyebrow. "Give up what?"

"Give up the ghost," Trainer said with a shrug, "means, well, die. Dead. Kaput. Now, if nothing is done, the effects gradually decay and the victims recover full use of their faculties. Takes half a day or so, much less with oxygen."

Aref stared at the monkeys, plainly impressed. He muttered something in a language Gil couldn't identify.

"A very important point," Trainer said, lowering his voice, "is that the gas leaves no trace in the system. None. We haven't yet found a test anybody could use to find out what happened. You can understand how important that would be in . . . in certain situations."

Aref nodded almost imperceptibly. "How would you transport it to these certain situations?"

Trainer dropped his voice so low that Gil could hear only fragments of his comments: "At the point of use, spraying from planes is . . . Bulk transportation . . . because of the pressure vessels and the volume needed . . . be done by rail rather than by truck. . . . could be loaded on ship at our end and off-loaded at your end. I can show you designs for rail tankers that we . . ."

Gil wanted to continue eavesdropping, but was distracted by the condition of the baby macaque. Cuteness was standing stiffly about three inches from one wall of the enclosure. As Gil watched she slowly lost her balance and tilted to the left until her shoulder was against the glass, a lifeless posture that brought her right foot an inch off the floor. Gil took a step to one side to look at her face: her stare was fixed on a distant point and a pale, translucent film had descended over her eyes. She looked like a stuffed toy that had been thrown against the wall of a closet.

Gil cursed silently. "Clem," he said in a strained voice, "I think Cuteness is in trouble."

"Oh, I doubt that." Trainer made a quick motion with his hand toward the oxygen tank. Gil twisted a valve and listened to a rising hiss as a needle moved to the right side of a dial. The sound of a door opening at the rear of the room made the men turn in time to see Vanneman, his face ashen, leave quickly with his hand over his mouth.

Gil looked at the general. "Looks like the agricultural consultant isn't used to seeing animals in distress."

"It does take some getting used to," Trainer said with a dry laugh. "He'd make a lousy combat soldier. Now, Colonel, watch this next phase carefully. Once oxygen gets into the lungs, the recovery is remarkable."

A minute passed. Two minutes.

Kong, the largest of the three macaques, showed faint signs of movement. He had been immobilized with his feet wide apart, his arms forward, and his fingers slightly curled. Now he was very slowly forming fists, as if checking to make sure his fingers weren't broken. His lips, drawn back to expose jagged yellow teeth, gradually closed into a straight line, then formed a small circle protruding oddly and far in front of his face—one of his characteristic expressions.

'Old Kong is almost back to normal already," Trainer said. "I'd recognize those kissing lips anywhere. Reminds me of my first wife."

Queenie was recovering as well. She took an awkward step forward and dropped both hands to the floor. After a few deep breaths she arched her back, waving her arms and sticking out her tongue. Her tail lashed from side to side like a whip. A minute later both adult macaques were testing their legs, lurching about drunkenly at first, then with growing control, ignoring their motionless offspring. Bumped by Kong, Cuteness toppled over, ending up with her face on the floor and her limbs twisted at bizarre angles. Kong and Queenie circled the enclosure, swinging and flexing their arms and chattering angrily, stepping over Cuteness as if she were a broken doll.

"We've lost her, Clem, goddammit!" Gil said. Turning to the control-room window, he said, "Everett, can you hear me? Looks like Cuteness is a goner. Send Stinson in with the wire cage."

"Put her in the freezer till the doc can take a look," Trainer said. "She was probably sick."

"She wasn't sick. You never know what this damned gas is going to do. It's one of the problems."

"Seems to me *you* are one of the problems." Trainer glowered at Gil, then guided Aref toward the door. "If we had used three monkeys the same size, they all would have recovered. With a given dosage, the animal with the smallest body suffers the biggest effect. Same as when three guys go to a bar and have a few drinks. The two big guys have fun, the shrimp passes out."

As they disappeared into the hallway, Gil heard Aref say, "The shrimp?"

CHAPTER 5

After the plane had left with Aref and Vanneman and the death of the monkey was confirmed, Trainer called Gil to his office. The moment Gil walked in the general was out of his chair and complaining, "That was some great performance you put on for the Arab. Whose side are you on, anyway? You were pulling the rug out from under me every step of the way. . . ."

Trainer was many things Gil was not—loud, sure of himself, aggressive—and on this day Gil found him threatening as well. The Mannequin project needs "company men," Trainer said, pacing and gesticulating, "men who can be counted on and trusted without question to support company goals." His face was pink with irritation when he said, almost spitting the words out, "Anyone not willing to work on my team maybe should start looking for another one. I wouldn't relish that, if I were you, not with your record. You are stuck with us. Trouble is, we're stuck with you too."

The office had a western exposure and, because the sun had not yet dropped below the ridge, the light coming through the window was blinding. Gil wouldn't have been surprised if Trainer had asked to see him when the sun was low as part of a deliberate strategy of intimidation. He shifted in his chair and shielded his eyes with his hand, wondering if he was about to be demoted, fired, or merely reamed out. Maybe he should quit before submitting to any of the three. Maybe he'd be happier pumping gas or selling shoes. At least in jobs like those mistakes didn't kill people. On the other hand, if he walked away he would lose all chance of learning Trainer's plans and of influencing—he cut himself off. He had fallen into the habit of examining all sides of every question so carefully, he couldn't act at all. Too much on the one hand and the other hand. Not like the old days, when things seemed clearer and he was known for making sharp, sound decisions without waiting for every last fact to be in. Maybe it was just chance that the decisions had almost always been good ones. What he thought was skill and insight might have been nothing but dumb luck . . . and then one day luck decided to catch up to him. No, that was foolish; luck was blind and didn't play catch-up. Flip heads ten times in a row and the odds on the next one are still fifty-fifty, unless the coin or the flips aren't legitimate. The issue before him at the moment, for example, couldn't be simpler: Mannequin was too dangerous to ship and Clem Trainer was a pompous fool. He should just come right out and say so. On the other hand . . .

Trainer ranted for several minutes about the importance of team play, allegiance, and a clearly understood command structure, and how he would not tolerate anything less. Gradually the anger in his voice melted away, as if he had decided to take another tack. He sat down and crossed his arms on the desk. In a conciliatory tone he said, "How long have you been with Draegler now, almost a year? You are a lot better than when you started, I'll say that. You were practically a basket case at the beginning, if you have forgotten. You quit going to the shrink, isn't that right?"

Standing, Trainer was like an old lion, slow-moving but still deadly. Seated, he was a cobra. Gil nodded, wondering how Trainer knew he had given up therapy. "Two months ago."

Trainer looked concerned. "Maybe you should start going again." He opened a folder on his desk, studied it for a moment, then laid it aside. "The Boston thing happened over a year ago, you stayed on the job with Brandon Chemical for another month, you were unemployed for two months, then you came aboard with us. After a year here you should know how we do things. Now, about today in the test room. Sure, there can be honest differences of opinion, especially in highly technical areas, but, my God, you don't air them before outsiders! Surely you can see that."

"Yes, I can see that, and I should have said nothing." Gil took a deep breath to bolster his courage. "I guess you know how I feel about the gas. It's too unpredictable. We don't know exactly how it works or what it can do even under laboratory conditions. As for transporting it, there is no way to do it safely. In my opinion—"

"Your opinion!" Trainer said in exasperation. "Your opinion isn't the only one. You aren't the only scientist or engineer around here. We don't know everything about Mannequin yet, I grant you that, but the consensus of my technical people is that it is no more dangerous than a lot of other things that are transported every day . . . like chlorine, or natural gas, or dynamite, or fireworks, or atomic bombs." He raised a hand to block Gil's effort to reply. "It makes sense that you are the most cautious one of the lot, after what happened in Boston. If I had the lives of twelve innocent Americans on my conscience, I'd be cautious too."

"So now it comes out. You think Boston was my fault."

"It was an accident that could have happened to anybody. You just happened to be the one on duty."

"I acted as anybody would have in the same position."

"Yes, anybody who had a little buzz on and who tends to freeze up in emergencies. You deny it? You think you are perfect all of a sudden? Look at today. We wouldn't have lost that monkey if you hadn't gone into a trance."

Gil flared up. "That's a rotten thing to—" He checked himself before losing his temper. Trainer was a dirty fighter, but there was painful truth in what he said. Gil couldn't escape at least some of the responsibility for the Boston catastrophe. He had been the engineer in charge, and, after Bhopal showed how trecherous methyl isocyanate could be, he should have tightened precautions more than he had and made sure his crew knew how to counteract even the most unlikely combinations of operator errors and mechanical breakdowns. He had held a few meetings and staged a few drills, but he obviously hadn't done enough. Part of the blame for what had happened was plainly his, and an army of psychiatrists would never make him feel otherwise. Errors of omission on his part had allowed the hand of death to caress a sleeping neighborhood, its silken fingers probing every bedroom in a ten-square-block area. In the aftermath his self-esteem had gradually dissolved, and then his marriage. He began having difficulty making love to his wife. He felt unworthy of her, not good enough for her, and so began the secret drinking, the self-absorption, the liaisons with lesser women. He was lucky Karen had stuck with him as long as she had. As for having "a buzz on" the night of the catastrophe, that was simply a damned lie. A couple of drinks at dinner was hardly having a buzz on, and he should never have admitted it to the board of inquiry.

Gil became aware of a dull ache on each side of his head, and he touched his fingertips to his temples. He thought of Cuteness dead on the floor of the glass cage—stiff, grotesque, staring. Would he have to accept the blame for her death as well? His mind had wandered for a moment, he remembered, and the result was that he might have started the gas evacuation a few seconds too late. How could he have let that happen? There was a distraction, yes, that was it: the pilot, the one they said was an agricultural consultant, had bolted from the room retching. Suppressed rage had made it hard to concentrate, too, rage at Trainer for using him, for keeping him in the dark, and for treating him like a child. As Gil looked across the desk at Trainer's long, jowly face, he felt nausea and could see only one thing clearly: he hated the man as he had never hated any person or thing.

"Mannequin," Trainer said soothingly. "I know how dangerous it is as well as anybody. But it's supposed to be! You can't kill rats with perfume! Certainly there would be risks in transporting it. That's what life is, isn't it, risks? You have to take them sometimes to reach certain desirable goals. Now you're a good man, Gil, in many ways. You certainly know the technical end and I'm glad to have a man with your experience on the team. I'd hate to lose you at this stage, that's for sure." He narrowed his eyes and leaned forward. "You know as much about Mannequin as anybody, maybe more than you really should. If you were to leave the company and . . . well, misuse what you know, it would be terribly damaging to, ah, what we are trying to accomplish. I can't let that happen."

Was there a touch of menace in the general's voice or was Gil imagining it? "You talk about the team, how you want team players, but you won't tell me the game plan. What is Mannequin? Is it a pesticide or is it a military weapon?"

Trainer drummed his fingers once on the desktop. "We don't know yet quite what it is, do we? That's why we are running so many experiments."

"The man we put on the demonstration for, Aref. Half the time you called him Mister and half the time Colonel. The other visitor, the tall one, mentioned 'the Ayatollah' at one point and implied that Aref was looking for something to use against him. Aref is a military man and he's from Iraq, am I right?"

"There are some things I can't tell you."

"I have Code Nine clearance."

"Not enough."

Gil raised and dropped his hands in a gesture of frustration. Trainer was a gang of one, using everybody and keeping everybody at least partly in the dark. Maybe generals are taught to hold back damaging information about planned operations to lessen the rate of desertions. "I shouldn't have said anything in front of outsiders," Gil said. "I apologize for that. But try to see it from my side. For years before joining Draegler I was part of a management team. I'm used to being consulted before important decisions are made. Here, though, I feel like an outsider, not fully trusted. I guess as far as you're concerned I'm on some sort of probation. That's new for me, and, well, I don't like it."

"Tell you what," Trainer said with some enthusiasm,

"I'll put your name in for Code Ten. Then I can tell you the game plan. Mannequin has military applications, I'm not giving away any secrets by admitting that. So does almost every chemical. Aref? I told you that he was the key to continued funding. You want more testing. Fine, but who's going to pay for it? Draegler is a private company. The money has to come from somewhere."

"Aref's government will pay for the research?"

Trainer smiled and shrugged. "No comment. Neither confirm nor deny. Colonel Aref's government, or I should say Mr. Aref's government, is not handicapped by the superpower treaties on chemical and biological weapons, if that's what you want to call a pesticide. Gil, I want you to promise me your full cooperation. There are larger considerations involved here that I can't tell you about, but believe me they fully justify the allegiance I'm asking of you." He rose from his chair and came to Gil's side of the desk. "We're both in this too far to back out. I can't tell you to forget what you know and give you my blessing to look for work someplace else. It doesn't work that way." He extended his hand. "I need your help, Gil, and I'm asking for it. Is it a deal? Can I count on you?"

You are a patronizing, smug, insufferable son of a bitch, Gil thought, and I'm going to screw up your plans if it's the last thing I do. I only wish I knew how seriously to take your threats about what might happen if I quit.

He took Trainer's hand and shook it with as much sincerity as he could muster. "I'm leery of Mannequin not because of what happened to me in Boston. Because of what it can do. I hope you'll think hard before letting it leave the plant."

Trainer walked with Gil to the door with his arm around his shoulder. "I mean what I told you before. Your views will be fully considered if we have to make a decision on shipping. If we did decide to send it somewhere, by sea would be the safest, don't you think? Then in case of accident or sabotage, the gas would be immersed in the one thing that neutralizes it—water. Good night, Gil. Not a word of this to anyone, understand? That includes your wife. Give her my regards, will you? A lovely girl, and talented too."

After a shower and a change of clothes at her downtown hotel, Karen retrieved her car from the garage and headed north on U.S. 101 toward Marin County. By the time she reached the middle of the Golden Gate Bridge it was six-thirty, and the evening rush-hour traffic had thinned out enough to let her risk a few glances at the view. On the left a red sun was low over the Pacific, and on the right, across an expanse of steel-gray water, rose the towers of San Francisco, as white and inviting as frosting on a cake. She wanted to stop and enjoy the view, but that would have been suicidal given the speed of the surrounding cars. How could the other drivers be so impervious to the splendor? She looked at them in wonderment. Most were gazing straight ahead with expressions as blank as store-window dummies. Never, she promised herself, would she become so blasé, even if she had to commute across the bridge a thousand times.

She ignored the first Sausalito exit, as the hand-drawn map instructed, continued through the tunnel with the rainbow portal, and took the exit at the bottom of a long downgrade. Just past the intersection with Bridgeway was a bait shop and a restaurant, and a block farther on was the end of the road and several rows of parked cars. Through breaks in a tall hedge she caught glimpses of houseboats lining piers that extended into the Bay.

After checking her makeup in the rearview mirror, Karen stepped out of the car, returning immediately for her leather jacket. Her brown tweed slacks and a heavy brown knit turtleneck sweater weren't going to be warm enough. The sun had dropped behind the Marin headlands, and the temperature was dropping along with it. June in the San Francisco area wasn't like June in Nevada.

The houseboats weren't like anything in the world. She pushed through a gate that was bracketed by at least twenty mailboxes and found herself on a creaking wooden walkway that zigzagged on pilings through the most diverse and whimsical neighborhood imaginable. Some of the floating homes were little more than large boxes on barges; others were fanciful collections of stained glass and shutters and shingles that might have been inspired by Hansel and Gretel or Dr. Seuss. In a jumble of architectural styles that was almost comical, beautifully designed and built structures were docked side by side with slap-dash huts that looked as though they had been made up as the carpenter went along. One looked like the caboose on the Toonerville Trolley, complete with a crooked stovepipe and window boxes full of flowers. Another looked like a steeple that had lost its church. Reading a newspaper on a tiny porch off the belfry was a man in a suit and tie who looked like a stockbroker; Karen had been half expecting to see an elf or a leprechaun.

She was not half expecting to see the man who answered her knock on the houseboat docked at Berth Nine. He didn't look like a stockbroker or a leprechaun, he looked like a professional football player, and he looked familiar.

"Mr. Eagan," she said, her face brightening, "I didn't expect to see you again so soon!"

"If you're going to rent my houseboat, you can call me Jim."

"You live here?"

"Welcome to my happy home. Come in, I'll give you the tour."

"Why didn't you tell me at the elevator the ad was yours?"

"I was going to, then I went berserk and asked you to dinner instead. When you stayed cool and said no, and refused to give me your phone number, I thought I better shut up. I didn't want to scare you off."

He led her down a narrow corridor lined with books into a small but attractive living room. Flames danced in a small fireplace. There was a spinet, a comfortable-looking sofa, a floor-to-ceiling bookcase, and a small deck beyond sliding glass doors. Across a hundred feet of water was another row of houseboats. In the air was the smell of books, of burning wood, of the sea.

"I can't stand it," Karen said, turning delightedly in a circle. "How much do you want, five thousand dollars a month?"

"For you there is a ninety percent discount. It's not a big place, as you can see. The bedroom is about the same size as the living room, and there is a tiny room at the top of a ladder in what used to be the wheelhouse when this was a tugboat. You have to like cozy."

"And you have to like cute. My God, I've never seen anything like it! Some of the boats are unbelievable, like the one that looks like a church steeple."

"That's what it used to be. The church stayed behind in West Marin and is now a Cajun Chinese restaurant."

Karen looked at Jim and frowned. There was something about him that was different. What was it? "Your mustache," she gasped, "you've shaved it off!"

"Well, yes, I did. Finished just as you knocked on the door. When you work for a big bureaucracy, you have to have a way of showing a bit of individuality. Now that I'm going to sail to the Caribbean, I don't have anything to prove. Besides, I saw the way you looked at my mustache when you walked into my office. You thought it was some sort of killer bat that might spring from my face to yours."

"It did scare me a little. You shaved it off because of me?"

"Not you only. Women in general. If I'm going to start asking women for dates again, I should come out from behind the shrubbery. I have nothing to hide except this big Irish mug."

She looked at him and smiled again. He was nervous and was standing six feet away from her, as if trying not to make her uncomfortable. To put him at his ease she asked for a drink.

"You look like the white-wine type."

"I'll have a beer, just to confuse you."

While Eagan was in the kitchen, Karen walked to the spinet and looked at the stack of music on the lid. Bach two-part inventions. Chopin waltzes. Early Mozart sonatas. Nothing too difficult.

"Do you play, Mr. Eagan?"

"Jim. The name's Jim. Yes, I play, if that's not too dignified a term for what I do. My soul soars, but not my fingers."

She sat down and turned to Mozart's Sonata in C, K 545, something charming to suit the surroundings. It was a piece her host must have worked on, judging from the notes penciled in the margins: "Slow down, deadly reefs ahead!" "Shit!" "Gimme a break, Wolfgang!" She played the first movement, taking it at a tempo she knew she could handle, concentrating on shaping the phrases and making the runs as smooth and liquid as possible. The piano had better action than she would have expected and was in good tune.

When she was done she let her hands drop gracefully to her lap and looked over her shoulder. Jim was standing a few feet away with his mouth open and a bottle of beer in each hand.

"That was beautiful!" he gasped. "That was terrific! I'll never play that frigging piece again!" He sat down heavily on the sofa and put the bottles on the coffee table. "You've got to go to dinner with me now," he said with a melodramatic gesture of helplessness. "If you don't, I'll kill myself. As for the houseboat, it's yours."

Karen laughed. "Jim, are you divorced?"

"Isn't everybody?"

"I soon will be. I accept your invitation. I hate it when grown men kill themselves. There are conditions, though. We won't talk about our marriages, okay? Or about hazardous chemicals. After dinner you'll drive me to my car so I can go back to my hotel. I want you to respect me in the morning."

He filled a glass of beer, twisting the bottle with a flourish at the end. Handing it to her, he said, "It's a deal. We'll talk about the terms of the lease."

CHAPTER 6

Although Sara Schuler wasn't beautiful in the classical sense—there was something hard about her face—the men at the plant had once voted her "Draegler Woman We'd Most Like to Be Trapped in a Vat With." It wasn't so much the prominent curves of her figure as it was her manner that set the men to fantasizing. There was an earthiness about her and a hint of something wild in her past that invited flirting and overtures, all of which she brushed aside with the practiced ease of a woman long used to them. Gil once heard a young engineer stop at her desk and say, "Why don't you come over to my place tonight, Sara? I've got something I want to show you," to which she replied, "No thanks, I'm too young to die laughing." She didn't flinch from eye contact, and the slight curl of her broad, full lips implied that not only did she know what men were thinking, but that they should be ashamed of themselves. The male employees of Draegler Chemical Corporation, particularly the younger ones, took it for granted that anybody lucky enough to crawl into her bed would be given a night he would never forget. The assumption was based on guesswork only, for the most any of them had ever gotten from her was a kiss on the cheek at the Christmas party . . . with the exception of Gil Ellis.

She rolled her eyes when Gil tried to compliment her on her looks, pointing out that her legs were too muscular, her buttocks and breasts too full, her mouth too big. On her cheeks were faint traces of adolescent acne. "You need glasses," she said when he told her she was beautiful. Once she slapped her hand on her bare thigh and said, "There is five years of burgers and fries. I don't have the shape I used to. Your wife, she looks like a movie star. I wish I looked like her."

"Too thin," Gil replied. "Always playing tennis and jogging and eating raw vegetables." Sara was five, maybe ten pounds overweight at the most, and he wouldn't have wanted her any other way. Her body was strong and significant. Encircled by her arms and lost in the softness of her breasts, he felt as warm and safe as a nursing child. Knowing nothing of his past, she couldn't compare him even subconsciously with what he once was. She loved him, or claimed to, for what he was now, and her unexpected availability was the one positive thing that had happened to him in a year. How could he not think of her as beautiful?

The timing couldn't have been better. Sara came into his life when he had been living in the motel for a month and feeling sorry for himself. He didn't question her sudden interest. Maybe she could see how depressed he was and felt sorry for him, maybe she never really noticed him before, maybe she had lost a lover and needed another. Whatever the reason, their first tentative kiss had almost immediately turned passionate, and before he knew it he was in the midst of an affair that was like a dream come true. She treated him like the most desirable man in the world. By sleeping with him she made him feel that he had won an undeclared contest with every man at the plant. He loved the way she behaved in bed: she left lipstick trails all over his body and she devoured him with her mouth and hands with wonderfully unrestrained lust. Karen was by no means inhibited, but she had become a reminder of derelictions he wanted to forget.

Sara was a fresh start, and she seemed to think of him in the same way. She expressed no interest in his past and Gil didn't ask about hers. He knew she was living with a dealer at one of the casinos, someone named Jamal. The relationship had problems, she told him, and she was thinking of breaking it off. He had seen them together once in a Reno restaurant. He was a tall, intense-looking man, Gil remembered, with a black mustache and the thin, sharp face of a bird of prey.

Sara Schuler was the Draegler Corporation's receptionist and switchboard operator as well as a typist and file clerk. She had been Jeremy Draegler's favorite secretary before the old man retired and now did much of General Trainer's routine work, though his confidential correspondence was handled by a male assistant he had brought with him from the Pentagon.

Gil's trysts with Sara were always at his room at the King and Queen Motel in Sparks whenever she could safely steal a few hours after work. The room was large, included a small kitchen, and was located close to Highway 445, which made the commute to the plant an easy one. It was there that he had moved "temporarily" after leaving Karen and the house, and it was there he still was three months later. There seemed no compelling reason to move.

It was to his room that Gil went after his confrontation with Trainer. Within minutes of Sara's arrival they were in bed together.

Gil was on his back with his fingers laced behind his neck and his eyes closed, trying without much success to enjoy the sensations that were radiating from the center of his body. She was working hard, moaning in a way that showed she was getting more out of it than he was. She was usually able to excite him if she kept at it long enough, but this time the odds were against her. His mind was tumbling with images he couldn't dismiss: Trainer pacing back and forth and making veiled threats, the meeting with Karen the night before, the rigid body of the baby monkey being slipped into a plastic bag. Always there were the thoughts about Mannequin that spread across his brain the way Mannequin spread across the walls of a glass box—silently, insidiously.

One thing was certain: at the moment he couldn't relax. Sex was out of the question. He buried his fingers in her hair and slowly pulled her head across his stomach, his chest, his neck, until her face was next to his. He kissed her on the lips. She asked in a whisper if she was doing something wrong.

"No, no, it has nothing to do with you." He kissed her forehead and hugged her reassuringly. "I can't seem to turn my mind off. It's spinning like a centrifuge. Trainer is driving me crazy. Mannequin is driving me crazy."

"You feel tense. Want one of Aunt Sara's special back rubs?"

Gil turned on the bedside light. "Sara, who were those two guys who came to the plant today? Was the foreigner from Iraq?"

There was a long pause before she answered yes. "I know things I'm not supposed to. Talking about them could cost me my job."

"Asking you about them could cost me mine. Trainer

is such a fanatic about security, he'd have a fit if he knew we were cheating on our mates. He doesn't know I left my wife, and I can hear him claiming that what we're doing could subject us to blackmail. You know the company rules—'Anyone becoming romantically involved with a company employee or an employee of a rival firm is liable to immediate dismissal.' "

"That's bullshit. They'd lose too many good people enforcing that. How would they find replacements willing to work in the boondocks like we do? The pay is not that great."

Gil went to the window and pulled the drape a few inches to one side. The room was on the second floor and there was a walkway outside the window. Across the parking lot was the motel office, dwarfed by a steel tower carrying the garish King and Queen sign, so large it was visible from Interstate 80 two blocks away. The sign was festooned with club, heart, spade, and diamond symbols, a motif that was carried throughout the entire three-story complex. The few scattered cars in the parking lot were empty and so was the small swimming pool. There was nobody in the pay phone booth.

"You think we're being watched? For doing what people have been doing for millions of years?"

"I don't know what I think," Gil said, returning to the edge of the bed and sitting down. "Sometimes everything seems treacherous, then I wonder if my imagination is getting the best of me. What about those security guards that Trainer has brought in? Is it my imagination or are they a bunch of assassins?"

"They remind me of the pit bosses at the casinos. Real swell bunch of fellas."

"Sara, do you know what's going on in Buildings G and H?"

"I don't have security clearance, if that's what you mean."

"You do some of Trainer's typing and filing and you know what calls he gets. You must know quite a bit."

"I hear rumors." The conversation was making her uncomfortable. "People talk at lunchtime. Gossip. We can't help being curious."

"How much do you know about Mannequin?"

"Only that it is something very dangerous. I've seen technicians in those suits that make them look like astronauts."

"Who is Aref? Is he a military man?"

She nodded slowly. "Colonel Ahmad Aref. A month ago I was in Trainer's office and saw references to him. He's with the Ministry of War for Iraq. Swear you'll never tell anybody I told you."

"I *knew* it! What about the other guy, Vanneman?"

"I don't know. Some sort of agent or broker. What's the matter? Is it so important?"

"I think Trainer is planning to sell Mannequin to Iraq to use against Iran. The thought of it in the hands of a nation at war makes me—it would be a thousand times worse than—well, I can't let it happen. I want no part of it."

"It's a gas? A poison gas?"

"I can't believe that old man Draegler knows what's going on. Has he been around lately?"

"He was in Hawaii for months, but he's back now. Supposed to start his weekly visits again pretty soon. I'd like to go to Hawaii. I've never been anywhere."

Gil said nothing. His chin was in his hand and he was lost in thought.

She stroked his hair. "You're like a pressure cooker! Why don't you tell me what's bothering you? Otherwise I'm afraid you're going to explode and ruin the walls and rugs. Talk to me. *Then* I'll give you a massage."

He lay on his back again and rested a fist on his forehead. He talked. He described how the baby macaque had died earlier in the day. He told her about Mannequin and the extraordinary precautions that had to be taken when working with it. He told her about his one and only visit to Building F, usually called "the Aquarium," an unsettling experience that still invaded his dreams. The Aquarium was a maze of water-filled glass tanks bathed in a ghostly ultraviolet light where research was done on the toxins and venoms of the world's deadliest creatures. He saw the baleful stonefish, a rare stingray from the Gulf of Thailand, a gelatinous, almost totally transparent jellyfish found only in one section of Australia's Great Barrier Reef, a bewildering variety of poisonous water snakes, eels, and crustaceans. His guide to this grotto of horrors was Draegler's stooped, hairless director of research, Everett Ordman, who was especially respectful before a tank labeled *crescas furas.*

"The devil clam of Madagascar," Ordman said in hushed tones, "and the source of Mannequin. I don't think the Russians have any of these. For one thing they're found only along a short stretch of rocky beach that ships can't get close to, and for another thing you can't get the natives to dive for them."

Gil had to stare at the sandy bottom of the tank to spot one of the animals, which matched the color and texture of the sand and was hardly bigger than a flattened golf ball. "A lowly bivalve mollusk," Ordman said, "but what a wallop it packs! A tiny sac in its pseudopod carries a drop of a venom so deadly, it could paralyze a whale. It took me fifteen years to track down this little critter, which most marine biologists think is only a tribal myth. When I found him I was so excited I . . . well, I could hardly speak for days. Think of what I had discovered! Venom far more powerful than anything that can be synthesized in a laboratory!"

Mannequin is a closely related derivative, the old scientist explained. As potent as it is, it is only half as strong as the real thing. He also explained the cloning method, which was a slow and painstaking process similar to growing crystals in a chemical solution. Several grams of devil-clam venom at precisely the right temperature were enough to start the reaction. "You know chemistry," Ordman said earnestly, "maybe you can think of a faster way."

Gil never returned to Building F, and he avoided Ordman whenever he saw him around the plant. The scientist later did find a faster way to replicate the venom, and to produce it in the gaseous form called Mannequin, though Gil didn't know the details. His tour of the Aquarium had taken place within a month after his arrival at Draegler; now, eleven months later, the technology existed to manufacture it in commercial quantities. A row of ten five-hundred-gallon pressure vessels were waiting in Building M, and more were being assembled. Gil had never been told directly that the tanks were intended to hold Mannequin, but they were inappropriate for any of the company's other products.

He had in fact seen the tanks only when he had once wandered by mistake into Building M, which was off limits to him.

Sara listened quietly to Gil's revelations, which were delivered in a monotone. When his voice finally stopped she asked quietly if there were an antidote. There was no answer.

Gil's eyes were closed and his lips were tight. "Is there an antidote?" she asked again, touching his shoulder. "There must be something victims can do—"

Gil rolled over and threw an arm around her. "You told me you live with a blackjack dealer. Do you love him?"

The question made her laugh harshly. "I hate him. I only recently realized it."

"Why do you stay?"

"It's a long story. He did me a big favor once. Getting

to know you has let me see him for what he is. You are the kindest, gentlest man I've ever known, while he is . . . well, I don't want to talk about him."

"Where did you grow up, Sara? What did you do before you came to Draegler?"

"All of a sudden you want the story of my life."

"I'll tell you mine if you tell me yours. I want to be closer to you."

"My story is a stomach-turner and you don't want to hear it. Maybe when I know you better, say in ten or fifteen years. What time is it?"

She held her wristwatch in the bedside light. "Seven? Shit, I've got to get going. My old man is getting off work in an hour and I'm supposed to feed some friends of his. A rat-poison casserole might be nice."

Gil turned on the overhead and they began dressing.

"Sara, keep your eyes and ears open at work. If you find out that any of the gas is going to leave the plant, even a sample, tell me immediately. Will you?"

"Yes. For you I'll be a spy."

CHAPTER 7

It was a small house Sara returned to after leaving Gil, only one bedroom and a bath, and it had other inadequacies as well: creaking floorboards, ill-fitting windows and doors, and sagging steps leading to an overgrown backyard. There were advantages. One was the rent. It was hard to beat three hundred dollars a month, even if the "hot" water was only a few degrees above room temperature. Another was the location: just eight blocks from the center of "The Biggest Little City in the World." Jamal could walk to his job as a blackjack dealer at Harrah's. She hoped he wouldn't get fired again, because he was at his worst when unemployed, by turns listless and abusive. Emerging from days of sulking, he would rage against the cruelty of "godless capitalism," sometimes right after collecting his unemployment check. On several occasions that were still vivid in her mind he had lashed out at her—apparently for not sharing his anger—hitting her on the arms and shoulders with his fists.

Yet she stayed. She was grateful to him for taking her in when she was a teenage runaway headed for a life of drugs, thievery, and prostitution. It was Jamal who had shown her how to fake the résumé and references that got her the job with Draegler. The episodes of physical violence, which were rare, were always followed by tearful apologies and pleas for forgiveness. Jamal was frightening at times and overly emotional, but he was magnetic as well, and she had never quite found the nerve to leave him. Leaving wouldn't be a matter of simply walking out; it would take careful planning. To avoid revenge she had to save some money he didn't know about, make a clean escape while he was at work, and go somewhere he would never find her. There was no longer any doubt in her mind that she would leave, and soon, and she thought about methods of escape every day. His interest in Islam and Iran had grown into an obsession that scared her.

Standing at the sink, Sara cursed the ridiculous kitchen. Doing the dishes was a real chore; there was no place to stack anything, the tepid water turned cold almost immediately, and now the sink drain was clogged. There were twice as many dishes as usual, too, because Jamal had wanted to impress the guests, particularly the man called Mahmed. Jamal's friend Alek, a cheerful man she liked, wouldn't have required special treatment, but Mahmed seemed to have the same power over Jamal that Jamal had over her and Alek. It was disgraceful during dinner—a vegetarian curry—the way Jamal deferred to Mahmed, pressing food and wine on him, laughing at his unfunny remarks, and boasting about his commitment to the Islamic revolution. It was almost as if Jamal were afraid that a false step would prompt Mahmed to pull out a gun and shoot him in the head ... an act which, as she thought about it, the husky, quiet visitor could probably perform without a twinge of regret.

Most of the talk during the meal had centered around impractical schemes Jamal and Alek had for stealing millions of dollars from the casinos for the war against Iraq. One would describe his plan, the other would point out the flaws, Mahmed would attempt a synthesis. It was idle talk, a kind of game. Alek's ideas were relatively harmless and involved signals a dealer could give a confederate while playing blackjack. Jamal favored armed robberies. Mahmed liked explosions and threats of explosions. After an hour of plotting that would have gotten them beheaded in Iran, they lowered their voices and switched from English to Farsi. That's when Sara left the table and busied herself with the cleanup in the kitchen.

Some strange Moslems Jamal and Mahmed were. They didn't eat meat, but smoking, drinking, and planning crimes were perfectly all right. At least Alek wasn't a hypocrite; he didn't pretend to be religious. Her thoughts drifted to Gil Ellis. What a contrast to Jamal he was! Gil was like a Boy Scout who had never grown up. She smiled to herself when she thought of him asking for her life story. How the blood would have drained from his face had she given it to him! How his mouth would have dropped open! Born in Stockton, California, to the worst parents in the history of the world; molested by her drunken father at the age of twelve while her mother watched; a runaway at fifteen to escape her father's further attentions; a street hustler and shoplifter in San

Francisco at sweet sixteen. She never went back home, not even two years later when she read in the paper that her mother had been jailed for shooting and killing her father.

Sara had a gun that she had bought on the street during her years in the gutter—a six-shot, .25-caliber Baby Browning that fit neatly in the palm of her hand. Jamal knew she had it and insisted that she keep it in her purse at all times. He saw how men looked at her and wanted her to be able to repel anybody who might try to take what he viewed as his personal property.

How could she tell a straight-arrow, vanilla engineer like Gil Ellis the story of her life? The poor man's heart would stop.

"Sara," Jamal called from the dining room, "come here."

Yes, *sir!* Right away, *sir!*

The men were still sitting at the table, brandy glasses full and smoke heavy in the air. On the wall was a portrait of a glowering Ayatollah Khomeini that Jamal had bought the day before at a novelty shop. Sara sat down and wrinkled her nose. "Whew!" she said, waving her hand back and forth in front of her face. "What are you guys smoking, rags?" To Alek she said, "You brought the cigars, didn't you? Thanks a lot."

"They're Turkish," Alek said with a laugh. "They are what we smoked as children. Notice that we don't have cancer. Nobody from the Middle East does. The reason is that Turkish tobacco kills cancer." Alek's smile faded at a glance from Jamal.

"We have serious business to discuss," Jamal said. "Sara, Mahmed came all the way from Los Angeles to be with us and is planning to move here to be close to the situation we have uncovered."

"That I uncovered," Sara corrected. To the stranger she said, "Do you have a last name? Or is Mahmed it?"

He was a powerfully built man whose muscular shoulders and arms were too thick for his gray silk shirt. Probably a weight lifter. His eyes were dark and his expression was one of amused curiosity, his lips parted in a half-smile. At the impertinence of her question the smile widened. "It is of no consequence," he said.

Sara had disliked him the moment he arrived. Another arrogant sexist like Jamal, she could tell. During dinner he had gazed at her, smiling his little smile as if to say he was looking forward to having her for dessert.

Had Jamal told him that she had sold herself a time or two in the casino lounges? She would never forgive him if he had. She was grateful to Jamal for saving her life, but she had more than paid him back with five years of fidelity. Passing along information from Gil Ellis was the last favor she would ever do for him.

"My apologies, Mahmed," Jamal said solicitously. "She is an independent woman who sometimes speaks more directly than she should. She means no offense."

"Maybe I do," Sara said under her breath.

"It is quite all right," Mahmed said. "We are in her debt. She is the one who learned that Aref was coming to Nevada."

Yes, she had mentioned to Jamal that somebody named Ahmad Aref, also called Haranji, also called Kahlan, was coming to visit the Draegler plant. She had seen the names while doing some filing in Trainer's office, wondered why the man would use aliases, and asked Jamal if the names were Persian. Jamal's excited reaction to the news had been startling.

Jamal prompted her. "Tell Mahmed what you have learned."

"What have you told him I learned? Maybe you've already told him too much." She looked coldly at Mahmed, trying to tell him with her expression that not all the flattery and charm in the Arab world would make her give herself to him.

Jamal smiled at her with seeming indulgence. "There is no need to hold anything back from Mahmed. He has proven many times that he is one of the great heroes of the Jihad. I have told him of the great sacrifice you have made to get the information we need."

"It is indeed a great sacrifice," Mahmed agreed, exhaling a plume of blue smoke, "one of the greatest a woman can make. It is not something we would have asked of you if you had not been . . . experienced."

"He told you I was experienced, did he? He had no right to tell you that. I hope the sewers of Calcutta back up into his breakfast."

Mahmed ignored the remark as well as Alek's appreciative chuckle. "If we can't reward you properly for what you have done, and what you still must do, then Allah will, in his wisdom and in his way."

"I can hardly wait."

"Miss Schuler . . . Sara . . . let us remind ourselves what we are up against. A poisonous gas of some kind—Mannequin, you say it is called—is being manufactured by Draegler Chemical Corporation. It has military applications, otherwise it would not have attracted an army official from Iraq. His visit poses a threat to our people. Indeed, to all the people of the world."

Mahmed went on in a pompous way about "global ethics" and the duty of decent citizens everywhere to resist evil wherever it is found. Sara glanced at Jamal. The hard glint in his eye carried an unmistakable threat. Respond to Mahmed in the right way, he was telling her, give him what he wants, or later I will make you sorry.

"Colonel Aref," Mahmed said, his dark eyes on Sara, "is one of the most evil men in the world. He is the man who has twice used poison gas against our troops in the field, as reported in your own newspapers. He will do it again, especially when he sees that the defeat of the Hassad regime is imminent. With your help, we can keep a weapon of the devil out of the devil's hands. You must try to learn the plan for shipping. The switchboard gives you eyes and ears. You also have the eyes and ears of Gilbert Ellis."

Sara brightened at the mention of Gil's name. "I'll tell you one thing, he's on our side. He's dead set against the gas leaving the plant, and he won't let it happen. He doesn't need the help of any blackjack dealers, if you don't mind my saying so. I take it you aren't a blackjack dealer, Mr. Mahmed. What is your line, diplomacy? Social work?"

"It is of no consequence. I have certain skills."

"I'll bet you do."

"It is inspiring," Mahmed said in a sympathetic tone of voice, "to see the faith you have in the ability of Mr. Ellis to upset the plans of the United States government. You are surprised? You think the government would not know about a weapon of great potential being shipped to a foreign country?"

"Nobody from the United States government or from the army has visited the plant. I would know if they had."

Mahmed shrugged. "General Trainer has long been an advocate of a large nerve gas arsenal. As a deterrent to Russia, of course. He would love to see Mannequin tested in battle where only Persian lives are at risk. Your Mr. Ellis may only be up against a large corporation at the present, but the government will be involved eventually, of that you can be sure. If he tries to upset the plans, he may find out that the men he disagrees with are not what they seem."

Alek Mirkafai, sitting directly across from Sara, winked at her. Several times he rolled his eyes and shook his head as if to say, "These guys are crazy, aren't they? How did we get mixed up with such a bunch?"

Mahmed continued the questioning. "You have told us that the gas has a paralyzing effect. Can you get more details on exactly how it works?"

"I'll try."

Jamal asked if there were an antidote.

"I asked Ellis about that and didn't get an answer. I didn't press too much because I didn't want him to get suspicious. As for shipping plans, he dosn't know. That's what he wants me to find out. Trainer is the one who calls the shots. Ellis is pretty far down the ladder."

"Could you get to him?" Mahmed asked.

"Who, Trainer?"

Mahmed nodded and blew another plume of smoke. "I do believe you could seduce any man in the world if you put your mind to it."

Sara laughed out loud. "Oh, God, anybody but Trainer! I would die first! Kill me now!"

Mahmed leaned forward and spoke with great earnestness. "We must know more about protective devices and antidotes. Watch your chance. Report to Jamal every day."

"Yes. I'll watch my chance." She would watch her chance, all right, her chance to escape to a different life, maybe with Gilbert Ellis. While she planned for that, she would have to play along. A trickle of information would make them think she was doing her bit for the glory of Islam. Then someday, and, dear Lord, let it be soon, she would be where Persia was only a name in a reference book.

"A graduate of Juilliard! No wonder you can play Mozart so beautifully. You say the piano isn't your main instrument?"

"The clarinet. I spent years with a chamber group in Boston. Then I moved to Sparks." Karen laughed at how foolish that sounded.

It was ten o'clock and they were in Jim Eagan's car on their way back from the Spinnaker, a waterfront restaurant in Sausalito, to the houseboat. Karen was feeling happier than she had in a year and was wondering what she would do if Eagan invited her in for a cup of coffee.

"I was following my husband," she continued. "It's a cross women have carried for centuries."

"You must have loved the guy."

"I did once, and I still do in a way. He was hit by a terrible tragedy a while back and just can't seem to shake the effects. Hey, we promised not to talk about that stuff! I want to know more about you. You got sidetracked after telling me you graduated from Sacramento State."

"Well, I found out that most employers weren't all that excited about people with degrees in English, so I became a cop for Mountain Pacific Railroad, where I had been working during the summers. I got tired of throwing hobos off freight trains, so after a few years I became a dispatcher, first in Sparks, then in Oakland. Finally I was kicked upstairs into the Operations Division in San Francisco, where you found me. There was a marriage and divorce thrown in there somewhere, I think, but my mind has blocked them out."

They arrived at the parking lot. Jim parked in his numbered stall and cut the engine. He turned to Karen and said, "You are welcome to come in for a nightcap or a cup of coffee or a shower."

"Jim, it's been great, but I better stick to my guns and go back to my hotel. The dinner, the wine, the conversation, everything was absolutely wonderful . . . and the view of the city across the water! Really, the whole evening was magical, and I thank you very much."

"When will I see you again?"

"As soon as I can arrange for some more interviews. I'll call you."

"Next time you can stay on the houseboat."

"I'm afraid I'm too old-fashioned for that. You'll have to give me more time."

"I don't mean we'd be there together. You take the houseboat, I'll stay on the sailboat. It's weathertight now. All I have left to do is finish the interior."

"I can't believe you built a boat from scratch."

"No harder than cooking a Thanksgiving dinner. Just takes longer. In my case, two years. Next time you're here we'll take it out on the Bay. The houseboat, incidentally, has just now been taken off the rental market until you decide where you want to live."

They walked to Karen's car. She hesitated before getting in. In unison they told each other that they had enjoyed the evening very much, and in unison they laughed.

He kissed her hand and then, softly, her lips. It was a perfect end to a perfect evening and a promise of many more.

Driving back to the city across the Golden Gate Bridge, she opened the windows and let the cool wind caress her face and tug at her hair. She felt as though she were already sailing.

CHAPTER 8

It was noon on the day the world came to an end for Gilbert Ellis. The heat in Sentinel Canyon was too intense for a pleasant lunch outdoors, but outdoors was the only place Gil and Sara felt safe from listening devices. On the shady north side of the Draegler administration building were several picnic tables, always deserted in the summer months. Gil used his handkerchief on the benches to wipe away a layer of dust and pine needles before they sat down. In the distance heat shimmered above the asphalt surface of the road leading to the plant, and an approaching car seemed to dance and quiver like a drop of water on a skillet.

Gil popped open two cans of soda and handed one to Sara. "What's up?" he asked. "You have some news?"

"They're getting ready to ship Mannequin."

Gil rose half off the bench. "You've got to be kidding . . ."

"I was in Trainer's office taking dictation when he got a call. While he was walking around with the phone, I had a chance to peek inside a folder on his desk labeled PERM. I saw a bill of lading accepting delivery of three . . . well, I think it said three . . . 'rail-mounted gas containment vessels.' I was so afraid he would see me, I was shaking."

Gil got to his feet and walked in a small circle with one hand against the side of his head. "Would that bastard let the gas go without telling me? That's exactly what he said he wouldn't do. Did he think I'd be too chicken to do anything about it?"

"He was talking to somebody named Mike. He said they were going to make a night shipment and didn't want any static."

"Maybe Mike Panozzo, the sheriff."

Gil sat down, took a drink, and brought the can down hard on the table. "This is absolutely unbelievable! Are you sure you've got it right?"

"After I left the office I walked over to the east side. Three tank cars are parked by Building H. They must have come in early this morning. Three silver tank cars. Aluminum or stainless steel."

"Stainless steel if they're for Mannequin; it's about the only thing other than glass that can contain it. Have they set a date?"

"I heard him say 'in a couple of days,' but I don't know if he was talking about the shipment. What are you going to do? You look so upset!"

"I'll think of something." Gil's eyes were diverted by the approaching car. When it reached the airstrip he could see that it was a silver limousine; a small American flag on the CB antenna identified it as Jeremy Draegler's. The uniformed guard at the gate waved it through. The limo turned right, cruised slowly past the parking lot, and stopped at the front door of the main building.

Gil watched as Carlos walked around the car and opened the rear passenger door. Jeremy Draegler, a tall spindly man in a blue business suit and gray homburg, climbed out like a praying mantis emerging from a hole. His legs seemed too long even for a limousine, and in a characteristic gesture he shook each one in turn as if ridding them of kinks.

Draegler had a weekly routine when he was in Reno and not at his Hawaii estate: he visited the plant, chatted with the supervisors, dictated rambling letters to friends, made a walking tour of the offices, reminisced with anyone who would sit still for it, and generally disrupted production and trains of thought. While he was busy with that, Carlos was in Building B, the garage, washing, waxing, and vacuuming the limo for the ten thousandth time. The joke among the mechanics was that if the waxy buildup were ever removed, the vehicle would float away like a balloon.

Gil usually didn't mind Draegler's visits. The old man was fuzzy-minded and boring at times and would waste your whole day if you let him, but he was sweet-tempered and had a certain humor about him. He was spry and sharp for his age—he must have been close to eighty—and Gil hoped he would be in such good shape himself if he lived so long. Draegler seemed to enjoy everything and everybody.

"Oh, no," Gil groaned. "He sees us. He's coming this way."

The old man was grinning and walking briskly toward

them with his distinctively light-footed and slightly bow-legged gait, his shoulders rocking from side to side. In his dark suit and hat, he looked like an undertaker from the Old West, or death himself.

"What are you going to do?" Sara asked again. "You worry me!"

"I'm going to raise hell with Trainer, that's one thing. What ticks me off is that he must have decided months ago to ship the gas. It would take that long at least to get the cars made. How long has it been since I had the talk with him after the monkey died . . . two weeks? He said no shipment would be made without consulting me. If he thinks he can do it in secret, he's in for a big, fat surprise."

"Don't defy him! He can't be trusted; nobody can around here. If he's got his mind made up, he's not going to care what you think. He'll kill you if he has to. . . . I'm sure of it."

There were tears in Sara's eyes, Gil was surprised to see. Cool, hard-boiled Sara Schuler was crying!

Draegler was upon them. "Well, by golly, isn't this nice! Having a little picnic, are we! That's why I put these tables here, for people to use, and they don't. Maybe we should hire some waitresses in bunny suits! That would bring the boys out, eh? Hah!" His single-syllable laugh was like a bark.

Gil and Sara said nothing, not wanting to encourage him. Draegler didn't notice the grim cast to Gil's face or the way Sara's eyes were glistening with moisture.

"All of the tables should be filled," Draegler said with a wave of his hand, "with happy young people like yourselves enjoying their breaks here in the goddamned heat before going back inside and giving a good day's work for a good day's pay. I know, we don't have a pension plan like some outfits, but what kind of wages do they pay? My idea is to pay a little more and let the workers take care of their own retirements, just like I did.

Isn't that right?" He squinted at Gil. "What was your name?"

"Gilbert Ellis."

"People expect their employers or the government to take care of everything. Sara! What a pleasure to see you! You get more beautiful every day, and that's a fact!" He kissed her hand with exaggerated courtliness, then turned back to Gil. "This girl is the world's greatest secretary! She can type like nobody's business and is smart as a whip! Never misses a trick! Cuter than anybody else, too, male or female, dead or alive. You take good care of her, son, because she is a real gem. What was your name again?"

"Gilbert Ellis."

"I used to be able to walk around the plant and know every single person. Every one! Now I see mostly strangers. People don't stay put like they used to. Of course my memory isn't the steel trap it used to be. Sara! By gosh, you are a sight for sore eyes! I hope you've dropped that A-rab and hooked up with this nice young fellow. That A-rab is no good for you, bad news, I always thought. You can see it in his mouth. Now you take an engineer like what's-his-name here, he'll be a good provider. An engineer can always get a good job, and that's as true today as it was seventy years ago when I decided to go right into business instead of wasting time in college. Hoo-hee, it's hot out here! Too hot for a picnic! You'd think so, too, if you weren't so much in love. Unless you were wearing Bermuda shorts or some fool thing, and even then. Always wear a business suit myself because it hides my legs, which are not my most attractive feature, according to my wife. 'You're a fine man, Jeremy,' she says, 'but your legs are like two sticks of beef jerky.' Hah! Goodbye. I'm going inside and sit on the air conditioner, and you would, too, if you had any sense. A picnic on a day like this is for people in the loony bin."

He walked away with a gingerly step, as if the sidewalk was too hot for his shoes.

Gil looked at Sara. "This roommate of yours," he said slowly, "he's an Arab? What kind of an Arab? Is he a citizen?"

Fighting tears, Sara grimaced and shook her head helplessly. "I don't know. I want to get away from him. I want to be with you."

"Have you told him anything about the gas? Dammit, Sara—"

"Don't look at me like that! Yes, I've told him about the gas . . . I told him about it months ago, long before you and I got together. He's the one who knew Aref was from Iraq. I mentioned the name one night and he recognized it."

"You never told me any of this."

"There's a lot I haven't told you because I didn't want to spoil the happiness I feel when I'm with you. I want Jamal out of my life, I want to get away from this place and this whole business about Mannequin or PERM or whatever it is. Can't you and I go away somewhere? The two of us? Forever?" Her shoulders shook as the tears came.

"Sure, just run away and hope somebody else does the dirty work while we smell the daffodils. I've run away from a few things in my time, or tried to, and I'll bet you have too. Running away, in fact, is what brought me to this shithole of a chemical plant in the first place. Well, no more running."

"Don't fight Trainer, please! You don't know what you're up against! God, why do men always want to fight—"

"I'll tell you why I'm going to fight Trainer," Gil said, his lips and voice tight. "Because I don't want him to think he can get away with lying to me and pushing me around like a piece of furniture. Because if a trainload of

Mannequin leaves this plant and there is an accident, I don't want it on my conscience. There's enough on my conscience as it is."

"Do you have to risk your life? We could go somewhere safe and with phone calls and letters you could—"

"If I left, who could I count on to stop the train, your Arab blackjack dealer?" Gil laughed contemptuously.

"Yes! My Arab blackjack dealer! Is it so hard to stop a train? A six-year-old could do it."

"Not so nobody got hurt." Gil stood up. "I need some time to think. Then you and I are going to have to talk."

"Yes, tonight at the motel. I'll tell you everything—about me, about Jamal. I should have from the start." She rose and clutched his arm to keep him from leaving. "*Please* don't make up your mind about me until you hear the whole story. We're good for each other, Gil! We should be together! If we went away and started a new life, I would be everything you ever wanted in a woman. I could make you happy, you know I could! Give me the chance to prove it. . . ."

Gil looked at her, moved by her uncharacteristic display of emotion. "I haven't ruled anything out. We'll talk tonight. There are some things about me you should know too." He took her hands. "I've never seen you cry before, or anything close to it. Looking at you makes me feel like crying myself, which is something I think I've forgotten how to do. You know, old man Draegler is a dingbat, but he's right about one thing. You are beautiful. If there weren't so many windows on this side of the building, I'd kiss you." He handed her his handkerchief. "Here, fix your face. The company needs a receptionist who looks like she's in complete control."

"Until a few minutes ago," Sara said, managing a small smile as she wiped the corners of her eyes, "I thought I was."

* * *

There they were, all right, three stainless-steel tank cars, so bright in the sun that Gil had to shield his eyes. As he walked toward them between two buildings, he heard a voice behind him: "Sorry, sir, you can't enter this area." Over his shoulder he saw one of Trainer's guards, a big man in a blue uniform.

"Is that so?" Gil said, not slowing down. "Try and stop me." He stepped on the bottom rung of a ladder at the end of the middle car and clambered to the platform. Eight steps on a second ladder brought him to the top of the tank.

"Get down off that car," the guard shouted. "Now!"

"What are you going to do, shoot me?" Gil said, examining a row of hydraulic fittings. "I work here. Call your boss on your toy radio and tell him Mr. Ellis is checking the Mannequin cars." He screwed a heavy-threaded cap partway into a connector, then backed it out. "Tell him the caps have to be machined to finer tolerances if he doesn't want to kill half the people in Nevada."

"Look, buddy, I got my orders. Get off that car or I'm gonna climb up there and throw you off!"

"It's all right," another voice said. "Mr. Ellis is my guest."

Gil looked down and saw Everett Ordman, the scientist who presided over the Aquarium. He was in a white lab coat, and his fingers were linked casually behind his back. Because of his stooped posture, he had turned sideways and was peering up at Gil through the corners of his eyes.

"Well, you should've told me," the guard said, moving away.

Gil came down the ladder and jumped to the ground. "I see you've found a way to make Mannequin faster than a drop at a time."

"Oh, my, yes. We can turn it out like Gatorade now. Simple matter of altering the structure of the seed crystals with a proton stream. Increases the potency and the cling time too. If those clams could talk, I'm sure they'd ask for the formula." Ordman's eyes were big behind his glasses and his thin lips were curved in a smile.

"You're going to ship it in these tankers, is that it?"

"That's it. Beautiful, aren't they? They cost a million bucks apiece."

"A million bucks apiece! For that kind of money you'd think you'd get hose couplings that fit. Fill those tanks with Mannequin and what you'll have is a death train."

Ordman chuckled. "A death train! Colorful, if a trifle melodramatic. The tanks aren't fully outfitted yet, Mr. Ellis. The caps will be tightened and sealed. The tanks will be given pressure tests. Everything will be as safe as it can be. Do you like the way the tanks are divided into compartments? That way if there is a wreck, or if some drunken hunter fires a random shot, the leak will be minimized."

"What about at the other end? Untrained people trying to empty these tanks, have you thought about them? Faced with Mannequin for the first time? They'll be dead ducks."

Ordman shrugged. "They'll be their dead ducks, not our dead ducks."

"How can you be so callous? You don't think Arabs are people?"

"Arabs! Well, now! What makes you think Arabs are at the other end? Have you been poking around where you don't belong?"

"You've created a weapon of war and you don't care where it's going to be used?"

"I care. I want our side to have it instead of the other side. I'm a scientist hired to do a job, Mr. Ellis. I did it, and if Mannequin were anything but nerve gas I'd be up for a Nobel Prize . . . and I still might be because it has a lot of uses other than on the battlefield. I'm not a politician or an expert on national defense, and I daresay you aren't, either."

Ordman moved into the shade of a building to get his bald head out of the sun. Gil followed, shaking his hands in exasperation as he talked. "You can't brush off responsibility that easily. There are moral issues here that you can't just hand to other people. When it comes to life and death—"

"Who the hell are you to talk about moral issues? You, a married man, screwing around with a bar girl! Spare me the righteousness."

"What the hell are you talking about?"

Ordman rolled his eyes tiredly. "I saw you at the picnic table this noon with Sara, as she calls herself now. My office window is on that side. She was crying and you were holding her hands. When a man and a woman think they are alone and the woman cries, they've been getting in each other's pants. I call it Ordman's Law. It applies 97.7 percent of the time, according to my rough calculations. But with a slut? Really, Mr. Ellis, I'm surprised at you—"

Gil lunged at Ordman, then managed to check himself.

Ordman backed up a step and raised an arm in self-defense. "Okay, okay," he said, "so she's a *former* slut, if such a thing is possible. Good grief, you are such an old-fashioned square it's hard to comprehend! Don't look so outraged! I screwed her myself ten years ago, though I'm sure she doesn't remember it, she was so strung out on dope all the time. It's the truth! She was notorious! Mary Ryan was her name in those days. I used to go downtown a lot and watch the lounge shows. She was always there. She'd get so hard up for a fix she'd do anything."

"You're lying! If that was true, you'd have her fired."

"Why would I do that? I like having leverage on people. I may want her services again sometime."

"Bastard," Gil said, turning and walking quickly away, "dirty, lousy bastard . . ."

"Who do you mean," Ordman called after him. "Me or her? Or you?"

CHAPTER 9

Gil pushed through the double doors and walked across the lobby to the receptionist's desk, his heels clicking on the tile floor. Sara's smile faded when she saw the dark look on his face.

"What's the matter?" she asked in a voice full of apprehension.

"Quite a con game you've been pulling on me. I feel like an idiot. At least now a few things are starting to make sense."

"What on earth—"

"First I find out you lied to me, you held things back from me, you blabbed to your roommate, now I find out you used to be a prostitute, or close to it."

"What? Who have you been talking to?" In a sudden panic, she checked to make sure all intercom circuits were off.

"Everett Ordman, one of your old johns. Isn't that the correct term?"

"Who? I never—"

"He said you wouldn't remember because you were always strung out on dope. Is that true, Sara? Or should I call you Mary? Mary Ryan, that's a nice innocent-sounding name. You're right, you can't trust anybody around here."

She stared at him speechlessly, her face white.

Gil turned away from her, shaking his head and looking at the ceiling. "My God, I've been played for a complete sucker. No wonder you wouldn't tell me about your life."

"I'm ashamed of it, ashamed of what I was! It was ten years ago, Gil! What difference does it make now?"

"The guy you live with," he said, facing her. "What's the deal with him? Is he your pimp or some damned thing?"

"For God's sakes! Just the opposite! He helped me go straight, he helped me kick drugs, he probably saved my life. I'll tell you everything tonight. Give me a chance to—"

Gil struck the desk with his fist. "You'll tell me *now!* What country is this Jamal character from? How much have you told him about Mannequin?"

"He's from Iran," Sara said in a rushed whisper, "he has relatives there, and he has even more reason to keep nerve gas from that part of the world than you do. Yes, I've told him what I know about Mannequin, and yes, I've lied to you. I have reasons and I was going to give them to you after work. The important thing now is that I want to get away from him. I want to be with you, Gil! I've told you a dozen times that I—"

"He put you up to it, didn't he? Told you to screw my brains out and get me to talk. You didn't care about the problems I was having in my own life, you just wanted to get some information."

"That's not true! I wanted information, yes, but not if it meant—when I got to know you I realized that I—"

"All the questions you had about the gas, and still I didn't get suspicious. You were obviously after something." He shook his fists in anger and frustration. "How could I have been so *stupid*?"

"Yes! I was after something! You! I love you! I've never said that to anybody in my life. I want *you,* not Jamal and not anybody else. Every terrible thing you might have heard about me in the old days is probably true, but so what? I would walk out of here right now if you asked me and go with you to anyplace in the world and spend the rest of my life with you. That's what I want more than anything else."

"Easy talk."

"Try me!"

Gil looked at her coldly. "You know what? Because of me, a lot of people got messed up in Boston—yes, I have secrets too—I botched my career, I drove away the best wife a man could possibly have, and now both my boss and you have treated me like a jerk. You know what I have half a notion to do? Kill myself."

"Don't talk like that! If anybody should think about suicide, it's me. You're the best thing that's ever come into my life. If I lose you over what I did ten years ago or because of what Jamal made me do now, if you won't even give me a chance to explain myself and prove what you mean to me, then I really will have nothing to live for." She struggled to hold back the tears. "God," she whispered, "crying twice in one day . . . that's a new record."

Gil took a deep breath. When he spoke again some of the anger had gone out of his voice. "Okay, come to my place after work. You've got a lot of explaining to do. Sara, I hope to Christ I'm wrong and that not everything we had going is a fraud and a joke. Whatever you say, the fact is, you used me and tricked me, and it's not going to be easy for me to get over it. Is Trainer in his office?"

Sara found a handkerchief in her purse and wiped her eyes. "I think so. Why?"

"I'm going to tell him that if he thinks he's going to ship Mannequin, he better think again."

"You should wait until you calm down. Threaten to make trouble, he'll get rid of you. Believe me, I know him." She blew her nose.

"He'd be doing me a favor if he canned me."

"I don't mean that. I mean he'll get rid of you literally."

"Kill me, you mean? Trainer may not be a nice guy, but I hardly think he's a murderer."

"He doesn't pull the trigger himself, no. Generals have soldiers to do that."

Gil dismissed her fears with a shake of his head and walked away. "You spent too much time at the bottom of the pit. Engineers and scientists don't murder each other."

"Don't trust the man," she called after him as he opened the door to the main corridor. "I know what I'm talking about. . . ."

"I doubt if I'll ever trust anybody again," Gil said, the door closing on his words.

Clement W. Trainer, General, U.S. Army (Ret.), sat at his massive desk like the driver of a tank. He was irritated by the interruption. "What the Sam Hill is the matter, Ellis?" he said, his jowls turning pink. "You don't just barge into my office like it's the men's room. We have protocol around here. March back to Corporal Percy's desk and make an appointment for tomorrow. I'm swamped right now."

Gil sat down across from Trainer and said, "I've seen the tank cars. The tank cars for Mannequin."

"You've seen the tank cars for Mannequin. Wonderful. I'll tell your optometrist there's nothing wrong with your eyes. Too bad I can't say the same for your brain."

The sun was in the windows again and Gil couldn't

look at Trainer without squinting. This time, however, he refused to let himself be intimidated. He strode to the venetian blinds and snapped them shut. Returning to his chair, he said, "Is it part of army management philosophy to make visitors stare into bright lights?"

"What's gotten into you? If this was the Army you'd already be in the stockade for insubordination."

"But this isn't the Army. It's a chemical company in what you probably call the private sector. Percy isn't a corporal, he's a civilian."

"Well, he used to be a corporal. It was the high point of his career. So you saw the tank cars. That's what you came here to tell me? Thanks for the news report and good-bye."

"You told me I'd be consulted before Mannequin was shipped."

"Hold your horses. I said your views would be considered. They were. At the last management meeting I said, 'Gentlemen, young Ellis thinks we shouldn't ship the gas,' and all my technical advisors said, 'Screw him! Why should we listen to that nervous Nellie?' It was a unanimous vote." He jabbed a forefinger at Gil and added, "Let's get something straight. Your title in this outfit is Assistant Chemical Engineer, Research Department. The kind of job a kid out of college would get. Hardly a policy-making post."

Gil pressed his knees against the desk to stop them from trembling. "Before I came here my title was Chief Plant Engineer and the company was bigger than this one. I'm used to being part of the planning team. In the beginning you used to ask my opinion. It's only lately that you haven't invited me to the management meetings."

"Right, because there is no telling what you might say. You are still so traumatized by Boston, you can't think straight."

"In the meetings, I gather, you want only people who share your views."

"Wrong. I want people whose judgment hasn't been muddled by something that happened to them personally."

Gil put his arms on the desk and leaned forward. "When a group of people is trying to develop a product or solve a technical problem, the best atmosphere is one of openness and trust. I never heard of anybody trying to do it with deception and misdirection and hidden agendas."

Trainer laughed out loud. "You never heard of the Manhattan Project? You think everybody at Los Alamos was kept fully informed of what was going on? Don't be a fool."

"There was a war on then."

"You think there isn't now?"

Gil composed himself before beginning again. "You had your mind made up six months ago about shipping Mannequin. It would have taken that long to design and build the cars."

"Prudence and foresight on my part. Wait until every little part of a puzzle is finished before starting the next one and it'll take forever. You'd understand that if you had more experience with the big picture. I started the tank cars down the pipeline a year ago, I'm proud to say, so they would be ready when we needed them."

"Needed them, for example, to ship nerve gas to a nation at war in violation of United States policy, not to mention any number of signed treaties and agreements." Gil's voice was wavering slightly when he added, "I can't be a party to that. I'm not going to let that happen."

Trainer pursed his lips and nodded slowly. "I see. You want to be a whistle-blower, the guy who throws the monkey wrench into the machinery. You know, I don't see the whistle-blower as the hero you apparently do. He usually has a very limited understanding of the reason for things. He usually has some sort of personality problem that stops him from going through channels. So he attracts attention to himself by going public. Most of the time the only thing accomplished is that he makes some money for a year or so lecturing to women's clubs."

"I'd go through channels if I could. The only channel open at Draegler is you, and you won't listen."

"I'm listening. I'm listening to a man whose career is already on thin ice talking about bad-mouthing his employer even though he doesn't have all the facts. You're a career man, Ellis. Running to the press, if that's what you're thinking of doing, just because you don't like me personally won't get you ahead. Whistle-blowers don't do well later in life, ever notice? Nobody will hire them. Besides, I can't let you do it."

"Can't *let* me?"

Trainer crossed his arms and leaned back in his swivel chair, studying the younger man. "I'm going to ask you a question and I want you to think about the answer for a few days before doing anything. Suppose you are in command of an army that is defending your country. Suppose it is vital to find out where the enemy lines are, and the only way to do it is to send a patrol forward until they draw fire. Somebody in the patrol might get killed, you know that in advance. Wouldn't you give the order? Sacrifice one man, say, to safeguard ten thousand? To save your country?"

Gil stared back without moving a muscle. Was Trainer saying that he would be justified in having Gil killed unless he kept his mouth shut? In the interest of national security as the general saw it? Gil saw no other interpretation, and it made his skin tingle. This was more than a contest of wills or a dispute over a technical point to be settled by argument and facts. He was dealing with a man who was so certain of the rightness of his cause that he would let nothing stop him. Gil decided to reply in a way that didn't show he had caught the threat. "Even if we were in a war defending the country, the decisions wouldn't be that clear cut or simplistic."

"Spoken like a man who has never commanded in battle. I want you to think about it, then we'll talk again. How about Thursday? Come back Thursday at, say, ten in the morning. Maybe your Code Ten clearance will have been approved by then and I can tell you some things that will change your mind."

Don't trust the man, Sara had said. Gil didn't need the warning. Trainer was buying time, he felt sure, trying to disarm him while he decided what action to take against him.

"All I want," Gil said in a parallel effort, "is a chance to give my side of the story to the rest of the staff. If they can counter my arguments about how hazardous the gas is and why there is still no way to ship it safely, I'll be satisfied. You have a way of bulldozing your opposition, General. You owe it to yourself to let your views be tested in open debate to make sure you're right."

"Good point. I guess I am a little overbearing at times. Probably a sign of deep-down insecurity or bad toilet training or something. What's the old saying? 'Uneasy lies the head that wears the crown.' " He stood up and extended his hand. "It's a deal then. You sit tight and I'll set up a meeting of the Mannequin team so you can have your say."

They shook hands. Gil apologized for barging in unannounced, and Trainer apologized for snapping at him. There were strained smiles and a lack of enthusiasm on both sides.

Gil's reception in Draegler's office, by contrast, couldn't have been more cordial. "Well, well, well," the old man said, putting aside a newspaper and uncoiling from a chair, "look who's here! Sal Willis! Mel Trellis!"

"Gil Ellis."

"Will Ellis! Of course! Sit down, sit down! God, pardon my memory. They say your legs are first to go, then your wind, and then a certain sexual organ celebrated in song and myth. With me it was names. The day I hit seventy-five and imposed compulsory retirement on myself, all the names in my memory bank went right out the window like a handful of spaghetti. Confetti! What did I say, spaghetti? My God, see what I mean? The other day I called my wife Spot, which is the name of a dog I had when I was in diapers. I pretended it was a joke that she just happened not to find funny. She prefers to be called Her Royal Highness. Care for a drink?"

"No thanks. Ever thought of coming back full-time and running the company again, Mr. Draegler? It would keep you young, and the company needs you."

"No thanks is right! I'm busy enough as it is. Most of my time is sucked up by traveling to the house in Hawaii and then traveling to the house here. Can't recall offhand whether I've ever spent any time *in* either place. Hah!"

The barklike laugh startled Gil even though he'd heard it a thousand times. "Well, I wish you were in charge instead of . . . other people."

"I built this business up from a lemonade stand in downtown Reno where Harrah's is today and I'm tired of it. I don't want to get involved in running it again. Fertilizer, pesticides, insecticides, and prepackaged mulch! Can't imagine how I buried myself in such stuff for so many years. Neither can Spot."

"Then you don't keep tabs anymore on the details?"

"Hell, no! Draegler Chemical is just a place I come to for the free typing and phone calls. I look at the P and L statement and if the P is bigger than the L, why then I smile like a wedge cut out of a melon."

"Mr. Draegler, I've been wondering just how much you know about what is going on here at the plant. General

Trainer has a management technique that is, well, not the best, if you don't mind my saying so, and I think he's taking the company down a very dangerous road."

The old man seemed not to hear Gil's words. "Trainer is a crackerjack, isn't he? When I was still in charge we were sinking deeper and deeper into the red. He turned that around right now! Hiring him was the best thing I ever did. The company was going under, I do believe. Retirement is sweet when you know that back at the plant there is a firm hand on the tiller."

"Yes, but where is the firm hand steering the ship? You built your reputation on providing products that help farmers grow food. Your name is one of the best known and most respected in the field. I've never read or heard any criticism of you or the company. Your life has been one long positive contribution."

"Thank you, son, I appreciate that. I'm sure the same can be said for you and your lady. Sara. Now why can I remember her name? I guess because she was the best secretary I ever had. I would have retired sooner if it weren't for her. I liked looking at her, so I stayed on. Jesus Christ, what a body! She was slimmer in the old days. I chased her around the desk a time or two, I'll tell you, until my legs gave out, and then my wind. Never caught her, though! Not only is she a terrific typist, she's quick on her feet! Hah!"

Gil waited patiently for Draegler to finish. "Has General Trainer been keeping you posted on Mannequin?"

"Mannequin? Oh, you mean Mannequin. The fumigant. Can't say that he has. Freedom from detail, that's the secret of happiness. What about it? Is there something I should know?"

"It is a very dangerous gas."

Draegler waved his hand. "I know that."

"There is still a lot we don't know about it."

"I know that."

"It has a way of eating through containers and valve seals, especially under vibration. Vibration also seems to make it more potent. We don't know why."

"I didn't know that."

"In other words, it can't be transported safely."

"Does Trainer know that?"

"He should; I've told him. He pays no attention to what I say. I'm just a junior member of the staff—I guess he figures I don't know what I'm talking about. Maybe other engineers are telling him something else. At any rate, he's going to ship the gas in three tank cars."

"No! To where?"

"I'm not sure, but I think Iraq."

"Iraq? You mean Iraq, the country?"

"A country at war. It has used poison gas in the past against Iran, according to some reports."

"Iran, now there is a great country, eh? Bunch of religious fanatics. When they looted our embassy and grabbed all those hostages, I was so mad I was pissing sulfuric acid."

"That was terrible, yes, but for Draegler to provide nerve gas to Iraq would be too. You didn't know about this?"

"No! Nobody tells me anything. I'm just a figurehead. Don't ever become a figurehead, Trellis. It's hell."

"Ellis. Mr. Draegler, I can't imagine that you would approve of what General Trainer is doing. A lot more research is needed before we can even think about shipping Mannequin, and shipping it to a country at war is, well, illegal for one thing, and immoral for another. I came to see you hoping that once you knew the facts you would take some action."

"What kind of action? I'm seventy-seven years old, for God sakes."

"You still own the company. Cancel the shipment.

Demand more research. Tell General Trainer to keep the company out of chemical warfare."

"Upset his whole program? Trainer is a top man! He is very well thought of at the Pentagon."

"Maybe he's taking orders from the Pentagon rather than you. It could be that the Pentagon wants Mannequin tested under battlefield conditions without taking the responsibility. They are more or less looking the other way and letting a private company do it. If it goes wrong, they'll deny everything and Draegler Chemical will take the blame. The name you built up will be ruined."

"Some theory! What if I don't believe you? What if I want to stay retired?"

"Then I'll stop Trainer myself. Or at least force his scheme into the open where it can be debated. All it would take is a few phone calls."

"You would do that? Defy Trainer? Get fired?"

Gil answered quickly and with obvious conviction. "Yes."

"You think the Pentagon is a bunch of bad guys, don't you, Ellis?"

Gil looked at the old man with surprise. The question, the tone of voice, the accurate use of his name, all seemed out of character. Even the expression on his face had changed. Where a moment before Gil had seen befuddlement there was now an air of calculation that was unnerving.

"No," he answered warily. "Good guys and bad guys, just like other large groups of people. It could be that the bad guys have General Trainer's ear."

"The Russians have a tremendous stock of chemical weapons. Don't you think it makes sense for us to keep one step ahead? If the government is crippled by ridiculous treaties and public opinion, don't you think a private company should help out if it can? Sometimes rules have to be bent when a democracy is facing a dictatorship."

Gil stopped breathing and stared at Draegler without speaking. He put his hand on the arms of the chair and uncrossed his legs.

Draegler picked up his phone and pressed a button. "Clem? Guess who's in my office? Gil Ellis. God, he's just as bad as you said he was. Hopeless case, in my opinion. Like talking to Eleanor Roosevelt, whom I once had the horrible experience of sitting next to as a punishment for voting for FDR. What do you want to do? Yes. Yes. I guess you're right. Pity. Okay. Right." He hung up and looked up at Gil, who had risen to his feet.

"Mr. Ellis, I want you go to your office and stay there till I call for you. The general and I want to have a little talk about what should be done in your case. The problem, you see, is that we can't let our work be disrupted. It is far too important. We have several options. We can put you under some sort of house arrest until the shipment is completed, we can tell you the whole story in the hope that you can be brought around to our point of view, or we can simply let you do or say whatever you want while we deny everything and make unkind statements about your mental health, referring reporters to your psychiatrist." He paused thoughtfully. "Maybe we should offer you a certain sum of money in exchange for a pledge of silence."

Gil wet his lips and wondered how much danger he was in. "How much is my silence worth?"

"Mr. Ellis, you seem to be edging toward the door. Were you thinking of making a run for it? That would be juvenile. You realize, of course, that I could have a couple of guards escort you to your office and make sure you stay there, but we are civilized men and surely don't have to resort to anything that heavy-handed. We have a disagreement and we'll work it out in a civilized way. I'm going to trust you to wait in your office until I call you. Agreed?"

Gil had no option. He nodded. As he turned to leave he said in a soft whisper, "You are a bigger snake in the grass than Trainer."

Draegler bowed and tipped an imaginary hat. His legs and wind may have failed, but not his hearing. "The snake," he said, "is an unfairly maligned creature. It does a lot of good in ridding the world of pests."

CHAPTER 10

Gil closed his office door behind him, walked to his desk, and sat down heavily in his chair. The confrontations with Ordman, Sara, Trainer, and Draegler had been exhausting. He leaned forward and lowered his head onto his arms.

He went over the last two conversations in his mind, trying to remember everything that was said. First he put the most innocent interpretation on every exchange, then the most sinister. It was no contest; there was no way to explain away the threats Trainer and Draegler had made. At best he was going to lose his job and probably his future as a chemical engineer, so there was no point in worrying any more about that. Both Sara and Karen would applaud. At worst he was going to be killed to preserve the secrecy of the Mannequin project. Would Trainer and Draegler really go to such an extreme? It was hard to accept, despite the things they had said . . . and the things they had concealed. How could they expect to get away with it? One thing they could do would be to put him on a military plane and send him to a remote overseas base where he would be safely out of the way for a while . . . and where an "accident" could more easily be arranged. Maybe they would simply give him mind-altering drugs and assign him to a psycho ward where his babblings wouldn't be taken seriously. But if those were rational fears, he should simply pick up the phone and call the police. He should have told Trainer he had written a report on Mannequin and his suspicions about the plans for it—no, then they might have tortured him to find out where it was hidden. He lifted his head and rubbed his face with his hands. Was his mind playing tricks on him? Had he lost the ability to see things clearly? The room was quiet. It was a pleasant Nevada afternoon. Perhaps the only signs of danger were in his head.

Better assume the worst. Sometimes paranoids *are* stalked by stranglers. He certainly didn't intend to sit passively while his fate was decided by people whose priorities were radically different from his own. He could imagine situations where he might be tempted to sacrifice his life for his country, but this wasn't one of them. There was, after all, a simple way he could protect himself against any wild plots Trainer might be hatching, and that was to tell others about his fears. Trainer wouldn't dare touch him then.

He put his hand on the phone, then hesitated. The police were a question mark—if the gas shipment had Pentagon or CIA approval, the police might be in on it. He could try calling a newspaper or a radio station, but would they believe such a complicated story over the phone? Even if he got past the switchboard operator he might be dismissed as a nut. Better go in person armed with a written report so they could follow his argument and get the facts straight. Still, it might be worth a try to call the Las Vegas *Sun*, a paper that had battled Howard Hughes and the Atomic Energy Commission and might be interested in another crusade.

Sara came to mind. Another question mark. She seemed more interested in escaping the mess than cleaning it up. He wasn't sure whose goals she would serve—his, hers, or the Arab she was living with. Karen. What about Karen? He hated getting her involved, but she was his best hope. She could be trusted to think clearly and do the right thing.

He glanced at his watch. Four o'clock. She was going to San Francisco again, she had told him, but not until after giving a three-thirty clarinet lesson. She might be at her studio or at home. He would start with her. He picked up the receiver and waited for a dial tone. Silence. He hung up and tried again. The phone was dead. There was another phone on a worktable on the other side of the room; it was also dead.

Gooseflesh touched the back of his neck like a cold breeze, and he became aware of a jump in his heartbeat. Had Draegler assumed that Gil wouldn't keep quiet and cut off his phones just in case? Was it rational to assume that a dead phone was ominous? He dropped to the floor and checked the wiring, wondering if perhaps he had kicked something loose; no, the phone jacks were solid. His mouth went so dry, it was hard to swallow, and a paper cup full of water from the cooler didn't help. He needed something considerably stronger than water. The leather flask of scotch was in his desk. There was barely a stiff shot left, and it went down his throat in a single, burning gulp.

He jumped when the buzzer sounded on his intercom. It was Sara, calling from the receptionist's desk in the lobby.

"What's wrong with the phones?" he asked her. "Are they all dead?"

"Trainer has cut the whole plant off. No calls can go in or out. What did you say to him? He's put the security force on alert and two guards are on their way to your office . . . they just went through the lobby with their radios squawking."

Gil cursed and felt his throat tightening.

Sara hurried on in a tense whisper: "Can you see your car from the window? They've put a guard there. Can you hide? I'll call the cops when I get a chance."

Gil whirled in his swivel chair and lifted the blinds. A uniformed guard in the parking lot was leaning against his Mazda and lighting a cigarette. To the right the chain-link main gate had been rolled shut—usually late in the afternoon it was left open for workers leaving the plant at the end of the day shift.

"Thanks for the warning, Sara. Listen, I'm going to try to get out of here. If I don't make it, well, then I guess it's up to you and your Arab to stop the train. Wish me luck. . . ."

He unlocked the lower right drawer of his desk and removed a small steel box. Two keys were needed to open it—one on his key chain, another in his desk. Inside the cotton-lined box was a rack holding three test tubes. Two were empty. He removed the middle one carefully and held it up. It was the color of the sky, an even, clear blue from the bottom to the top. The stopper was sealed in wax. Taped to the side was a typewritten label: "Danger! PERM—0.1 solution."

He laid the glass vial down and hurried to the water cooler, wrestling the inverted glass jug off its moorings. Water splashed energetically onto the carpet. He directed the lurching stream to the floor around his swivel chair, then replaced the jug on its stand. His shoes, socks, and trousers below the knee were soaking wet when he sat down again. There was a small bottle of oxygen in another desk drawer; he removed it and pulled out the safety pin. Footsteps were approaching in the hallway. Time for one more thing: he adjusted the blinds behind his desk to let the maximum amount of sunshine in . . .

might as well use Trainer's technique against him. The footsteps stopped outside the door. Two men exchanged brief words punctuated with the static of a two-way radio.

As the knob turned Gil hurled the test tube as hard as he could against the wall next to the door. It shattered on impact with the pop of a light bulb, and there was a tinkle of breaking glass as the slivers rained to the floor. Instantly the wall was tinged with a faint, translucent patina of pale blue.

Two uniformed guards stepped into the office. They glanced about before advancing, one staying several steps behind the other. Both were wearing holstered sidearms. Gil recognized the first one, an overweight, surly man named Brisson with whom he had several times tried to exchange pleasantries. Brisson looked quickly around the room, his eyes narrowing at the wet carpet that surrounded the desk. "Don't make a move, Mr. Ellis," he said, raising his hand.

Gil, his face white, opened his mouth to speak, but no words came. He cleared his throat and started again. "Do you normally walk into offices without knocking?" To explain the wet carpet he said, "I was changing the water jug and spilled half of it. What can I do for you?" The blue tint was spreading across the dry areas of the carpet behind them. It accumulated around their shoes, where it seemed to pause to gather strength before advancing up their legs. It reached their knees before weakening and sinking.

"Sorry," Brisson said, frowning slightly at the brightness of the window, "we're just following orders. I'm Sergeant Joe Brisson. We'll have to ask you to come with us."

"Go with you, Sergeant? Why? Is something wrong?"

The guard grimaced and moved his shoulders from side to side. "Just come with us. Orders from General . . . from General Trainer." He was having difficulty speaking. His companion was lifting one foot and then the other as if he had stepped in gum. The sun was so bright, neither of them could see the blue film on their shoes, their ankles, and the cuffs of their trousers. The layer of Mannequin was so diaphanous that to anyone not knowing what to look for it was invisible.

"Jesus, Eddie," Brisson said, stretching his arms and twisting his head from side to side, "I feel . . . I don't know, I . . . Are you . . ." He tried to look behind him but his neck had stiffened. Had he succeeded he would have seen his companion rooted to the floor, his hand on his gun, his face frozen and contorted. Brisson turned his eyes back to Gil, who sat motionlessly watching them. "What's happening to me?" he managed to say, forcing the words through clenched teeth. "What did you . . . shit, I . . . help me! Help me!" The last requests were uttered in a small and dwindling voice. A moment later the two guards were rigid, standing with their arms and heads at awkward angles like caricatures of cops in a wax museum.

"Just a small dose," Gil said quietly. "You'll be all right in a couple of hours." He hoisted the glass jug again and let water cascade on the rug as he walked to the door. He kicked it closed and locked it. Returning, he splashed the remaining water on the shoes of the guard closest to the door. Eddie was about Gil's size and his uniform would fit well enough. Gil worked swiftly, trying not to touch the guard's shoes, socks, or slacks, which had been contaminated with Mannequin. The blue film on the floor had broken up and retreated to the wall. Thirty seconds later the only traces of it anywhere in the room were concentrated around the broken test tube, where Gil could make out a blue halo.

Brisson's radio crackled. "Can you hear me, Joe? Come in, Joe." Gil lifted the radio from the guard's belt, careful not to knock him off balance. "This is Brisson," he said curtly, trying to imitate the voice. "We've got Ellis and will be down in a minute. No problem. Over."

"Take him to Building H," the radio voice said. "We'll meet you there. Over."

"Building H. Right. Over and out."

Gil turned the valve on the oxygen bottle and took several deep breaths as the cold stream played on his face.

Ninety seconds later, Gil, wearing Eddie's police coat, hat, black belt, and gun, was running down a service stairway at the east end of the administration building. With luck he could get out the back door and have to cross only a hundred feet of open space to Building B, the garage, where Draegler's limousine was parked.

Emerging at a run from the stairwell on the ground floor, Gil almost collided with a guard standing at the back door, a man he had seen several times in the company cafeteria.

"Hey, what's the hurry?" the guard said in alarm, catching Gil's arm to keep him from falling.

Gil took a step back. "Jeez, sorry! What building is this? I don't know my way around yet. . . ."

The guard looked at Gil as if wondering where he had seen him before. "This is A. Where are you supposed to be?"

"Building B."

"Are you night shift?"

"Yeah. Just started. Don't want to screw up. I'm already late." Gil kept an odd grin on his face as a disguise.

"Relax! You're too excited!" The guard pulled open the door and held it. "That's B right over there. Next building."

"Thanks," Gil said, pushing past him. "I just saw Sergeant Brisson. He and Eddie are taking Ellis down the front stairs."

The guard nodded and raised his radio. "Next time you see Joe," he called after Gil, who had broken into a trot, "tell him to get you a new cap. That one's about two sizes too small."

* * *

Coming from the bright sun into the gloom of the garage, Gil had to pause for a minute to let his eyes adjust. He was standing in an aisleway between bins of hoses and pipes that reached to the ceiling. On the far side of the hangarlike room two mechanics were talking at a workbench; as Gil watched they walked to opposite corners. One turned on a welding torch; the other raised the hood of a truck. Directly in front of him, no more than twenty-five feet away, was what he hoped to see: Carlos waxing the limousine. Because it didn't need waxing and because Carlos had all afternoon for the job, he was making small wiping motions in extreme slow motion, as if restoring an oil painting. He was in his shirt sleeves. His gray uniform jacket was draped over the back of a chair. The limo's radio was tuned to a Mexican popular music station and was turned up loud.

"Carlos!" Gil hissed in a loud whisper. "Carlos!"

Gil had to shout to be heard over an enthusiastic mariachi band. "Carlos! Over here!"

The chauffeur stopped polishing and peered into the shadows between the tiers of storage bins.

"C'mere! I want to show you something. . . ."

Carlos left his chamois on the roof of the limo and walked toward the guard he could see standing in the shadows, wiping his hands on a cloth. "What you want?"

"Look at this," Gil said, beckoning. "Have you ever seen anything like this?"

Carlos advanced, peering intently. When he got to within a few feet of Gil, he brightened. "Meester Ellis! What you doing in that hat and coat!" He smiled broadly, revealing more gold than ivory. "You look like Halloween!"

Gil reached for his arm and drew him deeper into the storage area. "I borrowed them from Eddie."

"Eddie loaned you his uniform?"

"Not exactly. I also borrowed this." The .38-caliber Smith & Wesson was in Gil's hand.

"Hey, don't point that thing! Jesus, man! Eet might be loaded!"

"It is loaded. Unless you do exactly what I say, I'll pull the trigger. Turn around and put your hands up."

"Thees a joke, eh? You try to be funny!"

Gil jabbed the gun in his face. "No joke. Turn around."

Carlos turned around. "What you want, Meester Ellis? My money? Santa Maria, I don't have much!"

"I have to borrow the limousine."

"You can't borrow the limousine! Boss man wants eet in ten meenutes! I have to—"

"I need it now. Please shut up." Gil reversed the gun in his hand. Holding it by the barrel, he hefted it a few times to get an idea of its weight, measuring it against Carlos's head. He had never tried to knock a man out and didn't know how much force to use. He didn't want to fracture his skull just to put him out of commission temporarily.

"Eet's my job, amigo! If the car isn't there when he wants it, he weel be peesed! He weel be totally peesed! We weel both be in very beeg trouble!"

"I'm sorry about this. I don't know what else to do." Gil raised the gun, but couldn't bring himself to strike.

"You are a nice man, Meester Ellis, I hate to see you make a beeg meestake! Can't I just give you a leeft somewhere?" The more alarmed he got, the heavier became his Mexican accent.

Gil took a deep breath and brought the gun down hard.

Not hard enough. Carlos clapped both hands to the top of his head and sank to his knees. "Sheet! Jesucristo!" His hand went inside his shirt and came out with a small silver revolver, but he was too dazed and in too much pain to lift it and aim. He toppled to his shoulder and dropped the gun, grimacing and returning both hands to his head.

Gil brought the butt of his gun down again, harder this time. The dull thud of metal striking bone almost made his stomach turn. Carlos went limp, and his mouth and eyes relaxed as if he were asleep. There was no time to find out if he was faking. "God, I'm sorry, Carlos. I hope you'll be all right."

Gil pocketed both guns and strolled to the limo as casually as he could, breathing like the winner of a footrace. The mechanics had noticed nothing. He took the chauffeur's jacket from the chair and tossed it onto the front seat of the limo, climbing in after it. The keys were in the ignition. He shut the door and sat still, waiting for his heart and breathing to quiet down a little. So far, so good, he thought, running the tip of his tongue around on his lips—it was the feel of cotton against cotton. There was probably a bar in the back seat. Maybe later he would have a minute to satisfy his thirst.

He shrugged off the policeman's jacket and hat and put on the chauffeur's. The fit was no better.

He turned the key. The engine awoke and purred quietly. Slowly, very slowly, he drove toward the garage door and glided into the sunshine of the Nevada desert.

He would have lived longer had the battery been dead.

CHAPTER 11

"Jessica!"

"Karen! Where are you calling from?"

"From my studio in Sparks. I had a three-thirty student cancel, so I'm leaving now for Sausalito. If I don't dawdle, I can get there before dark."

"Why Sausalito? Aren't you going to stay with us? When we had lunch two weeks ago you promised that next time you'd be our guest."

"That was before I met the most wonderful man in the world. I was down a week ago, too, for a couple of days and meant to call you, but I was so mesmerized by this guy, I couldn't stand to be away from him for even a minute."

"Oh, oh. This sounds serious. Have you seen a doctor?"

"I don't need a doctor, I need an anchor to keep me from floating away like a balloon. You'll see why when you meet him." Karen gave her friend the highlights of how she had met Jim, enhancing the story slightly to make it even more romantic than it already was.

"I'm worried," Jessica said. "You file for divorce and the next guy you meet knocks you over. Slow down, okay? Don't get carried away."

"We haven't exchanged body fluids, if that's what you're worried about. He's been a perfect gentleman and I've been a nun."

"He's gay, then. That's why he's not married."

"Not a chance. You should see the way he undresses me with his eyes. We even laugh about it. Tonight I think I'll let him do it with his hands. I think the tide will come in. Tonight a guy named Jim Eagan is going to get lucky and he doesn't even know it yet."

"And men think they run the world! Karen, listen, you've got to be careful. This is San Francisco and some things are going around. AIDS, for instance. God, I'm glad I'm not single."

"Jim was married for years and hasn't scored since, same as me. We're clean. Just to be safe, though, we're going to cover our entire bodies in latex. I stopped by the Army Ordnance Depot this afternoon and picked up some rubber sleeves they use to transport missiles. They slip over your head and shoulders and have a drawstring at the feet."

"That should do it. When can I meet Mr. Wonderful?"
"How about tomorrow for lunch? All four of us? I want to meet your husband too."
"That would be fun. I'll ask what's-his-name if he's free."
"Let's meet at that hideous black rock at noon."
"The banker's heart, we call it. Noon it is. See you then."
Karen ran to her car, certain that the next few days would be the happiest of her life. Her phone was ringing as she drove away.

"It's beautiful," Karen said, running her fingers along the hand-rubbed wooden railing as she descended the stairs. "Everything smells so new! I can't believe you built it all by yourself."
"From scratch," Jim Eagan said, holding the flashlight over her shoulder so she could see her footing. "Took most of my spare time for two years. All I started with was a set of plans and a pile of lumber."
"It's bigger than I thought! Seems too big for one person to sail, especially on the ocean."
"You're right. No problem when using the engine, but the sails are really too much to handle alone. When I started the project I still had a wife. We were going to sail it together to the Caribbean. After she left I kept working on it. Good therapy. Now I'm faced with the almost impossible task of talking you into going with me."
Karen laughed. "You made fun of me two weeks ago for leaving San Francisco for Nevada. You're preparing to leave for an empty ocean."
"For the adventure! I'm in a rut at work and need some excitement. Railroading used to be fun. Now it's so mechanized and routine it's mainly a matter of shuffling papers. Nothing ever happens. No more steam whistles wailing in the night and beckoning to small boys in farmhouse bedrooms."

"Were you one of those small boys?"

"Sure was. The whistle called me like the Pied Piper. I followed the call of the road and wound up as a cog in a faceless conglomerate. Besides, the ocean isn't empty. It's teeming with monsters, oceanographers, drunken yachtsmen, oil slicks, and kelp. A thrill a minute."

"Sail to the Caribbean . . . I don't think I have the nerve to do something that wild."

"Wild? Sailing is one of the most peaceful things imaginable."

"You just said it was a thrill a minute."

"Whatever. I'm trying to find the words that will get you to join me. Don't you crave a little adventure? Doesn't teaching the clarinet get a little dull? Somebody blows a few wrong notes and it's the highlight of the day."

"That's all the excitement I can stand at the moment. Getting a divorce, finding a job, getting to know you, that's enough."

"Well, you have a couple of more weeks to think about it, because it'll take me that long to do the finishing touches. For one thing, the electricity isn't hooked up yet."

Jim pumped a Coleman lantern, lit it, and hung it from the low ceiling. It was surprisingly bright, and Karen smiled at the way the shadows moved as the boat bobbed on the water. "Who wants electricity?" she said. "This is much more romantic."

"Got to have juice for my electronic keyboard. Can't take the spinet, and I don't want to make the trip without Bach and Mozart."

Earlier in the evening on the houseboat, Jim had demonstrated his skill on a sixty-key Casio keyboard. For a big man with thick fingers, he was surprisingly dexterous and musical. He didn't let a few mistakes interrupt the tempo, a skill she had a hard time teaching her young students. With more coaching and practice, she could tell, Jim would be quite a good accompanist. Next time she came to the Bay Area she would bring her clarinet—the Oakland Symphony and the San Francisco Ballet Orchestra had invited her to audition—and she would try some duets with him.

He proudly showed her some of the boat's more ingenious features. The galley, which at first sight seemed to lack counter space and an oven, was transformed by fold-down shelves. The oven was a microwave hidden under the sink. Under the stairs at the stern were two double bunks on each side and a row of horizontal windows above the water line.

"This is where you slept last time I was here," Karen said sympathetically, "while I luxuriated on the houseboat's king-size bed. Makes me feel guilty. Sorry I'm such a prude."

"It's not so bad. Watch . . ." From underneath one of the lower bunks Jim pulled a wooden frame that was fitted with a foam-rubber mattress and mounted on rollers. It was exactly as wide as the center aisle and locked into place between the two bunks like an extra leaf in a dining-room table. When it was in position he rearranged the sheets and blankets to make a comfortable-looking and inviting triple-width bed. "Voilà! The biggest, softest bed on the high seas. I'm lost and lonely in it." He took her by the shoulders and kissed her gently on the forehead. "It would be just right for two."

"Why, Mr. Eagan!" she said, pretending to be shocked. "Is this a proposition?" She looked up at him and fluttered her eyelashes.

"Just a news report."

Suddenly she was serious. "Jim, I . . . I want to thank you for not . . . for not pressuring me. The problem is that, well, I'm still technically married, and that makes me feel a little uncomfortable. I'm not used to the idea of going to bed with a new man." She shrugged helplessly. "I'm stuck with some old-fashioned values."

"Part of your charm. I can wait. When it happens I know it will be wonderful. When you love a person it's almost bound to be good."

"Oh, don't say you love me. You couldn't possibly know after so short a time."

"Let me rephrase that. I love you more than I've ever loved a woman after knowing her for only two weeks."

"That's better. I can accept that. But I know what you mean. It's amazing how close I feel to you. When I'm not with you all I can think of is the last time we were together . . . and the next time."

They kissed and clung to each other for long minutes.

"I can wait," Jim added in a whisper, "but it isn't getting any easier."

Karen sighed. "It isn't getting any easier for me, either."

They kissed again. Her lips parted and their tongues touched.

"Do you still make love with your husband?" Jim asked a moment later. "You talk about him with affection."

"No. It's been six months."

"Six months! Does that mean if we took off our clothes you would go out of control and attack me like a wild animal?"

Slowly her hands moved up the front of his shirt to his neck. She unbuttoned the top button. "Don't worry," she said softly, "I'll be gentle." She unbuttoned them all, from top to bottom, and when she was done she pulled the shirttails free and ran her hands around on the front of his body. "You have just the right amount of hair." She kissed his chest and pressed her cheek against it, holding him tightly. She looked up at his face and said, "In this light, with the lantern behind you, you look like Darth Vader."

"And you look like Princess Leia. Now it's my turn."

He threw his shirt aside and began undoing the buttons of her blouse. When it was off he kissed her bare shoulders and her throat, then moved his hands behind her and hunted for the clasp that would release her bra. As Karen tried unsuccessfully to suppress laughter, it gradually dawned on him that the clasp was in the front, between the cups. She raised her hand to help him, but he pushed them down. "I'll get it," he said, "just be patient. When you are unwrapping a gift you've waited all your life for, you don't want anybody helping you."

His fingers seemed too large to manipulate the tiny clips, but at last the bra was loose. Very slowly he drew the filigreed silk aside, breathing in pleasure when her ivory breasts were revealed to him. The nipples were already erect, and when he dropped to one knee and took them gently in his mouth, a shudder of pleasure ran through her body from head to toe. She laced her fingers through the hair on the back of his head and moved his mouth from one breast to the other, her eyes closed and her back arched.

They finished undressing each other in silence, and as each new place was unveiled they explored it lovingly with their fingertips and lips. Then they were on the bed with their arms around each other and their lips together and their legs intertwined. The thrust of penetration gave them both such a rush of pleasure that they gasped aloud. Holding each other close, they moved slowly, matching the rhythm of the waves.

"Oh, God, Jim, it feels so good . . . I knew it would. . . ."

He cradled her head in his hands and kissed her eyes and lips. "You're like a dream," he breathed, "and so beautiful, so incredibly beautiful."

"It's the dim light. You . . . you . . . you can't see. . . ."

The two glowing filaments of the lantern brightened and merged into a single ball of light at the moment of her ecstasy, then seemed to fade into distant pinpoints.

The glow of the lantern and the way it swayed with the creaking of the boat were the last things she remembered about the night, that and how safe she felt encircled by his arms.

She was asleep when Jim turned the lantern off and arranged the blankets over her. It was very quiet, and the only light was from an almost-full moon over San Francisco Bay.

It was also quiet deep in Sentinel Canyon. The moon had moved over the edge of the high rock rim and was casting more light than the saboteurs wanted. Total darkness would have made their operation safer, but they had to act when the tank cars were empty and unguarded. The next night might be too late; by then the tank cars might be filled with Mannequin and on their way across California. Alek helped Jamal and Mahmed climb the fence, then retreated to the canyon wall to act as a lookout.

"I don't like putting my life in his hands," Jamal whispered to Mahmed when they were alone and crouched in shadows. "He complains and worries like a woman."

"He knows if he betrays us, he is dead."

The two worked silently and quickly. Moving from one car to the next and reaching as far under the tanks as they could, they attached explosive packs to each compartment. Nestled against the support cradles, the packs would never be noticed.

There were fifteen in all, five for each car. Each one was no bigger than two decks of cards and consisted of a shaped charge of plastic, a battery, a detonator, and a radio receiver. The explosive, Mahmed had explained to an awed Jamal earlier, was called Semtex. It consisted of equal parts of RDX and PETN held together by a vegetable-oil binder and was covered by a tungsten-steel cone designed to direct the force in one direction. Because of the focusing effect of the conical shape, only two ounces of plastic were needed to punch a silver-dollar-sized hole through half-inch steel. Attaching the packs was simply a matter of peeling off a protective strip and pressing a patch of pressure-sensitive glue to the side of the tankers. After five seconds the glue was set so solidly that it would have taken a sledgehammer to knock them off.

"Made in Czechoslovakia," Mahmed whispered. "The latest technology." Mahmed had added an improvement of his own. Before leaving Reno he had sprayed each bomb with a metallic silver paint. When they were in place they matched the stainless-steel tanker walls so closely, they looked like they must have been installed in the factory.

Just as they finished they heard a faint clicking above them. It was Alek striking two rocks together as a signal that a guard was coming. Jamal and Mahmed flattened themselves on the ground behind a row of barrels next to the fence. The guard, having no reason to feel that three empty railroad tankers needed special attention, cast his flashlight beam idly about as he strolled by. The two men lay still until they heard Alek signal an all clear.

Minutes later they were running down a dry creekbed and climbing an embankment to the clump of scrub brush where the car was hidden.

"What's next?" Jamal asked when they were on the road. Alek, driving, pressed his lips together and kept glancing in the rearview mirror.

"As soon as Radio Shack opens we can get what we need to make the transmitters," Mahmed said, lighting a cigarette. "By tomorrow we should be ready to put them in place between Truckee and Oakland. I hope you can get by for a couple of days on a few hours sleep."

"A few hours? I don't need *any* sleep." Jamal showed Mahmed a small plastic envelope full of white powder.

"Ah, yes. Things go better with coke."

CHAPTER 12

"I told them I'd be in the office after lunch," Jim said when they had finished breakfast on the deck of the houseboat, "but if you'll stay the rest of the day, I'll take the afternoon off. There's a great walk we could take on Mount Tamalpais. A trail that circles the peak. On a day like this the views will be fantastic. Afterward we could—"

"Sounds marvelous, but I can't. There's an ad starting today in the Reno paper about the house and people will be calling to see it. What time is it now, nine? It takes four hours to get there, so I've got to get a move on." Karen took a final sip of coffee.

"You're not using an agent?"

"I'm home most of the time anyway, so I thought I'd try to sell it myself."

"Miss one day's calls."

"Now, Jim, the sooner I sell the house, the sooner I can put Nevada behind me and turn my full attention to you."

"Wait a minute, there's got to be a way around this. I've got it—call your husband and see if he can get off work a little early to deal with the flood of buyers."

"Hmm. I suppose I could do that. He still has a key. The house is half his, after all, and he should help sell it. Okay, where's the phone?"

Karen dialed Gil's office number and was surprised to hear an unfamiliar voice: "Draegler Chemical, Tom Percy speaking."

"Oh, sorry, I was trying to reach Gil Ellis."

"His calls are being directed to me. Can I help you?"

"This is his wife calling long-distance."

"Who? Mrs. Ellis? Oh my God . . . Listen, hang on, I'm sure the general wants to talk to you. . . ."

Karen waited, frowning.

"Mrs. Ellis? Clem Trainer. We've been trying to locate you. It seems that . . . well, I have to give you some terrible, terrible news. Your husband, I'll never know why, has . . . well, late yesterday afternoon he . . ." Trainer cleared his throat and began again. "Your husband is dead. He ran off the road in the canyon. For some reason he had taken the company limousine, why we don't know, and . . . it's not an easy vehicle to drive, and he must have misjudged . . . I'm terribly sorry, Mrs. Ellis. He was gone before anybody was able to reach him. Where are you now? Can we send a car for you? Hello? Hello?"

Stunned, Karen lowered the phone and looked at Jim. She opened and closed her mouth. "Gil is dead," she said, her voice trailing off, ". . . he ran off the road . . ." She burst into tears and her knees sagged.

Jim knocked over a lamp in his haste to reach her and ease her into a chair. She wouldn't let him take the phone; instead she threw her arms around his waist and squeezed him hard until she was able to get her sobbing under control. Trainer's voice kept asking if she was still there, if she was all right. Karen leaned back in the chair and raised the phone. "I'll leave right away," she managed to say into the mouthpiece. "I'm in Sausalito, near San Francisco."

"We could send a car or a plane to pick you up."

"I have my car. I'll be all right."

"Are you sure?"

"Yes."

"I'll be at your house to meet you at, say, thirteen hundred hours . . . that's one o'clock. I'll wait for you in front."

"Yes. All right." Her voice was toneless.

"We've made temporary arrangements, but of course certain decisions can only be made by you."

"I understand."

"I can't tell you how much this pains me, Mrs. Ellis. Gil was a special favorite of mine and he always spoke highly of you. We're all going to miss him. If there is anything that I—"

"There is nothing. Good-bye."

Karen pushed the phone aside and stared into space. Jim put his arm around her shoulders and tried to comfort her.

"Ran off the road," Karen said distantly. "In the company limousine. I didn't get the details. God, what next?" She put her head on his shoulder and cried quietly, finally straightening up. 'We were getting a divorce . . . it's not as if we were madly in love."

"You were once. Karen, I'll drive you to Reno."

"No, no, I'll be okay."

"You shouldn't have to drive. Let me—"

"Jim, thank you, but I'll be okay. I'd really rather be alone." She squeezed his arm reassuringly, then went to the bedroom to get her clothes together. "It's such a shock," she said as she packed. "One day he's . . . and then . . . I hope he didn't suffer. He had enough problems in his life lately without—oh, I guess I'll find out all about it when I get there."

"If you have any trouble on the way, if you can't keep your mind on the road, call me."

"I will."

"Just pull into a gas station. And call me when you get home so I'll know you made it."

"I will."

"Better let me drive."

"No. Then I'd be up there and my car would be down here."

"We could take your car. I'll take the train back."

"Thank you, but I better handle this myself. You'd be too hard to explain. I can hear Mrs. Yost next door saying, 'The poor man not cold in his grave and already she—' "

The words were choked off. She finished packing silently, double-checking the closet and bathroom to make sure she had everything.

"If you need a place to get away from it all," Jim said, "you have the houseboat. You can be alone whenever you want."

"I appreciate that. I appreciate you. Last night was wonderful." She embraced him and kissed him briefly on the lips.

He carried her suitcases to her car using one arm, keeping the other around her shoulders. He kissed her good-bye and told her he would stay by the phone until she called. He watched her drive away, returning her wave when she merged with traffic on Bridgeway and headed north toward the Richmond Bridge.

When Karen turned into the driveway she noticed two men in a Cadillac parked at the curb. Coming across the lawn from the house next door was Mrs. Yost, who had probably been keeping a vigil at her dining-room window. Karen's hair was uncombed, she was wearing no makeup, and her eyes were red from the crying she had done during the drive from Marin County. She no longer felt like crying, and she hoped that phase of grieving was behind her. Mind and body, she felt numb and dull. Not the best time to receive visitors. She wanted to go to the bathroom, make a sandwich, have a drink, and call Jim, after which she would have liked a nap and a few more hours of solitude. Instead she had three people to contend with, all of them overflowing with sympathy and solicitude.

She walked like a zombie to the back of the car and

opened the trunk. The two men had left the Cadillac and were coming up the driveway.

"Oh, Karen, I'm so *sorry,*" Mrs. Yost said. "Ever since we heard the news, Clyde and I have been just *sick*. Are you all right, dear? Don't you sleep in that house tonight alone. I'll stay with you or you can come over and stay with us. We have a room ready. You shouldn't be alone."

Karen looked at her and smiled wanly. "Thank you, Mrs. Yost. You're very kind."

"Don't even think about cooking. Cooking is my department. If there's to be a wake or reception or anything like that, I'll handle the cooking. Just say the word."

"I will."

"Mrs. Ellis? I'm Clem Trainer. We met at the Christmas party."

"Yes. Nice of you to meet me here."

"This is Jeremy Draegler, our company president."

"How do you do?" She shook hands briefly with both of them. To Mrs. Yost she said, "Thanks very much for your concern, Edith. I can't make any decisions right now, please understand."

"Of course. Talk to you later, dear."

Karen showed the two men into the living room and offered them a drink, which they refused. She excused herself and went upstairs. There was a phone in the bathroom, and she called Jim from there. He sounded tremendously relieved that she had arrived safely. Thank God for him, Karen thought. He's going to make everything a lot easier.

After fixing herself a scotch and soda in the kitchen, she sat down facing Trainer and Draegler, who were side by side on a sofa. She glanced briefly at Draegler and was struck by his appearance: thin and spindly with eyes like an owl behind rimless glasses and skin the color of chalk. Trainer was as she remembered him: well fed and pink of skin and with an overbearing manner he couldn't subdue even in the present circumstances. It was easy to understand why Gil never liked him.

Karen gathered her strength and looked at both of them. "Okay," she said with a sigh, "tell me how it happened."

Trainer shifted uncomfortably. "It's a bit bizarre," he said. "He went into the ravine about four miles from the plant, and he almost certainly was knocked out on the way down. Three or four hundred feet down. The limousine was badly crushed. It took our welder over an hour to—"

"The cause of death, then, was . . . ?"

"Loss of blood, the coroner thinks."

Karen winced and closed her eyes. In a small voice she asked where they had taken him.

"The remains are at the Siegert Funeral Home awaiting your wishes."

"He wanted to be cremated. It's in his will. He has relatives in Ohio. I'll ask if they want the ashes."

"If there's anything further we can do . . ."

"I came along," Draegler said, "to convey to you personally my deepest sympathy. I know what a blow it would be to me if my Mildred were to, well, if she were to . . ."

"Why was he driving the limousine?"

"That is a mystery," Trainer said. "If he wanted to leave the plant, he could have taken his own car, which was right there in the lot. I want you to know that none of this was given to the press. We told the police and the paper that he admired the limousine and wanted to take it for a ride, to which we gave our permission. We didn't mention the alcohol. Yes, I'm afraid there was alcohol involved. There was an empty flask on his desk. We also found traces of cocaine in a plastic envelope, but we don't know if he had taken any."

"The drinking I knew about," Karen said desolately, shaking her head, "the cocaine, no. That would have been something new."

"Nothing was said about his having been, until recently, under a psychiatrist's care. The paper mentioned his connection with the Boston disaster, implying that suicidal tendencies might have been a factor, but they didn't get that from us. Some reporter dreamed it up."

"The limousine was a thing of beauty," Draegler said, "with every convenience you could shake a stick at. It's reasonable that he might have wanted to take it for a spin. The Cadillac doesn't begin to compare."

Karen looked at the general in bewilderment. "It doesn't make sense," she said. "Even if he *was* drunk, or on drugs, it wasn't like him to steal a limousine and drive off a cliff. You must have some idea why he did it."

Trainer raised his hands and let them drop. "We were hoping *you* would."

"Who was the last person to talk to him?"

"I suppose I was," Draegler said. "He came into my office quite upset over a minor disagreement with Clem. He was going over Clem's head, you might say, hoping to get me on his side."

"A disagreement over what?"

Trainer answered with a shrug. "A minor policy thing."

"After hearing him out, I told him to go back to his office while I talked it over with Clem, then the three of us could have a meeting and make a decision. When he left he seemed agitated, as if he thought we were ganging up on him or something, but my word, I never thought he would—has he been acting strange lately at home?"

"Has he been depressed?" Trainer asked. "Under unusual stress? Did he do or say anything that suggested that he might be developing a persecution complex?"

"We separated three months ago and were getting a divorce."

"Ah. That would contribute."

"A divorce!" the old man said. "I had no idea! I saw

him at lunch the other day and got no inkling, no inkling at all. Divorce! My word!"

"We had a sort of argument two weeks ago," Karen said to Trainer.

"About his work?"

"Yes. He said he had to run a test with lab animals and I said he should refuse to do it."

"Hmm." The general nodded in understanding. "A nasty part of the business nobody likes. I knew it bothered your husband a good deal and I was thinking of moving him away from it."

"He told me little about his work, said there were restrictions on talking about it. That was part of the argument we had." Karen thought for a moment and added, "There was one other thing he mentioned last time we talked."

"Oh? And what was that?" Trainer leaned forward, interested.

"Something about a dangerous product, a gas I think he said, that he didn't think should be shipped."

"He said that? That there was a dangerous gas that shouldn't be shipped?" The general and the old man exchanged glances and shook their heads as if the idea was ridiculous.

"I wasn't paying much attention to the details," Karen said, "because divorce was what we were really talking about, and what we both should do with the rest of our lives."

"We've developed some new agents to use against rats and mice, but they are nothing to get excited about," Trainer said.

"Then why the security precautions? The pledge of silence?"

"Proprietary reasons. They will be quite profitable if we reach the market first. How much did he tell you about them?"

She tried to remember the conversation. Gradually it came back to her that Gil had urged her never to mention the gas to Trainer for fear that it would put her in some sort of danger. She looked at the two men, and suddenly wondered why they had come. Was it reasonable that the plant manager, whom she hardly knew, and the owner of the company, whom she had met only once and who was supposed to be retired, would visit the widow of a junior member of the firm? Draegler had a pleasant cast to his face and was looking around the room at the paintings. Trainer was staring at her intently, and it struck her that the sympathy in his face and voice could well be insincere. She decided that she had said enough.

"He gave me no details. Or if he did, I don't remember them."

"Do you know if he wrote anything about his work? A diary or a report or notes?"

"Not that I know of. If I find anything, I'll give it to you." Was that why they had come? To find out if Gil had passed along industrial secrets?

"Might contain a clue as to his state of mind. He seemed to be fantasizing about the products in the last few weeks, acting as if we were developing a secret weapon. Building conspiracy theories in his head. These delusions of his apparently reached some sort of peak, something snapped, and . . ." Trainer gestured helplessly. "He acted exactly as if someone was chasing him. Nobody was. We were amazed when we saw him racing through the gate in the limousine. I sent one of the men to trail him at a distance just to see where he was going. He was careening all over the road, almost hit a water truck, then went over the edge. Saddest thing I've ever been involved with. He was a good man. He was much loved. I have to think it had something to do with Boston. A delayed reaction. Like Vietnam vets who get along for several years and then snap. Well, Mrs. Ellis, we won't take up any more of your time. You have our utmost sympathy. These next few days will be the hardest, then I'm sure you'll find the strength and the courage to carry on. It's what Gil would want."

They rose and moved toward the door.

"I'll miss young Ellis," Draegler said. "I always enjoyed talking to him. Sorry to hear that you were getting a divorce. That's very depressing. If Mildred left me, I'd put my head in the oven."

"We've cleaned out your husband's desk," Trainer said. "I'll send a man over with a box. We'll get his car back to you too. Don't forget to call the funeral home. There are various details to attend to besides the cremation. The will and whatnot."

"I know."

"Well, good-bye, Mrs. Ellis. Please call if there is anything at all I can help you with. Anything at all."

When they were gone Karen made herself another drink and sat on the deck until it got dark. She phoned Jim and told him about the conversation and how Trainer in particular gave her the creeps. Jim urged her to spend the night with friends.

"Maybe I will. The lady next door has already invited me. It's going to be hard to sleep, though. There are things about Gil's death that don't seem right. I can't imagine him stealing or even borrowing the limousine. He was a passive sort of guy. I don't think Trainer was giving me the whole story. I have a notion to call some of Gil's friends at the plant and see if I can find out what really happened."

"Sure you want to do that? You might find out things you'd rather not know."

"Maybe, but loose ends are aggravating too. Gil was terribly worried about a gas he thought was too dangerous to ship. Mannequin, he called it. It's why I came to your office a hundred years ago. Trainer brushed it off when I mentioned it as no big deal, but I wouldn't trust him as far as I could throw my piano. Maybe the gas had something to do with it."

Jim offered a possible explanation. "Could be Gil had been caught drinking or snorting coke on the job. Trainer and the other guy, Draegler, threatened to can him or tell you about the drugs. There was an argument, he blew his stack and tried to leave, but they took away his car keys till he calmed down, afraid he would give away company secrets or kill himself on the freeway. So he stole the limo. You told me he tended to blow things out of proportion and look for conspiracies and so on."

"Could have been like that, I guess. I know he kept a flask in his office. He could have drunk too much and panicked in some way. There's more to it than I've been told, that I'm sure of. The drug thing is all wrong. He was too straight and old-fashioned for drugs . . . except booze."

"Sleep on it. In the morning, if you want to do some digging, I'll help. Remember, I used to be a railroad cop."

"All right. Maybe I'm—what's the word my mother used to use?—overwrought. Driving up here, I thought a lot about sailing to the Caribbean. That sounds better and better. Getting away from everything, a complete change of scene . . . might be just what I need. Especially since I'd have you all to myself."

"I'm ready when you are."

"I miss you, James J. Eagan. I can't wait to be out of here and back in the Bay Area. It's wonderful knowing you are there. If I can't sleep, I might call you in the middle of the night."

"I'll lie on top of the phone so I won't miss the call."

She stood in the living room for a while in the darkness. She couldn't bear to turn on the lights and be reminded of all the things she and GIl had shared. What a troubled man he was, more deeply troubled than she had imagined. Was his death a form of suicide? Was there something she could have said or done to head it off? If she hadn't become so engrossed in her own plans for the future, maybe she would have noticed telltale signs. No, she mustn't blame herself; she had hardly seen him in months. Somebody at the plant should have been more alert.

Mrs. Yost seemed surprised to get a call from her. "Edith," Karen said, "I can't stay in this house a minute longer. Can I come over?"

CHAPTER 13

Dawn came after a night of tossing and turning. Karen put on jeans and a sweater and slipped out of the house as quietly as she could, trying her best not to wake Edith and Clyde. She wanted to use the bathroom and take a shower in her own house. When she was cleaned up and dressed, she would drive down the hill to her music studio and pick up any messages on the answering machine there, then come back to the house and spend the day packing. She had decided during the night to turn the house over to a real estate agent and move to Sausalito as soon as she could.

The sun was low in the east and dew glistened on the lawns. In the clear morning air the Sierras stood out so sharply against the blue sky, they seemed only a few miles away. The gray granite peaks and a scattering of snowcaps reflected the sun's first rays while the foothills were still shrouded in blue shadows and patches of mist.

Karen felt good. Her spirit had returned and she was more than ready to take on the house and its contents.

She stood in the middle of the living room and looked around appraisingly. The furniture could go into storage along with the stereo system. Books and records would be a problem because there were so many; she would set aside a few dozen favorites and store the rest; moving them all onto the houseboat would send it to the bottom of the Bay. She could hire a mover to bundle up Gil's stuff and send it to his relatives.

There was a surprise in Gil's den, which had remained pretty much as he left it when he moved out. It had been ransacked. The desk drawers were upside down on the floor, the locked filing cabinet had been pried open and the folders strewn about, the shelves of the floor-to-ceiling bookcase had been swept clear, even the framed prints on the walls had been turned backward and sliced open.

Karen backed out of the room with a feeling of nausea. Ghouls, she thought, ghouls who read obituary columns and then . . . she looked behind her. The silent house, which had seemed innocently familiar a moment before, had taken on an air of menace. Whoever had done this might still be present, behind a door, in the next room, crouched behind a piece of furniture. Slowly she moved through the living room, dining room, and kitchen, all of which were undisturbed. She went upstairs to the master bedroom, walking softly, alert for any sign that she wasn't alone.

The drawers of her clothes dresser were hanging open. Gil's had been taken out and were stacked upside down on the floor and the contents scattered. Her bathroom was undisturbed, but Gil's was a mess. Even the lid of the toilet had been set aside.

After checking the rest of the house, Karen carried the telephone onto the deck, where she felt safer than inside, and called Jim.

"Karen?" he said sleepily. "God, what time is it? Six-thirty? You interrupted my beauty rest. . . ."

He listened as she described what she had found. Even Gil's small workshop in the garage had been turned upside down, she told him. "It wasn't money they were after," Karen said. "My jewelry box wasn't touched."

There was a moment of silence on the line, then Jim said, "Didn't you say that Trainer asked you if Gil had written anything about his work? You told him no, but maybe he didn't believe you and sent somebody to make sure. Maybe the gas the company is working on is so valuable he doesn't want to take a chance that somebody else will find out about it. The upside-down drawers, that probably means they were looking to see if anything was taped to the bottom. Any signs of forced entry?"

"None. I checked every door and window. Everything was locked tight and there are no broken windows or marks from pry bars or anything like that."

"Ever give a key to anybody?"

"Never."

"Did your husband have a key?"

"Yes. A lot of his stuff is still here."

"Do you think he had it with him when he died?"

"I suppose so. I think he had it on his key ring. General Trainer said I'd get his personal effects back today, including his car."

"Anything he had in his pockets when he died should come back to you from the police or the coroner's office, not from Trainer."

"What difference does—"

"Maybe the police gave Trainer your house keys, which they shouldn't have done. Maybe he used them."

"Now who's looking for conspiracies?"

"You'll have to call the police and file a burglary report. There could be fingerprints, though I doubt it."

"What good will that do? If Trainer is in cahoots with the police, then—"

"If you *don't* file a report, he might think you suspect

something other than a random burglary. Look, let me get dressed and go to the can and have some coffee. I have to wake up. I'll call you back in half an hour."

Karen hung up and stared vacantly at the mountains. The sun was higher now and had chased away most of the shadows and mist. Before calling the police, she decided she should check her studio to see if that had been ransacked as well.

Two miles separated her house on Westview from the studio, which was on Prater Way across from the middle school many of her students attended. She unlocked the door, switched on the light, and stepped cautiously inside. Everything looked in order. The red light on the answering machine next to the piano was shining steadily, not blinking, which meant that the message tape was full. She slid the rewind lever to the left and when the tape reached the end moved it to PLAY. She sat down to listen with a pad and paper.

The first messages were from her divorce lawyer, the mother of a student explaining why her daughter had missed a lesson, and a jogging companion, all asking her to call them back. She jotted down the phone numbers. Then came a rushing noise, static, a high-pitched, frantic voice, and the words "Draegler's limousine" and "they're going to kill me" and "tank cars" and "Arabs." The words were rushed and hard to understand against the background noise—my God, she thought, was that Gil's voice? Was somebody tormenting her by impersonating him? She rewound the tape and listened to the rambling, disjointed message again, writing down phrases she missed the first time until her hand shook so much that writing was impossible. "Shooting at me with a rifle," she thought she heard the voice say. "Trainer's going to ship . . ." What was the word? Sounded like "anagram" or "had a pin." Mannequin? "Nerve gas . . . Iran war . . ." Something that could be "Sara Schuler" and something about a train.

She locked the door and picked up the phone. Her hand was shaking so much she had to dial twice.

"Jim! The most fantastic thing . . . the most incredible . . . There is this message on my studio machine, could be Gil's voice . . . my God, he says somebody was shooting at him . . . a voice on my answering machine—"

"What? Slow down and start over."

She did, reading the phrases she had managed to decipher and jot down after listening to the tape several times. A lot of static, she told him in a shaking voice, and she couldn't even be sure it was Gil.

"Might be a joke," Jim said. "Some people have sick senses of humor. On the other hand . . . look, try this. Take the tape out of the machine and see if it fits in your stereo system. Do you have a stereo in the studio?"

"Not a good one, but I sometimes play tapes for students here."

"Do you have a graphic equalizer? A row of levers on the amplifier? Move the upper registers, on the right side, down. That might cut out some of the static. Go on, I'll hold."

The cassette fit. On the stereo the voice was much clearer. It was either Gil or somebody who knew him well and could imitate his voice. Still, she wasn't sure. The terrified, desperate tone she had never heard before. The volume rose and fell and the voice in spots was buried by rushes of static. The message lasted less than thirty seconds, and when she had listened to it three more times she read to Jim what she was able to reconstruct:

> "Aw, shit, Karen, they're going to kill me . . . I've stolen Draegler's . . . headed down the canyon . . . I don't think I'll make it to town . . . you've got to believe me and not whatever they tell you. . . . They're shooting at me with a rifle . . . the gas, the

> nerve gas . . . Trainer's going to ship by train . . . three silver . . . don't let them leave . . . don't let Trainer . . . a dealer, a casino dealer from Iran, is going to try to . . . Iran war . . . tell the police or the railroad . . . the gas, Karen, the Mannequin gas . . . Sara, Sara Schuler at the plant . . . is the Arab's name, don't let him wreck . . . state police, not local—"

"I'm not sure of a lot of this," Karen said, "but that's what it sounds like."

Jim listened carefully, and when he found words his voice and manner had changed. He usually sounded relaxed and amused, now he was crisp and businesslike. "The first thing to do is make a couple of copies of the tape. Keep one with you and hide the others. Do you have a safe-deposit box? Put one there."

"Should I tell the police?"

"About the burglary, yes, not about the tape. Let's check a few things out first to see what we're up against. The police might be part of the problem . . . and the whole thing might be a hoax. Who is the Arab?"

"I have no idea."

"I'm going to get on the phone and see what I can find out about Draegler Chemical Corporation and Trainer. I know a couple of detectives from my days in Sparks who can find out almost anything. I'll check to see if the company has asked the railroad to ship a toxic chemical. Of course they could mislabel a box or a tank car and the railroad would never know. Karen, listen. Don't take any chances. If it turns out that we're onto something, you've got to be careful. Nobody suspects you, so keep it that way."

"I understand. Suppose I have a look at the limousine? See if there are bullet holes in the back of it?"

"Better not. You'd be attracting attention to yourself. Good thinking, though. Just like a detective."

"What's the risk? A widow might want to see the wreckage."

"I suppose so. If there *are* bullet holes, we'd have to make sure the evidence isn't destroyed."

"I'll phone you the minute I find out anything."

"Don't try to be a hero . . . or heroine. One more thing—I'm coming up there tomorrow whether you like it or not."

CHAPTER 14

Just before noon Sara was surprised to see Alek Mirkafai come through the Draegler front doors and walk across the lobby toward her desk.

"Alek!" she said. "What are you doing here?" She had never seen him at the plant before, and she could tell by the look on his face that something was bothering him.

"I came to take you to lunch." He held up a red-and-white striped bag. "Colonel Sanders, the extra greasy recipe." The words were one of his jokes, but there was no humor in his voice.

The moment they were outside, Alek started talking, and by the time they had sat down in the picnic area—at the same table Sara and Gil had used two days earlier, just before Gil had driven to his death—Sara had turned pale and lost her appetite. The three silver tank cars, Alek told her, had left the plant during the night. Filled with Mannequin, they were in the Sparks railroad yard east of Reno. They would be added to the center of a freight train arriving from Denver that afternoon and sometime after nightfall would be on their way to Oakland. To give them an air of innocence, the words MILK: GREEN PASTURES FARMS had been stenciled on each one in two-foot-high letters.

"Jamal didn't tell me. Jamal hasn't told me anything in days. . . . I don't think he trusts me anymore."

"He doesn't, and he has doubts about me too. Mahmed has him hypnotized. Did he ever tell you who Mahmed is? Iranian secret police. He's an expert in sabotage, kidnapping, explosives, assassinations, you name it."

"I suspected as much. He's the scariest man I ever saw in my life. The train will be wrecked, is that it?"

The food was arrayed before them in its plastic and paper containers, but neither of them had taken a bite. Alek was frowning and twisting in his seat as he talked, as if struggling against a shifting pain. Sara hated seeing him in such distress; he usually was joking or smiling or winking at her behind Jamal's back.

"At first it was like a game. Jamal and I played at being spies. We made sure the visitor was Aref, we found out what he was up to, we got word back to Iran. Why not? I have cousins and grandparents there the same as he does. The war is bad enough without more poison gas. Then Jamal found Mahmed. They are going to bring the war here, here to the United States." He looked at her and with great emotion said, "I don't see how you can stand Jamal. The way he treats you! He'd like you in a veil and locked in a house. Honest to God, there have been times when I wanted to—" He tightened his lips and held up a fist. "Nobody should treat you the way he does."

Sara stared back, wondering if she should tell him that she had been planning for months to leave Jamal and that she had begged Gil Ellis before his death to run away with her. She hesitated. There was a chance that Alek had been sent to test her. Instantly she hated herself for being so suspicious. Alek was too good-hearted and ingenuous to carry off such an assignment, much less accept it. She had always liked him—alone among Jamal's few friends—and it had saddened her to know he was involved in a plot that might land him in jail, or worse. No, Alek couldn't fool her and would never try. The moisture that was shining in his eyes . . . there was nothing fake about that.

"Alek, what are you going to do about the train?"

"Don't include me. I'm getting out. Planning to wreck the train . . . that was bad enough. To think that I was helping to make plans to wreck a train—I have hardly slept for a week. We were going to block the track in the mountains and blow up the tank cars and send statements to the press. I might have been able to go along with that, but this *new* plan—no, no, Alek Mirkafai is not a terrorist. Alek Mirkafai will not take one more step down this path."

"What new plan?"

"You have been against Jamal and Mahmed from the start, I know, that's why I have come to you. I am going to stop them, Sara! I want you to help me, then I want you to go away with me where we can be safe. I know you don't love me the way I love you, but we could make a happy life together. I would treat you like a queen! I would—" He turned away as if fighting off an impulse to cry. Crying was for babies, according to Jamal.

Sara looked at him in amazement. The man loved her? She reached across the table and gripped his arm tightly. He was a good man, but she had never thought of him as a romantic partner, something he surely realized. She couldn't imagine what had driven him to declare his love and ask her to go away with him when he knew he would almost certainly be rejected. Something else he certainly knew was that any attempt to interfere with whatever Mahmed was planning could cost him his life, and hers, too, if she helped him. Mahmed was capable of cold-blooded murder, she had no doubt, and maybe Jamal was as well. She wanted no further part in the scheming, and while she was planning to leave Jamal, when she made her break it would be alone. She watched Alek as he noisily blew his nose and wondered how to refuse him gently.

Five minutes later she had changed her mind. When he told her what would happen later that night if they did nothing, she knew she would have to collaborate with him whatever the risk. If running away was required, there were advantages in going together, and she could do far worse in her choice of a partner than Alek.

Mahmed and Jamal had sabotaged the tank cars, Alek confided, two nights earlier, before they had been filled with gas, while they stood unguarded in the Draegler yard. Alek himself had taken part, acting as lookout and driver, which made him as guilty as they were. Plastic explosives and remote-control detonators had been attached to each of the compartments of the three cars. Mahmed and Jamal were out of town as they talked, planting transmitters along the railroad line in Truckee, Auburn, Sacramento, Benicia. When the cars passed the transmitters, certain of the explosives would go off, allowing gas to escape and spread through neighborhoods near the tracks as people slept. In Oakland, where a ship waited to take the gas to Iraq, one whole car would explode.

"They are insane!" Sara gasped. "Blowing up the cars in the mountains makes some sort of sense, but deliberately killing innocent people . . . what is the point? What possible good can it do?"

"Only if many people die, Mahmed says, will the American people feel outrage and stop the plan for chemical war. Thousands of our people, maybe tens of thousands, will be killed by the Mannequin gas. The United States government, Mahmed says, is willing to let Iranians die horribly as they sleep, so the same should be done to Americans. Many Americans must die. America must have its face rubbed in the war." Alek's voice was hollow as he repeated the phrases he had heard from Mahmed. "When Americans die in the way intended for the Children of Allah, then the United States will stop helping the forces of evil. Death must be met by death."

The blood had left Sara's face and she was afraid she would be sick. "That's what his religion teaches? That death must be met by death?"

"It is Jihad, the holy war. Death to the enemies of Allah."

Sara's face was contorted and her voice was weak when she asked Alek what he wanted her to do.

"Mahmed and Jamal are staying in Oakland tonight, they told me, to see the results of their work. They think I'm going to spend the afternoon addressing envelopes and making copies of the statement they have made up." He snorted contemptuously. " 'The Islamic Hammer of God,' that's what they call themselves. I am going to spend the afternoon instead typing out the truth about what is going on. What is on the train and why it must be stopped. Who Mahmed is. What he and Jamal are doing. After work, Sara, pack a suitcase and come to my house and look at what I have written. Make sure nobody can misunderstand. When I write in English, I stumble. Help me make copies and give them to the newspapers, to the radio stations, to the railroad, to the police. Then we will go away together. Do we have any choice? Whatever happens, we cannot pretend we weren't involved. The way Jamal talks against America at work, the police will suspect him soon enough. Then they will turn to me . . . and you." He added softly, "As for loving me, or living with me as my wife, that is up to your heart. All I ask is that you consider the possibility. I make no demands."

His glistening brown eyes rose to hers. "Will you come tonight? Will you help me?"

Sara nodded helplessly. She said, "I'll come. I'll be there."

"Follow me," said the uniformed deputy, beckoning to Karen. Karen rose and walked behind the counter, through a small anteroom where a tight-lipped, gray-haired woman at a desk glanced at her sternly, and into the office of Michael Panozzo, sheriff of Sutro County, Nevada. Panozzo, a square-faced man with curly black hair, was younger than Karen expected, no more than forty years old. His face was expressionless and oddly free of lines or wrinkles of any kind, as if he had never smiled or frowned in his life. He shook her hand and waved her to a chair.

"Sorry to keep you waiting," he said. "Lunch ran on a little longer than expected. I'm sorry about your husband. It must have been a shock. What can I do for you?"

"I was hoping you could give me a few details about the accident. Maybe it would be better if I just tried to forget about it, but there are so many questions in my mind about what happened, I just can't seem to put it behind me." Karen was wearing a black dress, appropriate for a grieving widow, and kept a handkerchief in her hand as if expecting tears.

"If I can help, I'd be more than happy to." Panozzo glanced at his watch. "However, I have an appointment in ten minutes, at two o'clock."

"For my husband to take the company limousine, or borrow it, or whatever it was he did, was not like him. Do you have any idea why he did it?"

"We didn't look into that. We were assured by the Draegler people that he had permission to be driving the limo, so we saw no reason for an investigation. It is in our records simply as a single-car accident."

"Could you tell me anything about the scene? I mean

were there skid marks? Were the brakes working? Was my husband drunk?"

Panozzo walked to a filing cabinet, opened a drawer, and fingered through the file folders. "There's a copy of the report here. Best I don't rely on my memory."

On a low bookcase behind the sheriff's desk were several small golf and bowling trophies, a half dozen seashells, and a number of framed photos of people Karen assumed were Panozzo's family and friends. One snapshot held her attention: four men in golfing clothes holding drinks in one hand and putters in the other. Two she didn't recognize, two she did. One was the sheriff, the other was Clement Trainer.

The sheriff returned to his chair with a folder and studied it for a moment. "Do you have some reason to suspect foul play, Mrs. Ellis?"

"No, no, none whatever."

"According to the report, there were no skid marks. The vehicle left the road along a relatively straight stretch where the sight lines are good. Your husband's blood-alcohol level was nearly point two, which is above the legal limit and would have impaired his judgment and reflexes, especially if he was speeding in an unfamiliar vehicle. Mrs. Ellis, sometimes there is simply no explaining automobile accidents. The driver takes his eyes off the road for some reason, maybe to get something from the back seat, or to adjust the radio, even to put on his safety belt. I'd like to know how many accidents are caused by people putting on safety belts after they're up to speed. Maybe a bee or a wasp got in the car. You never know. I can tell you that at the request of the Draegler people, and because your husband was a respected member of the community, the press was not told that your husband was driving under the influence."

By "the Draegler people," Karen thought, you no doubt mean your good friend and golfing partner Clem Trainer.

She would have to be careful not to give the impression that she suspected him of any wrongdoing. She held the handkerchief to her nose and sniffled.

"Who was first on the scene? I'd like some idea of what it was like, of what went on, instead of this terrible, terrible blankness. I know it's crazy. . . ."

"Not at all. We were notified by the Draegler people. Apparently one of the security guards was following your husband. Our deputies got there at about the same time as a Draegler welder, who helped my men remove the body from the wreckage. By then an ambulance had arrived. Because he was obviously dead, he was taken to the county morgue."

"I see. And the limousine? Is it still there in the canyon?"

"It was removed an hour later."

Karen wanted to ask him where the limo was now so that she could inspect it, but another question about the limo might make Panozzo think she suspected foul play on the part of his golfing partner. "Must have been quite a job to haul it out," she ventured to say.

"Not when you have the right equipment. Our men are well trained."

He may not have meant to, but he had told Karen that the removal was handled by the sheriff's department and not a private firm.

Panozzo glanced at his watch again and returned the folder to the filing cabinet. "I'm afraid you'll have to excuse me."

"Of course. Thank you for talking to me. It helped a lot, believe me, and I appreciate it."

"Anytime. Good-bye, Mrs. Ellis."

"Good-bye."

She was beautiful, and Joe Dori was impressed! He looked at her with open admiration, savoring the way she stood there with such pride and confidence and strength. She knew she was the best, oh yes she did, no question about it! He especially liked her graceful lines and the way they disguised her two hundred and twenty tons. Sixteen feet high she was, from track to stack, and eighty feet long, the biggest, strongest, newest, and prettiest diesel-electric locomotive in all creation: Federal Engine's Model 1000X, the X standing for experimental. Saber One, the maker also called her in an effort to make her seem more than just an efficient collection of parts; Saber because she was as strong and sleek as a sword, One because she was the first in a series of road locomotives of advanced design. Here in the afternoon sunshine she was even more impressive than when Joe had first seen her in Pennsylvania, where she was dwarfed by the hangarlike assembly building.

It was Joe Dori's job, as Mountain Pacific Railroad's chief road foreman for the Sierra Region, to evaluate new motive power and make recommendations to management. Earlier in the year he had spent an entire week at Federal Engine's Avonia plant, a sprawling complex of red brick buildings near the shore of Lake Erie, with thirty counterparts from around the country, listening to FE experts talk about the design, manufacture, operation, and maintenance of the new Saber line. One day had been spent crawling over, around, and through a dozen of the machines in various stages of completion, another in operating one on a four-mile test track. Despite the cold wind off the lake and a freezing drizzle that never let up for the entire week, Joe Dori left Pennsylvania elated, convinced, along with FE's engineers and publicity men, that the Saber was the locomotive of the future.

One touch he appreciated that had nothing to do with operating costs was that the machine *looked* good. Streamlining had no significant effect on the efficiency of a locomotive, but the new line's designers had departed ever so slightly from the usual boxy look—nothing radical or flashy, just a slight rounding here and there to suggest that here was something new, something . . . well, exciting. There were even bold white stripes on each side, like racing stripes on a sports car—a subliminal appeal to those who liked speed as well as power.

Standing quietly in the Sparks yard, Saber One was still warm from the thousand-mile run from Denver. It was on loan from the manufacturer, and for the next year it would work in regular service on Mountain Pacific's lines, its performance closely monitored. Joe felt sure that at the end of the trial period his faith in the machine would be justified by the cost figures and the company would order at least forty of them, maybe eighty or a hundred.

Joe Dori, a short, wide man with a conspicuous shock of gray hair and skin the color of the smoked salmon that was his favorite food, climbed the steps to the cab and turned to the engineers, firemen, and conductors who had turned out to inspect the new locomotive. "Operating and maintaining this sweetheart will be a cinch!" he said in his booming voice. "Every conceivable condition is monitored by automatic sensors and displayed on a screen in the cab. If something goes wrong, or is about to go wrong, you know about it right away. I want you guys to follow me up to the cab six at a time and I'll explain the new features. No crowding, please. It's two o'clock now, so I can give you an hour. Then I'm going over to the bunkhouse and get some sleep. She's due out before midnight and I'm going with her. You'll wish you were, too, when you see what she can do. This baby is a dream."

Joe's claim that automatic sensors—the locomotive had a hundred such devices, an unprecedented number—monitored "every conceivable condition" was one of his typical exaggerations. One condition, for example, that the sensors were not designed to detect was the presence of nerve gas.

CHAPTER 15

At three in the afternoon the phone booth was an oven and Karen felt like a bouquet of wilted flowers. The receiver was almost too hot to touch, and the Nevada directory was mounted on a swivel in such a way that it was impossible to read without backing halfway out and resting it on an upraised knee. Under the Sutro County heading were several listings for the Sheriff's Department. Karen dialed the number for Impounded Vehicles and told the woman who answered that she was with Allstate Insurance Company and asked if they were still holding the Draegler Chemical Company limousine.

"The which?"

"The limousine owned by Draegler Chemical Company. It went into a canyon the day before yesterday. Sheriff Panozzo told me it was brought to the county garage."

"Yes, it was. We've already had an insurance adjuster take a look at it. State Farm, he was with. You're with Allstate?"

"The carrier was changed in mid-term," Karen said glibly. "Now there is a question of which policy was in force at the time of the accident. The vehicle was totaled?"

"Completely. Looked like a ball of crumpled aluminum foil. The agent okayed selling it as scrap."

"I see. To a local junkyard? May I ask which one?"

"Take my word, the thing was totaled. You'd be wasting your time looking at it."

"I have to make a personal inspection. One of those

stupid policies. If you'll just give me the name of the yard—"

"Afraid I can't do that without an okay."

"I beg your pardon?"

"I've got the file up on my screen and there's a note to give out no information."

Karen protested. "This is official insurance business! We may be liable! We have every right to examine—"

"I just work here, lady. Call the sheriff, that's what sheriffs are for. What was your name again?"

"You're darned right I'll call the sheriff. I never heard of anything so outrageous in my life."

Karen hung up, pleased at how well she had carried out the deception. She wondered if perhaps she was in the wrong business. Private detectives made more money than clarinet and piano teachers. What would a real private detective do now? Call every junkyard in town, of course. First, she dialed Draegler Chemical Corporation, whose number she knew by heart.

"Draegler Chemical, good afternoon."

"Could I speak to Sara Schuler? I believe that's the name."

"This is Sara Schuler." The voice suddenly became guarded.

"This is Karen Ellis. My husband spoke of you."

"He did?"

"Yes, just recently. I'm hoping you can tell me something. The limousine that Gil died in, do you know what year it was, and the make and model? I want to take a look at it. Before I start calling the local junkyards, I'd like to know exactly what to ask for. Will you help me?"

"Well . . . I suppose I could call our garage."

"Tell them the insurance company is checking."

"All right. Please hold . . ."

After a minute of silence, Sara was back on the line.

"It was a Mercedes 560 SEL stretch limo, 1988. Mrs.

Ellis, you really shouldn't be doing this. It . . . it isn't safe."

"What do you mean? Looking at a wrecked car in a junkyard isn't safe?"

"Better try to forget what happened. There's nothing you can . . . I'm afraid that you might . . ."

"I'm simply trying to find out what really happened that day, and I'm trying to do it without attracting attention or making anybody nervous. Don't tell anybody I called. I have the feeling that you could clear a few things up for me if only you would. Then I wouldn't have to waste time snooping around on my own. Did you know Gil well?"

"We . . . in the last few months we had become quite close. I lost a very good friend. I can't begin to tell you the sense of loss I feel."

"Did you see him on the last day?"

"Yes."

"Did anything seem wrong? Was he drinking or on drugs?"

"He might have had something to drink. I don't think he took drugs." She was choosing her words with care, as if afraid the line was tapped.

"Was he in some sort of danger?"

"I don't know. I think he thought he was."

"Sara, I have the feeling you could tell me a lot. When you get off work, would you call me? Could we meet? I'd like to find out all I can about how Gil died . . . and why."

"All you need to know is that what Gil was trying to stop will be stopped. It is being taken care of."

"What is? What was he trying to stop?"

"You'll know tomorrow. I have to go."

Karen was holding a dead receiver. She was tempted to call back or even drive to the plant and confront Sara. Karen stood in the heat of the cubicle thinking hard, sweat rolling down her face. Maybe Sara would call her that night. If not, Karen would call her again in the morning and try to make a date to meet away from the plant. The woman obviously was afraid to talk from the company switchboard.

Back to the phone book. In the Yellow Pages, Junk Dealers were listed with cross references to Automobile Parts and Supplies—Used & Rebuilt. There were only a few in the Reno area. Swiveling the directory upward and holding it open with one knee while writing down the numbers on a notepad proved to be impossible, so she did something for the first time in her life—she tore a page out of a book. What the hell, she thought, this is an emergency.

The first two companies she tried were of no help. "Hello," she said to the man who answered her third call, "this is Stravinsky Car Parts of Fresno. I'm in town looking for limos, especially Mercedes. Got any late models in the yard, by any chance?"

"Got a 560 in yesterday. Pretty smashed up, though. You wanna look?"

Otto's Autos was on an edge of town where junkyards, dumps, corrugated metal buildings, and power lines shared a section of desert with fast-food franchises and mobile-home parks. City planning at its most absent.

A teenager hanging hubcaps on the wall of an office trailer seemed to be the only living thing at Otto's. His complexion matched the neighborhood—rutted, pocked, and dusty.

"It's in the back," he said with a toss of his head in answer to Karen's inquiry, "next to the pile of school buses. Silver. You can't miss it."

She found it lying in a pile by itself. It was so badly damaged that at first glance she couldn't tell the front from the back. There was no doubt it was the wreck she was looking for; on the left front door was the Draegler

Chemical Corporation logo: a small green tree and the letters DCC.

Her husband's coffin. She cringed at the thought of him trapped inside as it plunged to the bottom of the canyon. The roof was so caved in, it was obvious that nobody could have survived. For so much damage to be done it must have rolled over a dozen times. The front end was almost completely crushed, giving the wreckage a wedge-shaped profile.

Karen examined the rear body panels carefully. Next to the left brake light she found a round hole the diameter of a pencil, the edges bent inward as if it had been made by a steel punch. Small radial cracks showed no sign of rust. There was a similar hole in the middle just below the rear window. They were almost certainly bullet holes.

She moved slowly along the left side of the car. The metal there was so crumpled that bullet holes would have been obliterated. At the driver's compartment a panel was missing, outlined by a jagged black line that must have been made by the cutting torch used to cut Gil's body free. The dashboard and the leather seats were covered with bloodstains.

Instantly her stomach heaved and tears sprang to her eyes. Gasping, she turned to run . . . and almost knocked the teenager over. He grabbed her by the shoulders to keep them both from going down. "Hey, what's the matter?" he said, laughing. "Didn't find what you wanted?"

"Blood," Karen said, choking. "Somebody got killed in there. . . ."

The youth chuckled and watched her hurry toward her car. "You must be new in the business."

At eight o'clock the dusk was fast deepening. Alek's house was set back from the street behind an overgrown hedge, and when Sara parked at the curb behind his worn-out Chevy she could see that lights were on in the front room—the shades were drawn and the windows glowed like Halloween lanterns.

Everything had conspired to make her two hours late. First was the call from Gil's wife, which rattled her so much she couldn't concentrate on her work. General Trainer asked her to take a few letters after quitting time, and she made so many mistakes she had to do them over and over to get them right. Then she had to change a tire in the Draegler parking lot. Jamal wasn't around, fortunately, when she got home—apparently he and Mahmed were still out setting the transmitters. It took her longer than she thought to fill the trunk of the car with belongings and pack two suitcases and a cardboard box. She hoped Alek didn't bring too much stuff or her 1981 Ford would never make the freeway grades. She had phoned Alek twice reporting the delays, and they agreed that as soon as she arrived they would go to the library or a hotel lobby to finish their work. If Jamal or Mahmed came back earlier than expected and discovered their treason, they would likely be shot on the spot. Finally, she was stuck for an eternity at a railroad crossing next to Alek's house while a freight train rolled slowly to the east—the damned thing must have had a hundred cars.

Spending an hour with Trainer in his office after work had one advantage: from overheard fragments of a telephone conversation she learned something she could hardly wait to tell Alek. Colonel Aref was in town again and was going to join Trainer, Ordman, and Vanneman on a train ride to Oakland later that night. There was no further Amtrak passenger service scheduled, so they must be planning to ride on the Mannequin train. In the caboose? Maybe Alek would know.

The stuccoed bungalow was between the ruins of a burned-out supermarket and a ready-mix concrete plant. There were three other small houses in the neighborhood, one of them boarded up and covered with spray-painted graffiti. Sara made sure her car was locked, then unlocked it again to retrieve her purse—she didn't want to be without her gun. She paid no attention to a car parked half a block away; had she noticed it she might have recognized it and kept on driving.

Approaching the house along the shadowy walkway, she was surprised at how scared she was. Her heart was beating fast and every hair on her body seemed to be standing on end. It struck her as odd that when she was twenty years old she thought nothing of risking her life with drugs or selling her body to strange men . . . and some of them were *very* strange. But in those days she felt suicidal half the time and didn't care if she lived or died. Now that she was approaching forty she had become much more careful. She had more or less wasted the first half of her life and had made up her mind to do better with the second half. Yet here she was risking death again. Eight hours earlier she had been comparatively relaxed, making plans to leave Jamal and move alone to another state; now everything was desperate, frantic, and dangerous. She was going to do the authorities a favor by helping Alek warn them about the sabotaged train, even though the authorities had never done any favors for *her*. And she was going to run away more or less on the spur of the moment with a man she really didn't know much about. Jamal and Mahmed were crazy and maybe Alek was too. She would find out soon enough.

The door yielded to her touch.

"Alek?" she called, stepping inside. "Hello? Anybody home?"

Off the front hall to the left was an archway leading to the living room, where an overhead light and a floor lamp were burning brightly. Beyond was a small dining room. She could see Alek sitting at a table facing a typewriter. His back was toward her.

Karen advanced cautiously. "Alek? You asleep? Wake

up, I'm here! Come on, let's go!" She came up behind him. Something was terribly wrong. He was sitting stiffly in the chair with his arms hanging straight down. She put a hand on his shoulder. She saw then the hole at the base of his skull and the glistening trail of blood that ran under his collar. The sheet of paper in the typewriter was flecked with red. He had been shot from behind.

"Hello, Miss Schuler."

The words were spoken in a conversational tone, but they came as such a shock that Sara jumped a foot and shrieked as she whirled around. Mahmed was sitting on the living-room couch with his legs casually crossed and a slight smile on his face. In one hand he held a sheaf of typing paper, in the other a gun that was pointed at Sara's face.

"Al . . . Alek," she stammered, finding it hard to breathe, "is he . . . is he . . ."

"He is dead," Mahmed said with mock sadness. "What choice did I have after reading this?" He waved the papers. "He has described our entire operation, making himself and you great heroes while Jamal and I are villains. Can you imagine such a distortion? Those who risk their lives to keep a war from getting worse are made to look bad, while those with no sense of loyalty, who sell out their friends behind their backs, are made to look good." His smile widened. "What could be more sickening?"

Sara stared at the muzzle of the gun. "I don't know what he's written," she said in a strained voice she hardly recognized. "He called me at work and told me to pick him up and take him to Jamal's, that his car wouldn't start. . . ."

Mahmed laughed. "Please, Miss Schuler, you insult my intelligence."

"I swear he didn't tell me anything!" She thought about the gun in her purse and wished she could somehow get to it. She glanced at the archway and wondered what chance she would have if she made a break for it. Once out of his line of fire she might have time to unlatch her purse and—

Mahmed saw the movement of her eyes. "Don't even think about it," he said.

"We should get out of here. We shouldn't stay in a house with a dead man."

"No reason to leave quite yet. When the final explosion goes off in downtown Oakland, then we will leave. We were going to stay there overnight and enjoy the festivities, but we decided to come back because we didn't trust the two of you. Jamal will be over in a little while and we can have a party, just the three of us. You can repeat your funny stories to him. I have some cocaine. There is beer in the refrigerator. Our work is done for the night. Now is Miller time." He stood up and walked toward her, throwing the papers aside and keeping the gun trained on her face. His left hand dropped and began kneading the flesh of his crotch. "Take off your clothes."

Sara's eyes widened. "My God, Mahmed, have you no respect for the dead?" She gestured behind her. "This man was our friend!"

"No friend of mine. Jamal promised you to me, did you know that? As soon as we found out what you and Alek were planning. Oh, you going to cry? You going to shake with terror? Good! I like it that way better." He waved the gun and ordered her to drop the purse.

The nightmare for Sara Schuler had begun. When it was over she would remember the details only as a blur. She would remember dropping the purse on her foot so that the gun inside wouldn't reveal itself by knocking against the floor. She would remember trying to talk to him, protesting her innocence, offering to be his woman and make love to him all night long if only they could leave this house of death . . . and being struck across the face with a gun for her trouble.

"Shut up, you bitch whore," Mahmed shouted. "When I want you to open your mouth I will tell you. Take off your clothes! *Now!*"

Whimpering, Sara took off her blouse and folded it, laying it on the floor so it half covered the purse, unsnapping the latch as she did so. She took off her skirt and draped it neatly over the blouse, opening the mouth of the purse with her fingertips.

Mahmed laughed. "You think you are going to need your clothes again? When I am through with you, when Jamal is through, you will wish you were dead. Maybe I will grant your wish. Traitor! Fucking bitch whore!"

He shifted the gun to his left hand, and with his right undid his trousers, stepping out of them when they fell. Sara took off her half-slip, and when she laid it down she gave the purse a half turn; now she could see the handle of her gun. All she needed was something to distract Mahmed's attention for a couple of seconds.

He was out of his shorts, fondling himself as he watched her take off her bra and smiling at the fullness of her breasts. He was bigger than Gil or Jamal, and his erection looked as hard and gnarled as the root of a tree. With his free hand he grabbed a handful of her hair and roughly forced her to her knees and rubbed himself against her face. "Open your mouth now, fucking bitch whore!"

At the moment of orgasm, Sara thought, then maybe I can reach for my purse. He will be distracted then, all right, and if he is like other men, he will close his eyes. He probably doesn't suspect I have a gun. In Iran women probably aren't armed and dangerous. She cried out in pain at the force he was using to press the muzzle of his gun against the side of her head. His fist in her hair had tightened so much, she was afraid he would pull a handful out by the roots.

As she was about to take him in her mouth, he took a step back. "Lipstick," he said, bending her head so she had to look at him. "Paint your bitch-whore lips! When I am done with you I want my cock covered with the color of your mouth!"

She was sobbing, but hope was rising in her heart. He was giving her an excuse to reach for her purse! He held her hair in an iron grip, forcing her to grope blindly. She found the purse and slipped her hand inside. Too risky to try anything at that moment, she decided. The muzzle of his gun was still pressed hard against her temple and might go off if she fired a shot. She took out the tube of lipstick, slipped off the cap, and drew it across her lips.

"Smear it! Make your mouth a red wound!" He released her hair and took the lipstick from her, rubbing it hard all over the lower half of her face. "Painted she-devil," he shouted, "painted American whore! Suck me now!"

She did as she was told, crouched in front of him, breathing through her nose and trying not to gag. As she moved her mouth on him, she dropped her right hand to the floor, found the purse, and slid it behind him and out of his view. The gun was in her hand at last. She raised it slowly to his thrusting buttocks, careful not to let the cold steel touch his skin. She moved her other hand to his testicles, fondling them to make his climax more intense.

Still too risky to shoot him. She would get her chance in a few seconds . . . just a few seconds more. She worked on him with her mouth, slowly at first, then faster and faster when she heard his quickening breath. He was shouting at her, cursing at her, in English at the beginning, then in the language of his childhood. She looked up and watched his face. His eyes began to lose their focus as his climax approached. His gun slowly strayed away from her head as the first spasms began deep inside his loins.

She didn't want to give him the satisfaction of an

orgasm. She waited until the last possible instant, then spat him from her mouth, grabbed the barrel of his gun and twisted it aside, and fired a shot from below into the soft flesh under his chin. The bullet coursed upward through his brain and he collapsed as if he had been guillotined. Sara had to throw herself backward to escape the falling body.

His head came to rest on her clothes, the eyeballs staring, the mouth open. On the top of his scalp was a ragged exit wound. There was the noise of air escaping from his lungs.

She pulled her clothes aside and, still kneeling, felt herself getting sick. Her stomach heaved and seemed to turn over, and as the acrid fluid rushed from her mouth she made no effort to turn away.

When the retching was over, she struggled to her feet and put on her clothes, smeared and spattered with Mahmed's blood. She had to get out of there. . . . Jamal, or the police, or neighbors from across the street might show up at any minute. Where should she go? Who would believe her story? Certainly not the police, not with her record.

She went to the front windows and turned back the edge of the shade. The street was quiet. On the sofa were the papers that Alek had typed. She scooped them up and jammed them in her purse.

On the way out she tried not to look at Alek, still facing the typewriter like an author stuck for a word. She couldn't avoid Mahmed, who blocked the archway. She carefully stepped over the body. To her amazement, he was still erect; if anything, his swollen member was bigger in death than it had been in life. She aimed her gun at it and thought about trying to separate it from his body, then decided not to waste the bullets. If Jamal caught up with her, she would need them.

CHAPTER 16

Jim tried Karen a few more times. Still no answer. It was eight o'clock in the evening and he was beginning to get a little worried, not having heard from her all day. It could be that she had tried to call him and gotten busy signals; he had been on the phone almost constantly. He was anxious to tell her what he had learned from newspaper and police friends of his from his days in Reno and Sparks. Most of what he had dug up was consistent with Gil Ellis's conspiracy theory.

Something suspicious was definitely going on at the Draegler Chemical plant. A couple of years earlier, shortly after Clem Trainer was hired as manager, at least twenty private policemen were brought in from the outside, which irritated the local labor brokers who supplied security personnel to the casinos. An airstrip was built. Tours for schoolchildren were stopped and a chain-link fence put up. The plant went to three shifts, even though sales figures didn't seem to justify increased production. There was, in fact, no evidence of increased production, at least not as measured by the number of Draegler rail shipments.

As for Trainer, Jim learned that he was a former general in the Chemical Corps, well known in Washington before taking early retirement as an advocate of strengthening America's capability for waging chemical and biological warfare. Nobody knew what he was up to at Draegler. Government contracts? None had been announced. Old man Draegler was still around, but neither he nor Trainer had given an interview in a long time.

Paradoxically, Jim had the most trouble trying to find out whether or not the company had asked Mountain Pacific Railroad for permission to ship a hazardous chemical. People in the railroad's Reno office, even people he knew, were evasive about it. Apparently an inquiry had been made, but nobody would tell him the nature of the chemical, the type of handling that would be required, the date of the proposed shipment, or even whether there would *be* a shipment. The head of the Sierra Region, Leon Magnus, a man Jim had met several times and who was based in Oakland, hadn't returned his calls.

There were three ways of hauling hazardous substances. The simplest was to put warning signs on the cars carrying it. If the substance was exotic or posed special problems, technical experts who knew how to deal with it had to travel with the load, either in the caboose or a special passenger car. The third method was called "Green Line," which the military sometimes used when certain weapons were being transported—nuclear bombs, say, or missiles. Technicians rode on the train, but the car was left unmarked . . . or was misleadingly marked; that way pranksters, psychotics, spies, and saboteurs were given no clue that anything unusual was being moved. Green Line trains were given priority over all other kinds of freight traffic. Speed controls were relaxed and restrictive labor regulations were waived in order to complete the trip as quickly as possible. It wasn't necessary, for example, to change crews every few hundred miles.

Jim wondered if the gas Gil Ellis was worried about had government backing and if Green Line status had been granted for the move. That would explain his inability to get the details.

He opened a beer and walked onto the deck at the rear of his houseboat. The sun was down and the breeze off the water was cool. He was wearing Bermuda shorts and thought about changing into slacks.

"Hello, Jimbo! How's it hanging?"

"Hi, Alan. No date tonight?"

Alan Loomis, Jim's next-door neighbor, was relaxing on his power boat, a drink in his hand and his feet up on the steering wheel.

"Sure I got a date. Are you kidding? On a full-moon night like this? She's a model with the Ample Woman agency. Wait till you see the tits on her."

"I can hardly wait. Don't you worry about doing too much pelvic bumping? You might rub your little dinky off."

"What a way to go! Hey, want to take a spin? Helga's not due for an hour."

"No, thanks. I had a powerboat once and hated it. Sailing, that's the ticket. Running free with the wind, at one with nature, a poem slicing through the foam."

"Oh, yeah? No wind and you're stuck at the dock. I'd sure love to give you a ride. What I've got here is a thirty-three-foot Sonic with a three-hundred-horse Evinrude, or have I told you already? I can do seventy miles an hour in this sucker! When I take off my cheeks sag like an astronaut at blast-off. I tell you, Jim, you'd love it!"

"I'm not going to take a ride on your goddamned stinkpot, now or ever. I wish you'd trade those six hundred horses for a pair of oars; then we could all get some sleep around here. If I had my way, every belchfire on the Bay would be—"

The phone rang inside and Jim ran to answer it.

"Karen! You okay?"

"I'm fine, but exhausted. Been out all day and just got back from a fabulous dinner at Jack-in-the-Box. Called you quite a few times and always got a busy signal. It's so good to hear your voice! Do you have any news?"

"A little. How about you?"

"A lot. You go first."

Jim sat down and recounted what he had learned from

a day on the phone: the changes at Draegler Chemical, Trainer's background, the possibility that a shipment might be in the works with a military clearance, in which case it would be almost impossible to stop. "One thing I learned is that we'll have to be leery of the sheriff, Panozzo or whatever his name is. Drives a Porsche and lives in a mansion on a salary of forty thousand a year. Thinks that Russia is going to invade Nevada at any minute."

"I met him," Karen said. "There's a picture of him with Trainer right in his office. Apparently they're old buddies."

Karen told him about her talk with the sheriff, the subterfuges she used to find the limo, and her discovery of the two bullet holes.

"How do you know they're bullet holes? Have you ever seen one?"

"I'll bet anything that's what they are. Gil said on the tape that somebody was shooting at him. We've got to go to the police. But which police?"

"Wait a minute. You said you weren't sure that *is* your husband on the tape. What if it turns out the holes were caused by flying rocks? We should be sure before we go public with the claim that your husband was murdered."

"How about hiring a private investigator?"

"Might be a good idea. Let's talk about it when I get there in the morning. I'll make it by ten."

Karen told Jim about her brief phone conversation with Sara Schuler and how Sara had tried to warn her away from tracking down the limousine. "She also said that what Gil was trying to stop will be stopped. 'It is being taken care of' were her words. She said I would know what she meant tomorrow."

"That's interesting. Maybe the company has decided against shipping anything toxic. Maybe a colleague of Gil's succeeded where he failed."

"Do you suppose we're getting excited over nothing?"

"Could be. The limousine, though, that definitely bears looking into. Karen, you're not going to stay alone in that house tonight, are you?"

"No, I'll be at the Yosts. We're going out to a movie. I'm hoping I can get my mind in neutral for a few hours."

"Glad to hear it. Call me when you get back. I'll be up. I'm going to call a couple of lawyers I know and find out what we should do about the limo wreckage. We don't want anybody destroying physical evidence like that either accidentally or on purpose. When I get there in the morning maybe we should buy it and haul it away to a safe place. I'll find out about the rail shipment, too, if any, tomorrow. People will tell me things in person they won't talk about on the phone. Maybe I should drive up there right now; that way we could get an early start and I wouldn't have to spend another night worrying about you."

"I can take care of myself, Jim. I'm not a little girl."

"Yes, but I'm a little boy."

"I know, and it's one of the things I love about you. Talk to you later."

Karen hung up and looked at her watch. There was no time to shower and change clothes. She would have to join the Yosts as she was. She walked into the downstairs bathroom to check her makeup and comb her hair.

Brakes squealed in front of the house. There was a quick knock on the door, then desperate pounding.

Karen's heart skipped a beat. "Who is it?" she called, walking into the hallway. "Who's there?"

"Far out," the fireman said. "This looks like the cockpit of a 747!"

Tommy Talbot's official title was Assistant Locomotive Engineer. In the good old days he would have been called a fireman, so that's how Joe Dori thought of him.

Joe also thought of him as a goddamn hippie because of hair that flowed over his shoulders, jeans with colorful patches on both knees, and a tiny diamond in the lobe of his left ear. An earring! Joe tried not to look at it because he didn't like the feeling when his blood curdled. This was the guy the Reno Division picked out for training on Saber One? American railroads were going to hell in a hand basket. Well, nothing to do but swallow his disgust and do his best to teach him a few things.

"Not as complicated as it looks," Joe said. "Same controls as on the switcher you're used to, just presented in a little jazzier way." There were three large levers, one under the other, in the center of the panel. Joe touched them in succession. "The master controller is exactly the same. Dynamic braking on top, moves from left to right. The throttle in the middle moves from right to left, with the same eight notches of power you're used to. The reverse handle is on the bottom. On the left here is your air brake, up here is your horn valve, over here is your sand switch."

"What's this?"

In the darkness of the cab, Joe rolled his eyes. "That's the windshield wiper."

There was a metallic thud from the rear that made the locomotive shudder. Two auxiliary locomotives, joined, had moved up behind Saber One and bumped it hard enough to link the couplers. Too hard to suit Joe, who leaned out of the side window and shook his fist in the air.

"What are you trying to do, Tony," Joe shouted, "break it?" The headlight of the trailing unit made it impossible to see into the cab, but a blast from an air horn showed that Tony had seen his gesture. Joe could imagine Tony laughing his ass off knowing how pissed he was at getting a hippie as his running mate. Very funny. Ha ha.

Tommy Talbot curled his lip. "It's not all that shit I'm

worried about," he said, dismissing the operating controls with a flick of the hand. "I know all that shit. It's this shit up here that gets me." He moved his face close to a computer display screen and wrinkled his nose in disapproval.

"That's the best part," Joe said. "Sensors keep track of everything. Look . . ."

Joe demonstrated. Under the glass screen was a list of code numbers and a numeric keypad. Punching in 2005 displayed the engine speed in rpms; 2012 displayed the traction motor average current in amps. To get the intake air manifold pressure in psi, all you had to do was type 3001.

"Oh, man," Tommy said, watching the ghostly green readouts come and go on the screen, "that's creepy!"

That's not creepy, you jerk, Joe thought, that's progress. You're the one that's creepy. You've got hair like a girl, an earring like a drag queen, and patched clothes like a circus clown. You should be in a rock band, not a locomotive.

"I hate computers," Tommy said. "They're not human. I like old-fashioned equipment. Don't you think railroading was better in the old days, Mr. Dori, before all this tricky stuff?"

Joe gazed at him. In the old days, he thought, the railroad police would have run a hippie like him off the yard at the point of a stick. Still, the kid had called him Mr. Dori, a term of respect he hadn't expected from an aging flower child. If he felt nostalgia for the great age of railroading that ended before he was born, maybe he wasn't all bad. "Computers are just tools," he said gently, trying not to look at the earring, "to help us do our jobs better. With the computers we have here, for instance, we can tell how everything is doing without dragging our butts all over the place, which is no picnic when you're doing sixty miles an hour. They also buzz when something is heating up, shorting out, breaking down, or going dry, and they make a record for the mechanics to look later. Put that in your bong and smoke it."

Tommy looked at Joe and smiled broadly. "My *bong*? First time I ever heard a man your age or dressed like you use that word. You're all right, Mr. Dori!"

Joe was dressed the way a railroad engineer was supposed to be dressed: a nice pair of black slacks, a peaked cap, a plaid wool shirt, and steel-toed shoes. If he thought he wouldn't be laughed at, he would wear pinstripe overalls and a red bandanna, as God intended. In his pocket was a gold pocket watch on the end of a gold chain. It was the same watch his father had used in the glorious days of steam and worked as well now as it did then, a comfortable, old-fashioned watch with two hands that went around in a circle and pointed at twelve different numbers. Old-fashioned was fine in its place, and so was high technology, a point he would try to make the lad understand on the run to Oakland.

There was more jostling and bumping as the freight cars were coupled in position behind the locomotives—piggybacks, mail and UPS cars, auto racks, cars carrying chemicals, coal, flour, and wheat, and three silver tank cars from the Draegler Chemical Corporation bound for a pier on the Oakland Estuary. Joe and Tommy went through the test sequences to make sure the three engines were interconnected properly. All of the electrical and air lines that tied the train together checked out perfectly. The signal at the west end of the yard turned from red to green.

Spence Kesson's voice came over the radio from the yardmaster's tower. "This is MP Sparks tower to seven six six one west. You're clear to highball, Joe. Final count is forty-nine cars. Bud Shieving is your conductor in the caboose, riding with three pieces of brass. Green Line to Oakland, Sixteenth Street. Hope you and Tommy have a lovely trip. Over."

Joe radioed back, "MP seven six six one west to MP Sparks tower. By brass do you mean rabbits in the bush?" The slang phrase meant inspectors. "Over."

"MP Sparks tower to seven six six one west. No, I mean outsiders on board because of the three tank cars in the middle of the string. Not milk, as labeled. That's why you're Green Line. Over and out."

Joe slowly moved the throttle from idle to notch one, notch two, and notch three. Behind him the hum of the powerful diesel engines grew deeper and louder. So smoothly did the locomotives ease forward that it was impossible to tell exactly when the motion began.

"That's nice," Tommy Talbot said. "I'm impressed."

"Give the horn a couple of toots, Tommy my boy, we're on our way,"

To the rear they could hear the metallic clicks as the slack in the couplings was taken up. The three linked engines had advanced ten feet before the caboose, almost half a mile away, began to move.

Bud Shieving checked in on the radio from the caboose: "Everything looks good, Joe. Open her up and let's see what she'll do highball."

With a smile of satisfaction, Joe moved the throttle all the way to the left, to notch eight, maximum power, then settled back in his seat to enjoy his newest toy. The sound of the engines, the vibration set up by the churning pistons and the rolling wheels, the smell of diesel fuel and well-oiled machinery, the sweep of the headlight from side to side, the sense of motion as he was carried ahead faster and faster, there was nothing like it in all the world.

He intended to have a lovely trip even if he did have to share it with a goddamned hippie.

CHAPTER 17

Karen stared open-mouthed at the woman at her front door. Her hair and eyes were wild, her clothes wrinkled and smeared with blood, and her breath so ragged that her first rush of words was incomprehensible. "I'm Sara Schuler," she said, "Sara Schuler from Draegler . . . please . . . I—"

"My God," Karen gasped, letting her in and locking the door behind her, "what happened? You're bleeding . . ."

Sara's eyes darted around like a terrified animal looking for an escape. "No . . . I'm sorry, I didn't know where to—Jesus, I had to shoot a man! He was—oh Christ, I think I was followed. . . ."

"What on earth—"

"Was that a car? Did you hear a car?" Sara peered through the narrow leaded window beside the door. "I think Jamal was following . . . he'll kill me. . . ." She whirled and said, "We've got to get out of here . . . turn out the lights, no, leave them on so he'll think we're . . . he'll see my car! Can we use yours? Can we get to the garage without going outside?" Her voice rose to a whine. "But where can we go? He'll track us down! I should have waited at Alek's and shot him too. . . . Where's the garage?"

As she tried to push by Karen took her by the shoulders and shook her roughly. "Sara, what are you talking about?"

"We've got to get out! Jamal will kill us both! I shouldn't mix you up in this, but I couldn't go to the cops after killing . . . Now Jamal will—but I have a gun! I have a gun! You let him in and then I'll . . ."

"No guns in this house!" Karen pulled open the front door and gestured at an empty yard and a quiet street. "See? Nobody there. Now will you settle down and—"

Sara hurled herself against the door and slammed it shut. "No! He could be hiding! Circling the house!"

Karen marched resolutely into the living room. She sat down and said as calmly as she could, "Sit down and get control of yourself and tell me what's going on."

Sara reeled into the room grimacing. She glanced worriedly at the windows to make sure the blinds were closed. She sat down suddenly on the edge of the sofa, took a deep breath, and told Karen that three tank cars full of nerve gas were in the Sparks railroad yard ready to be taken to Oakland, maybe were already on their way.

"The compartments are wired with explosives," she said, making an effort to speak plainly, "and they'll go off when the train goes through towns. It's all explained in papers in my purse. We were going to warn the police, Alek and I, now he's dead and I . . . I got in my car and started driving, as fast as I could, just to get away, then I thought I couldn't let them win, I couldn't let all those people die. . . . I owe that much to Gil, to his memory and what he was trying to do. Now we've got to get out of here, Mrs. Ellis! Jamal might be—"

"There's nobody outside. I'm going to make a phone call." She picked up the phone from the end table and dialed Jim's number.

"No time! We should go right to the railroad yard and try to stop the train before it leaves . . . then we can go to the police if you want. I'm innocent. I shot Mahmed in self-defense." Sara went to a window and lifted a slat of the venetian blinds. "There's a car out there! I think it's Jamal's!"

Karen cursed under her breath when she got a busy signal, then frowned. She clicked the cradle with her finger. "That's funny, it went dead. . . ."

"Jamal!" Sara said in a trembling voice. "He followed me and now he's cut the phone wires! Look . . ."

Karen dropped the phone and went to the window. Squinting through the opening Sara had made in the blinds, she saw a car parked across the street.

"See?" Sara whispered in her ear. "That car wasn't there a minute ago, was it? I think it's Jamal's!"

"There's a kid across the street with a car something like that. Could be his. As for the phone," she added, her voice betraying a lack of conviction, "they've been working on the lines lately. There've been a couple of outages already this week, and . . . who is Jamal?"

"A crazy man! He sabotaged the train . . . I killed Mahmed—I had to!—and now Jamal will kill me . . . and you, too, if we don't get out of here. . . ." Sara opened her purse and took out the gun. Karen made no effort to stop her.

"If he comes anywhere near either of us," Sara said through clenched teeth, brandishing the weapon, "he's dead." She took Karen's arm. "Come on, which way to the garage?"

"Is that thing real?"

The door chimes sounded. The two women gasped and stared at each other.

"It's him!"

Karen tried to swallow. "Probably Mrs. Yost from next door," she said weakly, "with a bowl of popcorn."

"Shout that you're coming, then we've got to make a break for it in your car."

Karen turned pale and gaped at the door, unable to find her voice.

Whoever was outside turned the knob and rattled it, then pounded on the door with a fist. "Open up, Sara! Do you hear me? Open it!" The door shuddered with the force of a kick or a shoulder.

That was enough for Karen. She led Sara through the

dining room and kitchen, through a small laundry room and into the garage.

"Thank God," Sara said when she saw Karen's 280ZX, "a sports car. He'll never be able to keep up in his jalopy."

Karen got behind the wheel. Sara took the passenger seat and made sure the window was down. They both fastened their seat belts. Sara rested her gun hand against the bottom of the window opening and nodded that she was ready.

The garage-door activator was clipped to the sunshade. Karen touched the button and at the same time started the engine and shifted to reverse. The moment the door had risen far enough to pass the car, Karen revved the engine and let out the clutch. With a screech of tires, the car shot backward out of the garage, up the driveway, into the street, over the opposite curb, and into a cluster of lilac bushes. Karen slammed the gearshift into low, pulled the wheel hard to the left, and roared forward. Out of the corner of her eye she saw a man running toward them across her front lawn with his arm raised. There was a flash of light, a thud against the side of the car, and the sound of a firecracker.

Despite being thrown against the back of the seat by the acceleration, Sara managed to get off a shot. "I got him!" she shouted. "I think I got him! He's down."

"Jesus, Mary, and Joseph," Karen breathed, her face as white as chalk. She kept the gas pedal floored and streaked down the East Prater Way hill past the Sparks Family Hospital at fifty miles an hour.

In the next five minutes Karen Ellis broke more traffic laws than she had in her entire life. She drove on the wrong side of the street, went twice as fast as the posted speed limit, ignored stop signs and lights, made turns on two wheels, and generally behaved like a maniac who was both homicidal and drunk. Sara rode shotgun, kneeling backward on the passenger's seat with her small handgun pointed toward the rear window. She alternately reported that she thought she saw Jamal's car and that they had lost him.

Between tire-squealing turns and roaring accelerations, the two women exchanged fragments of what they knew about the gas, the train, the sabotage, and Gil Ellis's last hours. Karen first headed for the downtown Reno police station, then decided instead to take Sara's suggestion and go to the railroad yard in Sparks with the hope that they could keep the train from leaving. Karen had boarded a train there once for a trip to Sacramento and remembered seeing a control tower of some sort and an office of the Mountain Pacific Railroad Police.

"He'll probably think we're headed downtown," Karen shouted over the roar of the engine, "and will try to head us off." She took a corner so fast, the car skidded sideways and bounced off a curb. The wheels spun briefly before grabbing and sending the car rocketing forward again. A light rain had begun to fall and the streets were getting slippery.

"I see him!" Sara screamed. "He's gaining!"

"Shit!"

"No, I guess not! I think we've lost him!"

After a zigzag course around several blocks, Karen found herself going south on Pyramid Way. She zoomed through the I-80 underpass and turned left on East Nugget at a parking lot full of campers and mobile homes. They were heading east now, separated from the rail yard by a fence. In the darkness the idle locomotives and freight cars were visible only as massive shadows. On the left, on the other side of the freeway, was the towering sign of the King and Queen Motel—"water beds and closed-circuit TV." On the right, beyond the tracks, was the four-story brick building that once housed Harrah's famed collection of automobiles.

"Jamal won't expect us to come down here," Karen

said, winded from the effort of wrestling with the car. "He'll think we'll try to stay as far from the gas as possible. See him?"

"No, but maybe he's driving with his lights out."

The rain suddenly increased in intensity. Water came down in heavy sheets for a minute or two, then eased off and stopped.

Karen looked to the right and saw a two-story wooden building in the middle of the rail yard. The roof sloped upward on all sides to a glassed-in room like a forest ranger's lookout. The dispatcher's office, she thought, and made a right turn onto a road that bumped across five sets of tracks.

"Look!" Sara said, pointing. "There's a freight pulling out now!"

Between a row of flatcars loaded with truck trailers they could see the dark shape of a train rolling slowly west. Karen turned right and stopped next to a one-story building with a small sign in a window: POLICE—PLEASE USE FRONT ENTRANCE. On the left was the Amtrak passenger station with the control room on top.

"If that's the train with the gas," Karen said, "tell the cops to stop it. I'm going to try to catch up to it. . . . If I see the silver tank cars, I'll block the track with my car if I have to."

Sara jumped out and ran toward the police office. Just beyond, the caboose of the departing train rolled past.

"I'll meet you back here," Karen shouted, stepping on the gas. The force of the acceleration slammed the car door.

Sara wasted no time watching Karen begin her chase. She ran between the two buildings looking for a way inside. "Police!" she shouted. "Police!"

Before turning the corner onto the loading platform, she glanced behind her. A car was turning off the frontage road into the rail yard. Her fingers went inside her purse and closed around the handle of the gun.

The road Karen was on went down the middle of the yard with rail tracks on each side. With the gas pedal floored, she quickly gained on the caboose, but before overtaking it the road ended between converging tracks. She had to turn around and go back. She was about to turn north on Fourteenth Street when she saw a railroad worker a hundred feet away. He was holding a white lantern, and as Karen lowered her window she could see him set it on the ground and strike a match. The flare of the flame briefly illuminated his face and the pipe he was lighting.

"Hello!" Karen shouted. "Is that train headed for Oakland? Hello, can you hear me?"

Apparently the rattle and rumble of the receding caboose were drowning out her words. Karen set the brake, shifted to neutral, and jumped out of the car, leaving the headlights on and the motor running. She picked her way across several sets of tracks in the darkness, stubbed her toe on a rail, and fell once to her knees on the rain-soaked ground. "Hello! Can you hear me? Can you stop the train?" The workman didn't respond.

The man stood stiffly, his pipe protruding from clenched teeth, his hands raised to his face. He was holding the burning match several inches away from the bowl of the pipe as if having second thoughts about smoking. He didn't move when Karen came up beside him.

"Is that the train with the three silver tank cars?" Karen asked breathlessly, grabbing his arm. "It's sabotaged! It's got to be stopped! Is there some way of changing the signals or calling it back?"

What was wrong with him? Was he deaf? Was he playing games? Karen stared into his face and shook his arm. "Emergency!" she shouted. "The train has to be stopped!"

The man's arm felt rigid and she could hear labored breathing. His eyes were swinging from side to side, but he seemed unable to move anything else. Then Karen noticed the flame. The match he was holding was a large wooden one and the flame was licking his hand. The entire length of the match was on fire and the yellow tongue was wrapped around the ends of his thumb and forefinger, yet he made no effort to drop it. Either he was oblivious to the pain or unable to loosen his grip or both. When the smell of burning flesh reached Karen's nose, she reflexively slapped at the flame, trying to knock the match out of his hand. She succeeded, but also knocked the man off balance. She clutched at his sleeve to keep him upright, then lunged to embrace him as he fell away from her.

He didn't try to straighten his arms and break his fall. He went down as woodenly as a department-store mannequin, landing hard on his side and coming to rest with one leg slightly raised and his body across a rail. The pipe remained fixed between his teeth.

Karen dropped to her knees and rolled the man onto his back. In the dim light she looked into staring eyes, wide and round and full of panic. "You'll be all right," she managed to say. "The train is carrying a gas, and you got a whiff." She hoped it was only a whiff. From what Sara had just told her and what she could remember from earlier conversations with Gil, she knew that anything beyond a light dose would make more and more of his muscles freeze until finally his eyes, his lungs, and his heart would be immobilized and he would be dead. At least now she knew that the train that just left was carrying the gas and that it was already leaking.

Karen dragged the man off the rail with difficulty and rolled him over, lifting his head with one hand to keep the pipe from being pushed into his mouth. Better leave the pipe between his teeth, she decided, to keep him from biting his tongue. She positioned him safely between two tracks, her skin crawling at the deathlike stiffness of the body. "Just lie here," she said. Could he hear her or was he gone already? "Don't try to move until you're sure you can get away from the tracks. I'm going to stop the train, then I'll send help for you."

She ran back to the car and threw it into gear, revving the engine and releasing the brake. She breathed a silent prayer that Sara had convinced the railroad police or whatever other workmen she had found that the train had to be stopped.

Looking down the tracks to the west, she saw the swaying lights of the caboose in the distance and heard faint warnings from the locomotive's horn as it nosed into downtown Reno. She knew the tracks passed close to Harrah's casino and crossed dozens of city streets. It would have to go slowly for quite a few miles. She was sure she could beat it to the edge of town.

Karen sped north on Fourteenth, crossed under the freeway, made a squealing right turn onto B Street, and raced east to the Pyramid Way on ramps, her headlights flashing on the wet pavement. Once she was headed west on I-80, it took only seconds for her Z to reach speeds of eighty and eighty-five miles an hour. If she attracted the highway patrol, she thought, so much the better.

CHAPTER 18

Sara threw herself against the door of the railroad police office. It was locked. "Police!" she shouted, shaking the knob and knocking. "Help! Let me in!" She cupped her hands beside her eyes and peered through the door window, a square of glass reinforced with wire mesh. She could see a counter, a desk, a chair. She could see a slit of light beneath a door at the end of a dark hallway. Was the cop on duty in the john? She pounded on the door as hard as she could with the side of her fist. "Police! Police!" Why was the door locked? Were even the police afraid of burglars?

She turned away and ran along the concrete platform looking for a sign of life. Next to the police office was the old station, a barnlike wooden building on top of which was a small room with outward-sloping windows. No lights showed at ground level. By backing away and looking up she could see a dim glow through the angled glass overhead. Sara stepped off the curbing of the platform to get farther away from the building and to get a better view of the rooftop room. When she was standing in the middle of the second set of tracks she could see a man's face eerily lit from below.

"Hello up there! Can you hear me?"

There was no response. She shouted again, this time as piercingly as she could, still with no effect. She clambered back across the rails, stepped onto the platform, and tried a door. Locked. Back to the tracks and down on one knee to feel for a piece of gravel she could throw at the window. Holding her purse in her right hand, she touched the ground with her left. There was gravel, all right, but it was tightly packed. Surely there was a loose piece somewhere. . . .

Fifty feet away, the door of the police office opened with a loud squeak and a man was silhouetted in the rectangle of white fluorescent light. "Hey, lady!" he called, walking toward her. "What the hell are you doing? Was that you hollering and pounding on the door?" A holstered gun at his hip bobbed with each step.

Never before had Sara Schuler been glad to see a policeman. "Oh, thank God!" she said, stepping onto the curb. "The train that just left, is there some way to stop it? Three cars of nerve gas have been sabotaged and—"

She saw Jamal too late. He was little more than a shadow between the two buildings, but there was enough light from the open door to reveal the gun he was aiming at her.

"Jamal, no!" she screamed. The hand she raised instinctively was no protection. The first bullet tore through her palm and slammed into her shoulder, knocking her hard to the ground. She rolled over twice in a futile effort to escape and felt herself falling off the curbing to the gravel roadbed six inches below. She managed to get her hand inside her purse, but before she could make another move a second bullet pounded into her. Pain blinded her like a splash of acid.

Jamal turned his attention to the policeman and fired again. Sara tightened her hand around her gun and found the trigger with her forefinger. She forced her eyes open and lifted her head above the edge of the concrete. Jamal and the cop were facing each other like wrestlers across a ring. The cop was doubled over, apparently shot in the stomach; his hand was on his holster. He took a small step forward to keep his balance, then pitched forward onto his face. A weak effort to regain his feet was ended by Jamal's fourth shot, delivered as coldly as a man putting a rabid dog out of his misery.

Sara watched as Jamal turned toward her. In the semidarkness he couldn't see that she had managed to raise her gun. With an effort of will fueled by hatred, she held her arm still and squeezed the trigger. The gun kicked, and a bullet struck Jamal in the center of the throat—his head fell to one side and he collapsed like a rag doll. She was able to send two more bullets into his crumpled body before pain overwhelmed her. Her fingers went limp and her gun clattered to the pavement. She felt strength and consciousness slipping away. It's up to you now, Mrs. Ellis, she thought. Karen. May I call you Karen? I think we could be friends. Then there was no pain anymore, just a heavy, crushing blackness that pressed her into the ground like a blanket of iron.

Racing down the freeway and threading her way through slower-moving traffic, Karen was torn by the options facing her. Should she head for the city police station? Should she go back to the railroad yard and make sure Sara got the message across to the workers there? Maybe she should find a phone booth and call Jim, or call an ambulance for the man she had left lying on the ground. She shuddered at the memory of the flames burning his fingers and the woodenness of his body as he toppled over.

The sky over Reno was clear except for a cluster of clouds directly overhead that were drifting away from the Sierras toward the desert. A renewed rain squall forced her to turn her wipers on again. She eased up on the gas and leaned forward, knuckles white on the wheel. It rained hard for twenty seconds—big, warm drops that exploded against the windshield—then stopped as suddenly as it had started. Great, she thought, just enough to make driving treacherous.

She considered taking the center off ramp and blocking

the train with her car in downtown Reno where the tracks passed between the Amtrak station and Harrah's, but she let the exit pass. Best let the train get through town and stop it in a rural area. Half sobbing, she wished she knew the city better and where the freeway went in relation to the railroad. Exits for Wells and Virginia came and went. What about Keystone? Keystone intersected West Fourth Street at a point where it was close to the railroad tracks and the Truckee River. She had only been in that part of town once, and she dimly recalled that it was an area of light industry rather than homes. She couldn't remember if there were any places where streets crossed the tracks, but she decided she better find out. Staying on the freeway too long might leave her without any point of access to the tracks.

The 280ZX cornered well, but a hard left from the off ramp onto Keystone almost turned it on its side. She ignored the traffic lights at Fifth and made her right turn on West Fourth with only a slight squealing of tires. The tracks were on her left, but out of sight behind a row of small businesses and storefronts. At Stoker, just south of Mountain View Cemetery, the street was adjacent to the tracks but on top of a five-foot-high embankment. On the right was a sign for the Tombstone Motel. A tombstone, Karen thought, that's what I'll probably need when this night is over. She lowered her window and tried to see if she was ahead of or behind the train. At a point where she had a clear view to the west, she saw the red lights at the end of the train.

She stepped on the gas and within a minute had pulled even with the caboose just as she shot through the McCarran Boulevard intersection. A glance at the speedometer showed that the train was doing forty-five miles an hour. Hoping to bring somebody out onto the rear platform, she honked her horn but without effect, partly because the street was seldom on the same level as the tracks. Sometimes the train was below and sometimes above, but always so tantalizingly close that she could have hit it with a rock. What would she do if the conductor appeared, she asked herself in despair, exchange waves with him?

She turned on the speed again, hoping to overtake the engine while the road and tracks were still next to each other. She gained ground steadily, and twenty-five rail cars from the caboose she saw the three silver tankers marked MILK, swaying and trembling, as ominous and threatening as giant bombs. She closed the window and held her breath until they were well behind her. Hitting speeds of sixty and seventy, Karen gradually pulled even with the three linked locomotives in an area where the freeway, the highway, the rail line, and the river were squeezed into a narrow valley.

Luck was with her—the highway and the tracks were side by side at the same elevation and a full moon in the east was casting a dim light. She lowered the window and leaned her head and shoulders into the wind. She waved her arm frantically at the engineer she could see sitting at the side window of the leading locomotive. "Stop!" she screamed. "Stop the train!" Her words were swept away by the wind and drowned out by the hum of the locomotive engines and the roar of hundreds of steel wheels on steel rails.

The desperate waving of her arm was answered by the engineer with a toss of the hand as casual as the Queen of England's. The highway diverged from the tracks then in a curve to the right, and Karen had to slam on the brakes; the wheels locked, the tires protested with a shriek, and the car slid sideways onto a gravel shoulder and came to rest a few feet from the edge of an embankment. She shifted to low and surged back onto the road, shooting through an underpass and making a hard left onto the freeway. That was the end of West Fourth Street. Now she was on Interstate 80 racing a train she could no longer see.

Her mind was racing as well as she tried to think what lay ahead. There were a number of exits before the city of Truckee, she remembered, exits she had never taken. They probably led to small towns along the river. If she could get well ahead of the train, she would get off the freeway and hope that the towns were on the same side of the river as the tracks.

Several minutes of speeds between eighty and ninety miles an hour brought her to an exit marked Verdi. She let it pass because lights on the mountainside indicated that the town was to the right of the freeway while the tracks were below her on the opposite side. The freeway swung in a broad curve to the left and crossed a bridge over both the tracks and the river—a quick glance to the left showed that she was now ahead of the train. All she had to do now was find a grade crossing.

The freeway crossed above the tracks again just as she passed a sign reading LAST NEVADA EXIT ONE MILE. Another sign announced that Truckee, California, was twenty-two miles away. Karen made up her mind to block the train at Truckee or before because farther into the mountains the freeway and the tracks drew miles apart; at Donner Lake, she knew for certain, the freeway was on one side of the water and the railroad on the other. If she failed to stop the train by Truckee, she would find a phone and call Jim, the railroad, the police, anybody she could think of.

Sacramento 125 mi.

Welcome to California!
Watch for snow removal equipment

Rock slide area next 10 mi.

The giant green highway signs came and went quickly in the night. When Karen saw that Floriston was one mile ahead, she made her decision. A mountain slope rose on the right, so close that a heavy chain-link fence was needed to keep rolling rocks off the traffic lanes. That meant Floriston had to be on the left, on the same side as the river and the railroad. She cut her speed and took the Floriston exit. At least the road here was dry; apparently the earlier rain squall had been confined to Reno.

The road angled down and under the freeway, then crossed over a narrow bridge above the river. She slowed to a crawl to pass through two short, one-lane tunnels that were made of corrugated metal and just barely big enough for a car. She sounded her horn as a sign instructed, though at night her headlights would alert anybody coming in the other direction. Beyond the tunnels the road rose steeply, then leveled off. Farther on Karen could see a group of wooden houses, none with lights showing. The railroad track was twenty feet away on the left. She stopped the car next to a billboard intended for freeway travelers:

B.L.'s Radiator Service
The Best Place in the State
To Take a Leak

Probably Floriston's leading employer. No time to try to find B.L. and ask to use his phone—coming toward her from the east was the train, the headlight of the lead locomotive sweeping back and forth like a blind man's cane. It was no more than thirty seconds away.

Karen swung off the dirt road, crossed a patch of rough ground, and bounced the front tires over both rails. She set the brake with the car straddling the track, jumped out, and began climbing the side of the mountain to get as far away from the collision as possible. The sound of the air horn was startlingly loud when it split the night silence, and the way the dancing headlight beam swept across her made her feel like an escaping convict. The engineer wouldn't stop the train just because she was waving her arms, but hitting a car should do the trick. Her beautiful car . . . Would Allstate, she wondered, replace it even though she had sacrificed it deliberately?

Breathless from the sprint up the slope, Karen wrapped her arms around the rough bark of a tree and looked down over her shoulder. The ground trembled as the train thundered past—on another track. The two short tunnels she had driven through carried the road under two tracks, one eastbound, one westbound, and she had blocked the wrong one.

She scrambled back down the slope, got in the car, and rolled up the window before the three silver tankers rushed past. She backed off the track and, holding her breath again, retraced her path through the narrow tunnels to the freeway. Truckee was the last chance.

Joe Dori sat at the controls at the right side of the cab with his elbow resting on the sill of the open window and Tommy Talbot sat on the left. Joe kept the speed below fifteen mph through downtown Reno, touching the horn as he approached every intersection.

"In a few years," he said to his partner, "the computer display will give you a picture of all three locomotives and let you monitor everything from here. Of course the others aren't equipped with the sensors, so if we lose power or something goes wrong, we'll still have to climb back there."

"There's the Sands," Tommy said, pointing to the left. "I lost fifty bucks there last night. Son of a bitch." He waved at some tourists on the sidewalk.

A sudden blast of rain cut visibility to almost zero. Joe

turned on the windshield wipers and both men slid shut their side windows. "Everything is recorded on the computer's memory," Joe said, "so that when we pull into Oakland four or five hours from now, the mechanics can punch a few buttons and tell exactly what needs looking at. Jesus, it's raining drops as big as horse turds."

"What bugs me is that when you win, you're supposed to give the dealer a tip. When you lose, does the dealer toss a few bucks your way? Hell, no."

"I suppose eventually headquarters will be able to *run* the train from the office. Not that the union will let them."

The rain stopped and they opened their windows again. Joe moved the throttle to notch six and watched the speedometer needle climb to forty-five.

Tommy looked across the cab at the older man. "Let computers run the train? You got to be kidding! They thought they could do that when they built the San Francisco subway system. Holy shit, if the state had let them, they would have killed a thousand commuters a day."

"Plenty more where those came from," Joe said, and they both laughed. "All the same, you got to admit that computers are getting better and better."

"Yeah, and people are getting worse."

"Take train control." Joe looked idly at the road paralleling the track. A white sports car was pacing the train. "Before long it will all be done by transmitters on the train and satellites in orbit. The dispatcher will be able to tell within a gnat's pecker the position of every train on the line at all times. With the block system we use now, why, Christ, they only know where you are within five miles. Five miles! That's a pretty big margin of error when you consider the damage potential." The woman in the sports car was waving her arm, her hair streaming behind her in the wind. "Hello, Blondie," Joe said, lifting his hand. He watched as the road she was on ended and she skidded to a sideways stop. "Dizzy dame," he said, shaking his head.

"Just to give you an example," Tommy said, "take the dealers. They used to be a lot friendlier. Last night when I emptied my wallet, that cold fish of a dealer gave me a 'tough shit' little smile that frosted my ass. I damn near stuffed my fist in his mouth."

Joe stood up. "Here, stuff your ass on this seat. Get the feel of running this baby."

They traded places, Joe taking the seat at the left window. "Take her up to notch seven," he told Tommy. "We can do sixty through here. Nothing but a couple of little bergs, Verdi and Floriston, before we hit the state line and Truckee. Don't be afraid to toot the horn. We don't want anybody to get too much sleep."

Tommy moved the throttle to the left and smiled at the way the engine responded. "I know what you mean," he said. "Too much sleep and you wake up logy."

Joe relaxed and watched the scenery go by. He was never more at peace with himself than when his ears were filled with the purr of a locomotive diesel and when he could feel the vibration in his bones. The sound of the wheels on the quarter-mile-long welded rails was a steady hum; the clickety-click of thirty-nine-foot rails was a thing of the past, at least on main lines. Looking to the rear, he saw no signs of sparks or hotboxes. Twice, as the train cruised down straightaways, he caught glimpses of the red caboose lights as the last cars came out of curves. Ahead, the side-to-side sweep of the oscillating headlight and the endless approach of the rails were hypnotic.

A half mile in the distance he saw the stab of an automobile's headlights. The car was making a left-to-right turn, and for a split second was aimed directly at the train. The driver seemed to be trying to get over the tracks, then stopped or stalled. Joe frowned. There was no grade crossing at that point. How the hell did a car get on the right-of-way?

"Hit the horn, Tommy. Look like we got a daredevil."

Joe squinted. The east- and west-bound tracks were gradually moving away from each other, and it was impossible at a distance of two thousand feet to tell which one the car was stopped on. At a thousand feet he could see that the car was parked across the east-bound tracks. Was that intentional or the mistake of somebody trying to commit suicide?

"Goddamn stupid idiot," Joe heard Tommy say between blasts on the horn.

As the locomotive hurtled past the car, missing it by no more than ten feet, Joe noticed that the headlights were on and the driver's door was open. "For God's sakes," he said, staring to the rear as the car receded in the distance, "that's the same car that was racing us a few miles back!"

He got on the radio. "MP seven six six one west to Sparks tower. This is Joe Dori. Hey, we got a drunk or a suicide trying to play tag with us. Sports car, white, maybe Japanese. Driver is a woman in a white blouse, blond with long hair. She just about totaled herself in Reno racing us along West Fourth. Now I see her again in Floriston parked across the east-bound tracks. We barely missed hitting her. Over."

Spence Kesson's voice crackled back, "Sparks tower to MP seven six six one west at Floriston. Sounds like a railroad buff. I'll tell Clay. Over."

"Do that. Highway patrol should pick her up before she kills somebody. Over and out."

"I hit a car with a switch engine once," Tommy said. "I'll never forget the look on the guy's face. He was stalled at a crossing, and he looked up at me as if he couldn't believe what was happening. Made no effort at all to jump out of the way. Scared shitless."

"One? Is that all? I've hit at least a dozen over the last twenty years. Makes me sick every time. Once I saw a gasoline truck parked smack across the track no more than five hundred yards ahead and the driver running for dear life across a cornfield. I was in notch six at the time, doing about sixty."

"What did you do, jump?"

"Better to ride it out. I threw it into notch eight and hit the floor. Well, my God, there was the biggest explosion you can imagine, orange flames everywhere, but I didn't singe a hair. It took me a mile to stop. The locomotive and the first few cars were solid black from one end to the other, but not a hell of a lot of damage otherwise. They were picking up pieces of the truck for months. You know what? The driver never showed up. He's probably still running."

"Why do people do it? What is it about a train that makes people want to race you or beat you across an intersection?"

"Wish I knew. The pleading look they give you just before you hit them, that's what gives me nightmares. They turn their big eyes up at you as if to say 'Don't hit me. I have enough trouble in my life.' "

Tommy bit into an apple with a loud cracking sound. "People are weird," he said, pushing the words through a full mouth.

For several miles she raced the train, which was to the left of the freeway and traveling at a little over sixty miles an hour. Gradually the two rights-of-way drew apart, and by the time she reached the Truckee exit she had no idea whether or not she had arrived first.

At ten o'clock at night on a Wednesday, Truckee, a town with a population of fifteen hundred souls, was largely deserted. The main street was only a block or two long, with a line of old brick buildings on the left and the railroad tracks on the right. The Chevron station was closed, but she spotted a pay phone she could use if she had to. A couple of bars seemed to be open . . . probably phones there also. She drove slowly, craning her neck to look east and west down the track. No sign of the train. A city street crossed the tracks to the right; it would be easy to block the train there if it hadn't yet arrived. Also on the right was a turn-of-the-century train station that looked newly renovated but was obviously closed for the night. The station agent probably went home after the last Amtrak passenger train went through late in the afternoon.

Karen was about to make a U-turn and go back to the phone she had passed when she spotted a small café. It was the size and shape of a railroad passenger car and was called Dwight's Depot Diner. Karen could see several patrons inside sitting on a row of stools and a cook with a white chef's hat behind a long counter. They all seemed to be leaning forward attentively, as if listening to a radio report. They would know if the train had come through or not. The diner was so close to the tracks that a speeding freight would shake a coffee cup off its saucer.

Karen parked and ran toward the entrance. The streetlights and a full moon were bright enough to reveal a faint blue mist that clung to the ground beside the railroad tracks like the last remnants of a morning fog, that flickered along the base of the diner, that delicately colored the knob on the door.

Nobody moved when Karen burst inside. "Did a train just go by?" she called. "In the last couple of minutes? Headed west?"

With growing horror she gaped at the three seated men and the cook behind the counter. They were staring at each other with twisted expressions on their faces, as motionless as statues in a park.

CHAPTER 19

No more work was scheduled in the Sparks yard that night, so Spence Kesson would act both as yardmaster and Reno Division dispatcher. Such doubling would never have been permitted in the old days, but now, when the railroad was losing more and more freight business to trucks every year, the unions were forced to make one concession after another.

He flipped the intercom switch and pressed the button that sounded Special Agent Clay Corman's buzzer in the building next door. While waiting for the policeman to answer, Kesson watched the electronic screens. One was a schematic of the Sparks-Reno yard showing the position of every string of cars; two others displayed the main line and sidings from Winnemucca in the northeast to beyond Donner Summit in the west; a fourth gave the condition of every signal and switch in any block he wished to highlight. As he watched, a red, inch-long segment representing the west-bound block from the state line to a point near Truckee winked off and the next segment winked on. Joe Dori's train, assigned road number 7661 for the trip to the Bay Area, had left one block and entered another. A printer behind him clattered as it automatically noted the time the train left the state-line block and entered the Truckee block. Kesson picked up a pen and noted the same information on his train sheet; federal regulations required that he make a manual note of everything that happened and every step taken. You never knew when the computer-generated record would be garbage. He would be able to follow 7661's progress block by block until it reached Emigrant Gap, when it would disappear from his view and appear on screens in Sacramento. Beyond Fairfield, near the upper end of San Francisco Bay, the train would be monitored by the dispatcher in Oakland.

Because it had Green Line status, 7661 would be insulated by keeping at least two blocks empty ahead and behind. It would be allowed to travel at passenger train speeds. It wouldn't have to stop at Sacramento for a crew change, either, which was required under normal union rules. Joe, Tommy, and Bud would be able to run for twelve hours without relief if the trip took that long. No delays were anticipated, though, and the estimated time of arrival in the Oakland yard was 4:30 A.M.

Kesson, a friendly-faced man of sixty, frowned and pressed the buzzer button once more and waited, wondering if the intercom was on the fritz again. After half a minute passed he gave up and reached for the phone, dialing the police office number. No answer. Where the hell was Clay, anyway? If he didn't show up pretty soon, he'd have to call the highway patrol himself; otherwise the woman in the sports car that Joe was worried about would be long gone. He tried to reach him on the two-way radio that the policeman always carried on his belt: "MP Sparks tower to Special Agent Corman. Clay, this is Spence. Can you hear me? Come in, please, over." Only static in response.

"Goddammit," Kesson muttered, leaving his chair and walking to the west window. With his hands on the sill, he could see that the lights were on in the adjacent one-story building and that the door was wide open. Clay would never leave the door open unless he was close by. Kesson had heard some commotion earlier, popping sounds and shouting, but had dismissed it as kids with firecrackers. He was talking to the Sacramento dispatcher on the phone as well as Joe Dori on the radio at the time and hadn't paid much attention, figuring Clay would handle it. Maybe Clay had chased the kids away or had them by the ear and was giving them a talking-to.

The dispatcher gave his terminals a quick glance to make sure everything was as it should be, then jogged down the stairs and outside.

He saw the woman first, her head and arm on the concrete, her legs across the near rail of Track One. "What the goddamn hell . . ." Was she drunk or what? He couldn't leave her like that . . . the freight coming in from Salt Lake would cut her in two. He took her under the arms and dragged her onto the platform, shouting for Clay as he did so. Good grief, there was a small silver gun on the curb. Was it hers? He felt something wet, and straightened up and looked at his hands. Sweat? No, it was thicker than that. Vomit? He turned his palms up and held them toward the light coming from the open door of the office and saw hands so covered with blood that they looked like shiny red gloves.

As his lips drew back from his teeth in shock, his eyes were drawn to a shape on the ground near the corner of the police building. He fought against the evidence that his eyes presented him. It was a trash bag, he tried to tell himself, a pile of laundry, a roll of canvas, not a human being, not the policeman who had been his friend for twenty years. But it was a human being, a man in the uniform of the railroad police, lying facedown with his feet apart, one arm extended, the other at his side. Ten feet away was another body, a man lying faceup with a gun in one hand, his legs curled under him and eyes staring from a head bent backward at an impossible angle.

Kesson lurched to the body of the policeman, leaned down and touched his shoulder, and began to cry. "Clay, no," he whispered, choking, turning him over, "aw, shit, no . . ." He saw the face of his friend streaked with blood and mutilated by a bullet fired at close range.

There were more than four victims of Mannequin in the diner, Karen soon discovered. There was a couple in one of the booths slumped down on the padded seats, and at the end of the counter was a teenage girl who had apparently slipped off a stool and was lying on her side with her legs drawn up in a sitting position. Karen ran from one to another trying without success to revive them or at least elicit some response. They were stiff as boards and glassy-eyed, though all had heartbeats and were still breathing . . . except for the teenager, who was able to purse her lips slightly and whose eyes were darting wildly back and forth. She was farthest from the door, Karen thought, maybe she didn't get as large a dose. One thing was for sure—Truckee must have been one of the places Mahmed had chosen for an explosion. My God, how much damage had been done? Had the whole town been blanketed by gas?

"You're going to be all right," Karen said with mock confidence, not knowing if her words could be heard. "I'm going to call for help. You've been hit by gas that's leaking from the train that just went by, but you'll get over it. . . ."

There was a pay phone on the wall. Karen fumbled in her purse for change and could find only two nickels. She went behind the counter and squeezed by the cook, careful not to knock him down, and pushed the cash-register keys at random until she found the one that popped open the drawer. "Just a loan," she said in case the cook could hear her. "I'll pay you back when this is over."

She scooped up a handful of quarters and noticed a stiffness in her fingers. Probably from gripping the steering wheel too long and too tightly, she thought, making her way back to the phone. She was in good physical condition generally from jogging and tennis, but her hand muscles were one thing she never bothered exercising; the piano and clarinet kept them limber. There was a stiffness in her neck and upper back, too, which she tried to shrug off by moving her shoulders up and down . . . the muscle tension of handling a speeding car was catching up to her.

Christ, she couldn't remember Jim's number. Were the last three digits 769 or 976? 796? She fished out her address book and looked through it frantically. There it was, 769; she was right for the first time. When she dropped a couple of quarters on the floor, the realization hit her that she had gotten a dose of the gas herself.

She felt a touch of dizziness, and when she tried to move her feet wider apart they wouldn't respond and she had to lean against the wall to make sure she didn't fall over. She could feel her back stiffening as if her spine were changing into a cold steel bar.

"Please deposit a dollar thirty for three minutes," an operator said.

Karen pushed coins into the phone with hands curled into claws, dropping half of them on the floor. She tried to tell the operator that there was an emergency, but her teeth were locked together and her tongue wouldn't form the words.

"I beg your pardon?" Karen heard the operator say. "I'm sorry, I can't understand you. Your call is going through." The operator left the line despite Karen's high-pitched noises of protest, and then there were ringing signals.

With appalling swiftness, Karen felt her hands and feet immobilized by invisible forces, then her arms and legs, then her stomach and chest. She tried to move and twist and speak to keep the invader at bay for just a minute more, but it was already too late. From head to foot she was in the tightening coils of a snake, and when she heard Jim's voice on the line she could only make strangling sounds.

Tighter and tighter the coils drew until breathing was nearly impossible. She bared her teeth and tried with all her might to form the words "gas" and "Truckee," but nothing came out. Suddenly, forming words seemed trivial compared with breathing, with staying alive. She fought to throw off the monster that had her in its grip and that was squeezing her into unconsciousness. Only her eyes obeyed. Looking down, she saw the eyes of the terrified teenager staring back; looking up, she could see the dingy ceiling, streaked with delicate, flickering, gossamer lines of blue that gradually faded and reappeared, each time coming back more weakly until finally they didn't come back at all.

Karen screamed in her imagination, screamed as loudly and long as she could, saw herself screaming, heard a scream of terror in her mind that expressed her fear of death and her hope that death could be held at bay. Cold hands closed around her neck, choking off the whimpering sounds she was managing to make. Now she couldn't even move her eyes, and as her vision was obscured by upwelling tears she was aware only of the growing pressure that worked on every part of her body at once, growing, growing, growing until it seemed she would be squeezed to nothing. She felt the receiver slip from her hand and fall away. Was she falling as well? She couldn't tell.

"Hello? Hello?" she heard Jim say as if from outer space. She also heard the receiver knocking lightly against the wall as it dangled, twisting, at the end of its cord, but she couldn't tell if the sound was coming from above or below.

"Lousy connection," Jim said. "I'll hang up and you try again. No hard feelings. 'Bye."

Click.

* * *

Jim settled back in his easy chair, picked up the book he was reading, and adjusted his glasses. He stared at the phone for a minute, half expecting it to ring again. Every month or so he got a call with a connection so bad he couldn't hear the other party or the other party couldn't hear him. The odd thing this time was that while the connection seemed to be good, all he could make out was a diminishing sound that made him think of someone trying to gargle and moan at the same time. Probably pranksters. He had made enough crazy calls himself when he was a boy in Iowa. "Hello, this is the phone company," he remembered saying in as deep a voice as possible to people who had answered his random dialing. "We are blowing out the lines today in your neighborhood. Please put a paper bag over the phone so that dust won't get all over the house." The challenge was to deliver the lines in a deadpan manner while the other kids in the room were convulsed with laughter. Whether anybody ever followed orders or not he never knew, which left him with an ache of curiosity that persisted for years.

The book he was trying to get through was one he had bought that afternoon at the Book Depot in Mill Valley, a store well stocked in such areas as war, women, nature, investing, poetry, interior decorating, and massage. The title was *CBW: Deadly Threat to the Biosphere,* the CBW standing for chemical and biological warfare, and he hoped it might help him understand what Draegler might be up to. The publisher was something called the Committee for Global Sanity, whose members believed, if Jim understood the preface correctly, that America's best hope lay in throwing all of its weapons, from handguns to H-bombs, into Lake Erie, which had already been ruined by corporate greed. A totally disarmed America would present such a stunning spectacle to the world that combatants in the Middle East, Africa, and Central America would look at each other sheepishly, shake hands, and throw a party, followed by a strong rally on the stock market. When Mother Russia saw a smiling Uncle Sam, she would relax and turn her full attention toward finding disease-resistant strains of cabbage and beets. The argument, so naive that it was almost endearing, was confined to the preface. The body of the work was a dry recitation of facts gathered mainly from government sources.

A depressing bunch of facts they were too. One appendix, titled "Agents Causing Death or Very Serious Injury," featured a list that had Jim shaking his head and considering making a contribution to the Committee for Global Sanity.

1. *Blister Agents (Mustard Gas, Lewisite)*—On contact with skin cause burns, blisters, conjunctivitis, blindness, edema. Currently stocked by Russia and the U.S.

2. *Blood Gases (Hydrogen Cyanide)*—Interfere with cell respiration. Rapidly saturate gas-mask filters.

3. *Lung Irritants (Phosgene)*—Widely used in World War I. Incapacitates at low levels. Gas masks provide total protection.

4. *Nerve Agents*—Cause uncontrollable muscle activity and death through respiratory failure. Immediate effect. Odorless and colorless. V and G exist in Russian and U.S. inventories, other types in laboratories.

a. *G Agents*—First nerve gasses, developed in late 1930s by Nazi chemists.

Effects occur through inhalation. In group are GA (Tabun), GB (Sarin), GD (Soman), GE and GF. GB is stocked by U.S., GD and GA believed to be stocked by Soviets.

b. *V Agents*—Absorbed through skin, necessitating complete body protection. Main types are VE and VX. VX is in U.S. inventory.

5. *Binary Nerve Gas*—Two-part chemicals that are mixed inside bomb or shell on way to target. U.S. began production in 1987.

6. *Incapacitating Agents*—Effects last from hours to days, generally nonfatal. Psychochemicals, like BZ and LSD, cause mental disorientation. Physiochemicals, like CX (phosgene-oxime), can cause paralysis. Unpredictable and expensive.

7. *Toxins*—Disease-causing bacteria. Production and possession banned by the Biological and Toxin Weapons Convention of 1972, but alleged to have been used in Laos, Kampuchea, and Afghanistan.

Jim forced himself to review the list. From what he knew and could guess about Mannequin, it was odorless, colorless, and fast-acting, like other nerve gases, absorbed through the skin like the V agents, and capable of causing paralysis or death, like the physiochemicals. Looked like somebody at Draegler had found a way to put all the best features into a really swell new product. Better living through chemistry.

Flipping through the book, Jim's eye fell on a familiar

name: General Clement Trainer. Backtracking a few paragraphs, he found the beginning of a statement made by Trainer before a congressional committee when he was still with the Pentagon. Speaking in 1985 in favor of a Reagan Administration plan to resume production of nerve gas, which had been halted by Richard Nixon in 1972, Trainer argued, in effect, that the United States should be paranoid because Russia is. Not only did Russia have every horrible chemical and biological weapon that we did, they might be developing some new ones, so we should, too, to maintain "parity" and "leadership." Furthermore, they had defensive equipment far in advance of anything in the United States, ranging from hand-held to truck-mounted. He spoke with envy of "rapid combat vehicle decontamination systems" and portable shower stalls for troops.

Trainer admitted during questioning that the existing United States stock of nerve agents weighed between 30,000 and 40,000 tons, but said that the armed forces no longer had weapons to deliver it, that most of it was stored in aging and in some cases leaking containers too dangerous to handle, and that in any case the Soviet arsenal was twenty times larger. He stressed that the Soviets had a dangerous lead because of the experience of using CBW agents on battlefields in Laos and Cambodia.

Trainer's assertions were disputed in footnotes. Nobody knew for sure what the Russians had or were working on. They had built up a strong chemical capability after World War I, when they suffered 500,000 chemical casualties, but their efforts seemed defensive in nature. Nobody knew what exactly happened, if anything, in obscure Third World conflicts. The main evidence from Laos, for example, was a leaf with yellow spots along with tales from the natives of planes spraying mist. Pentagon scientists said the spots were evidence of a toxin gas. Independent scientists, though, dismissed anecdotal material as unreliable and contradictory and said the spots were nothing more than bee feces.

Jim threw the book down and went to the kitchen. Bee shit! Good God, the world was going mad! Inside the refrigerator was a package of sliced ham, half a loaf of bread that was getting stiff around the edges, and an elderly head of lettuce that possibly had an edible core. How about a ham sandwich? Before meeting Karen he would have started constructing one at once, lathering mayo on the bread like plaster on a wall. Now, though, he hesitated. Hanging from the inside of the refrigerator door was a large mirror he had put there to give himself a clear view of his waist, which was making a forty-inch belt look cruelly small. Written on the mirror in grease pencil was a question he wanted to ask himself at moments like these: "Do you sincerely want to be fat?"

Somebody at Draegler had developed a new type of nerve gas while working on insecticide, maybe that was it, Jim thought, his eyes straying to a desiccated orange and back to the ham. Trainer was sent in by the Pentagon to help develop it with the help of government contracts. Maybe the gas was so terrible, or maybe its development was such a treaty violation, that the government wanted to have—what was the term Washington politicians used?—plausible deniability. Or maybe Draegler was doing it on his own as a commercial venture while the Pentagon winked and looked the other way.

Eliminating the mayo would cut the calorie count. He could hold the bread as well and just fold a slice of ham around some lettuce. No! He slammed the door in an unprecedented displax of discipline. Pounds of flab had to be eliminated, and not eating a ham sandwich was easier and quicker than running two miles. Karen was as slim and trim as an aerobics instructor and would no doubt prefer him that way too, although she was too polite to say so. For her he would do anything.

Let's see, Jim mused, Gil discovered that the gas he thought was an insecticide was really nerve gas. He tried to block a proposed shipment and was rubbed out for his trouble. Pretty melodramatic scenario. Where did Draegler want to ship it? Karen said she thought she heard the words "Iran" and "Arab" on the tape but couldn't be sure. Iraq had been accused of using gas against Iran and maybe was thinking of doing it again. Or was it the other way around? Jim couldn't think of a country he disliked more than Iran. Not that Iraq was a bargain. Some said that in World War II the Allies delayed the Normandy invasion to give Russia and Germany more time to beat each other's brains out. Should he and Karen, who were allies if not Allies, do any less for Iran and Iraq? Jim smiled wryly and shook his head at how strange his speculations seemed. Alone on a houseboat under a full moon in Sausalito, it was hard to take the whole thing seriously.

He opened a broom closet and rummaged through the debris on the floor. He found what he wanted behind a dustpan and held it up by one end—a jump rope. Positioning himself in a clear area, he began skipping vigorously, the rope occasionally hitting the ceiling. Amazing what love would make a man do! He did love that woman. What a doll she was, what a sweetheart, what a wonderful companion! Smart, educated, and talented. Exactly the kind of woman he had always wanted, and it was exciting that she seemed to find him attractive too. He stepped up the pace of the rope until his feet set up a drumbeat on the wooden floor and beads of sweat ran down his face. What the hell was she doing investigating a possible murder and getting involved in a war in the Middle East? It was ridiculous. In the morning he would tell her to get off the case and turn it over to professionals. But would she listen? She had a stubborn streak.

After five minutes he threw the rope down and collapsed in the easy chair, puffing like a steam engine. Not much of a performance, but okay for a start. He vowed to keep at it until he could skip rope for half an hour or his belly button touched his spine, whichever came first. He leaned forward and turned on the television. An old Cary Grant movie was playing on Channel 9. Good, he'd watch that. By the time it was over it would be eleven o'clock and Karen would be home and he could hear her voice again.

Ten minutes later he was asleep.

CHAPTER 20

Battery-powered transmitters were concealed close to the tracks in Truckee, Auburn, Sacramento, Fairfield, Benicia, Richmond, and Berkeley—one for each town. Another was tuned to set off the eight remaining bombs and was hidden in a telephone pole south of the Sixteenth Street Station in Oakland, where more than half a million people lived within a radius of two miles. A gentle breeze off San Francisco Bay would guarantee a tremendous loss of life and would give America an unprecedented taste of war.

The first charge exploded prematurely as the train pulled out of Sparks . . . set off, investigators guessed later, by a stray signal from a two-way radio or garage-door opener. Gas under pressure jetted downward onto the gravel ballast along the track like steam from a ruptured pipe. When the rain struck a blue sheet had spread a hundred yards away from each side of the train, sliding under boxcars parked on sidings and sweeping around the storage sheds on the edge of the railroad yard. In the sudden downpour the advancing blanket of gas was punctured in a million places by raindrops, beaten back, torn into unrelated patches, and finally obliterated. The only casualty at that location was switchman Pete Undiks, who was so concerned about lighting his pipe in the rain that he didn't notice the luminescence that climbed over his shoes and up his legs.

In a quirk in the weather, the storm missed Truckee, sheltered in a canyon at the foot of the Sierras. As the train rolled through town at thirty miles an hour, patrons of Dwight's Depot Diner heard a sound resembling a shotgun blast over the locomotive's horn and the roar of the wheels. Gas boiled out of the silver tank car and rolled over the café like surf, then collapsed into a film that slid silently across the pavement toward the buildings lining the north side of Main Street.

Only three downtown businesses were still open at that hour of the night, the diner and two bars. Minutes before the train passed through, the proprietor of The Honeybucket came outside and hosed the sidewalk where an unwell customer had lost his dinner. While he was at it he sluiced away dog droppings and gave the entire Old West front of the building a bath, hoping to remove wasp nests, cobwebs, and peeling paint. It was an uncharacteristic act of sanitation that his customers would thank him for later.

Merrymakers at The Mine Shaft, a block away, shouting to each other over the blaring jukebox, weren't so lucky. The film crossed the dry street faster than a man could run, wrapped the outside walls in a diaphanous embrace, and, after a moment's hesitation at the open door, spilled inside like ground fog. Voices and laughter gradually faded away, leaving only music.

"Holy Toledo, it's really coming down now!" Joe Dori opened the window on the right side of the cab and peered into the storm. Cold rain assaulted him like spray from a nozzle. He slammed the window shut and wiped a sleeve across his face. "Auburn is around here somewhere, but I sure can't see it. It's late June, for chrissakes! The rainy season is supposed to be over." He moved the throttle handle from notch six to notch five and shifted to dynamic braking. No sense trying to set speed records in a monsoon.

The fury of the storm was impressive. Wind and water lashed and clawed at the train as if Mother Nature were trying to keep it from blundering into some terrible danger that lay ahead. In the old days, Joe thought, the days before World War II, his father would have had to slow to a crawl in weather like this, maybe even stop. Back then communications weren't so good, and neither were the drainage and the roadbed. Radios weren't standard equipment. In the night you never knew when you might find water on the tracks, or rocks, or a washout, or even a missing bridge. Today, why hell, you could go full speed in a rainstorm if you had traction and hardly be taking any chance at all. The engineering and the equipment were that good.

"We're in Auburn," Tommy Talbot said. "The marker just went by and I can see lights." He pointed through the shimmering curtains of steel-gray rain.

"You're right." The hippie had young eyes, the son of a bitch. Joe sounded the horn and radioed to the dispatcher in Sacramento, twenty-five miles down the line.

The response was immediate: "MP Sacramento dispatcher to MP seven six six one west. Hello, Joe, how you doin'? Over."

"MP seven six six one west to MP Sacramento. Slow but sure, Larry . . . mostly slow. Coming through Auburn at the moment and it's raining like Niagara. Well, it's easing up a bit now. Wet down there? Over."

"Sacramento to seven six six one west. Dry as a bone.

We could use a sprinkle. How's the new locomotive working? Over."

"Like a Swiss watch. We're behind schedule, though. Fighting a head wind like you wouldn't believe. Can you hear it howling? Hey, the sky is clearing! I'll be go to hell if the moon isn't coming out! Over."

"MP Sacramento to seven six six one west. That's the mountains for you. If you don't like the weather, wait five minutes. Over."

Joe pulled out his gold watch and squinted at it. It was dark in the cab and he had to hold it in the light of the instrument panel. One-thirty. "We'll be passing through in about half an hour, I guess. Two o'clock. Not bad, considering. Over."

"MP Sacramento dispatcher to MP seven six six one west. Twenty minutes late. That's better than Amtrak by about a day. Going to stop for coffee? Over."

Joe laughed. "Not this time, Larry. We're highballing it all the way to Frisco. Should make it by four in the morning. Over."

"Don't call it Frisco. Besides, you're going to Oakland . . . unless they put tracks across the Bay Bridge and didn't tell us. Over."

"MP seven six six one west to MP Sacramento dispatcher. Frisco, here we come. Over and out."

Joe turned off the windshield wipers. The air was clear now and the headlight was stabbing hundreds of yards ahead, reflecting off the wet, shining rails that converged and disappeared in the distant gloom. The endlessly approaching rails made Joe think of fishing lines being reeled in at high speed.

"Did you hear that?" the kid asked. He had his head out the left window and was looking to the rear.

Joe hadn't heard anything beyond the sounds of the storm and the locomotive's constant rumble and hum.

"It was a bang," Talbot said. "Like an explosion."

"Probably thunder."

"Not thunder. A shotgun, maybe."

Joe got on the radio again, this time to the caboose. "Hello, Bud. How's the weather back there?"

"Raining," was the tinny reply on the loudspeaker.

"Really? It's clear up here and the moon is out. Say, my colleague just heard something go bump in the night. Sort of a boom."

"More like a bang," Tommy corrected. "A kind of a thump."

"More like a bang or a kind of a thump," Joe said. "Did you hear it or feel it?"

"No. There are detector signals a couple of miles ahead."

"Hope they're dark. Hate to stop in this rain."

"Hey, it just stopped raining back here."

"How are your passengers doing?"

"Serious card players, all four of them. Been playing poker for an hour. Big stakes, too. You'd think we were still in Nevada."

"Stay out of the game and tell them we'll arrive in Oakland about four. I'm going to make up time going across the valley."

Bud climbed the stairs to the cupola, which was odd in itself because mainline cabooses usually didn't have cupolas. Typical of Mountain Pacific to pair a brand-new locomotive with an obsolete caboose. This certainly wasn't your routine night run to Oakland.

He looked ahead over the tops of the cars. The moon and a few lights from Auburn enabled him to see twenty or thirty cars, all of them trembling and swaying normally. No sign of fire or sparks. For a second he thought he saw a faint blue glow on the roof of a boxcar, but when he squinted it disappeared. Probably just a trick of light.

Returning to the foot of the stairs, he slipped on a pair of safety glasses and slid open the door to the front platform. On the left side he leaned over the railing as far as he could and with the wind in his face studied wheels and undercarriages for a full minute, then did the same on the right side. No sign of hotboxes, no smell of smoke.

The bank of detector signals came and went; no indication that anything on the train was too high, wide, low, or hot. A flashing light would have meant stopping the train and examining every one of the goddamn cars. He assured Joe on the radio that everything was fine.

There were detectors for everything, Bud thought as he went back to watching the card game, except the one the railroad needed most: a shit detector. The guy who invented that would make a fortune. Of course, it was hard to detect something you've been buried in for years. He suppressed a smile and tried to imitate the frowns on the faces of the poker players.

An odd bunch, these four guys. One was called "General" and another "Colonel," but they didn't seem to belong to the same army. On the general's right was a tall, gray-haired gent named Vanneman who was trying to pretend he was a cowboy or rancher: Western clothes from head to toe, all of it too expensive to do any real work in. Opposite him was a hunched-over baldy with Coke-bottle glasses who reminded Bud of caretakers who open squeaky doors in horror movies. Dr. Ordman was how he had been introduced. An egghead who looked like one. Doctor of what, Bud wondered, potions and spells? They were all getting pretty well lubricated from two fifths of scotch and bourbon that Trainer had carried aboard in his traveling bag. Bud told him that alcohol was strictly against railroad regulations. "Don't drink any, then," Trainer had replied, waving him away. Bud decided not to make an issue of it, though it would have been well within his rights. Alcohol was strictly forbidden.

The four men had something to do with the three silver cars in the middle of the string, but he didn't know exactly what or what was in the tankers. All he had been told was that they were technical experts who would be helpful in case of emergency and who were under contract to accompany the shipment. Whatever was in those cars must be important or the train wouldn't have been given Green Line status, that's for sure. Nothing dangerous, the crew had been advised, just something secret. The Atomic Energy Commission sometimes sent short trains down the mainline carrying mysterious loads shrouded in canvas. Shrouded in canvas, okay, but not in tankers labeled MILK. Something fishy was going on. Bud's guess was that the load was just as dangerous as it was secret and was being called milk to escape the high freight charges for hazardous materials. The whole thing stunk, the more he thought about it. Somebody at headquarters got paid off, he would bet. One thing he knew for sure was that no payoffs had been offered to *him*.

Bud slowly circled the table to glance at everybody's hand, but as he passed behind each one they pressed their cards against their chests. What a bunch of suspicious assholes! As if he couldn't be trusted! He had half a mind to turn the whole bunch in to the railroad police because of the booze.

"Roseville and Sacramento coming up, gentlemen," he announced. "The storm slowed us down, but we are still estimating arrival in Oakland on time."

The big guy, Trainer, nodded curtly in acknowledgment, but the others were too absorbed in the game to respond. There was a lot of money on the table, and somebody was going to get hurt.

* * *

Jim Eagan watched a dozen noblemen with elaborate white wigs and satin britches arrange themselves around a harpsichord as if awaiting the young Mozart, but it wasn't tiny Wolfgang who sat down and waited for silence, it was Karen! She looked more like an angel than she did in real life, her skin shining like pink cream and the feathers on her wings beautifully groomed. As she lifted her hands over the keyboard, the walls of the room began to writhe and undulate like a Dali clock! A bulge grew alarmingly in the floor and burst to reveal the hideous face of . . . Old Lady Heed, his fifth-grade teacher! "You'll never amount to a hill of beans, Gooch," she hissed, using his childhood nickname, smoke rising from her nostrils and her head filling the room, "unless you cut out the tomfoolery."

Jim woke with a start, cold sweat on his forehead. On the television screen was a black-and-white test pattern rampant on a field of snow. Quickly he grasped the fact that he wasn't in eighteenth-century Vienna or back home as a ten-year-old in Dickeyville, Wisconsin. He was on his houseboat in Yellow Ferry Harbor in Sausalito, he had fallen asleep in his chair, and it was . . . ten minutes after twelve! Why hadn't Karen called? She had to be back from the movie by now. Had a ringing phone failed to penetrate his nightmare? Had she gone to bed forgetting she had promised to call?

Jim went to the bathroom and splashed cold water on his face, wondering what he should do. He could wait a little longer. He could turn in and call her in the morning. He could phone her now, even though there was a chance she was asleep. The more he thought about her silence, the odder it seemed and the more worried he got. Had she done more snooping than she should have, getting into something she couldn't handle? He tried to shake the cobwebs from his brain. Maybe her ex-husband had indeed been murdered . . . that meant there was a murderer on the loose. If somebody thought Gil Ellis had to be blown away, maybe Karen Ellis was a candidate too. The possibilities seemed more ominous in the middle of the night than they had in daylight.

Jim dialed Karen's number, fidgeted while the ringing signal sounded four times, and cursed when her machine came on.

"Karen, this is Jim," he said at the sound of the beep. "It's half past twelve and I still haven't heard from you. Call me the instant you get in, no matter what time it is, okay? I'm worried about you and I love you, which I guess is redundant."

He walked onto the deck and looked across the water toward Corinthian Island. A full moon hanging in the sky cast a trail of busy light across the Bay. One thing he had learned by living on a boat was that the moon left a trail only when the water was agitated. When there was no wind and the water was smooth as glass, rare for the Bay, the surface acted like a mirror and reflected a single image. It was very quiet, and all but a few of the neighboring boats were dark. The only sounds were the creaking of wooden pilings and a rhythmic bumping from Alan Loomis's boat next door. Apparently the Ample Woman was helping him get through his continuing post-divorce sexual frenzy.

Jim found himself trying to recall the names of Karen's neighbors, the people she said she would be with at the movie. She had mentioned them before, the boring old duffer and his motor-mouth wife. Clyde and Edith Something. Despite their flaws, Karen said, they were concerned about her and had been of tremendous help and comfort. She was quite fond of them. Clyde and Edith . . . Yost! Yes, that was it.

Thank God, Jim thought, going inside and dialing Reno information, senility hadn't yet ruined his memory.

When he reached a sleepy Clyde Yost he came right to the point.

"I'm a friend of Karen Ellis. She told me she was going to a movie with you tonight, but she's not back yet, or at least isn't answering her phone."

Jim could almost hear Yost trying to wake up and organize his thoughts. "Karen? Karen Ellis? A movie? Tonight? What time is it? God!" Jim heard him explaining to his wife that someone was asking about Karen.

"I'm terribly sorry to wake you up," Jim apologized, "but Karen was supposed to call me. It's not like her to forget. She's been under a lot of stress lately, and I can't help worrying about her."

"The movie, yes, we were going to go to a movie—a documentary at the college on the world's great fishing streams. She never answered her phone, so we finally went without her. There were lights on in her house when we got back, so we assumed she just forgot."

"When was that? What time?"

"About ten, I think. Who did you say you were?"

"Did you phone her then?"

"No, we figured if she had forgotten, it would embarrass her. You are who, again?"

"Jim Eagan. Listen, would you mind seeing if she's home? I'm afraid something might have happened. See if her car is in the garage."

"Eagan. The fellow with the houseboat? She's mentioned you." There were muffled words as Clyde consulted with Edith. When he came back on the line he asked for Jim's number and told him he'd "mosey over to Karen's and have a look-see."

Five minutes later Jim's phone rang and Edith Yost, taking charge, was on the line. The lights were still on, she reported in a breathy, nervous voice, the front door was ajar, Karen's bed made, the garage door open, the car was gone. It was a deeply unsettling litany.

"She's had an accident," Jim concluded, trying to keep his voice even. "I'm going to make some phone calls. You watch the house and let me know if she returns. I'll call you back and tell you what I find out."

With a growing sense of dread, Jim called the Reno police, the medical emergency switchboard, and the Reno *Gazette.* It took him thirty minutes to learn that there had been some sort of disaster with scores of casualties and at least a few deaths. Victims were still arriving at area hospitals, with Reno General on the west side of town carrying the main load. Either nobody knew exactly what had happened or they were unwilling to tell him over the phone.

Jim called Reno General and claimed to be a doctor. "I think I know what happened," he shouted at a harassed switchboard operator. "Put me through to the physician in charge." What he got was an emergency-room nurse, which was good enough."

"What are the symptoms," he asked her, "stiffness? Coma?"

"They're stiff as boards," she said. "Stiff as rigor mortis. Some can move their eyes. We don't have a diagnosis yet. You are doctor who?"

"Look, I think I know what you're up against. It's a type of nerve gas."

"Nerve gas?"

"Get hold of somebody with Draegler Chemical—they might know what you should do. Is one of the casualties a woman named Karen Ellis?"

"I'm too busy for names at the moment. Are you kidding? Call the Red Cross. Draegler, huh? We'll try them."

The Red Cross had established a hot line. Yes, Jim found out after waiting through fifteen minutes of busy signals, a Karen Ellis was one of the casualties, but not one of the fatalities. She was at Mercy Hospital. Handling emergency admissions there was a doctor named Ernie Crowley.

More busy signals, then Crowley was on the line. Karen Ellis was in intensive care, he told Jim, at least a woman was in intensive care who was carrying a purse belonging to Karen Ellis. Jim asked if she was blond, about thirty-five.

"How the hell should I know?" Crowley exploded. "We've had fifty admissions in the last half hour."

"All with the same symptoms? Stiffness? Paralysis?"

"Who is this?"

"There's been a gas leak, I think. A nerve gas made by Draegler Chemical. Maybe somebody there can help. There's a guy named Clem Trainer, the plant manager. If there's an antidote, he'll know about it. Where was Karen Ellis found?"

Jim could hear Crowley paging through a notebook. "Nerve gas, you think? Wrong symptoms. These people are rigid, not limp."

"It's something new that Draegler's developed."

"Truckee. Karen Ellis was one of the ones in the restaurant. Most were in a bar across the street."

Truckee? What in God's name was Karen doing in Truckee when she was supposed to be out with the Yosts? Jim asked if the restaurant was near the railroad tracks.

"Everything in Truckee is near the railroad tracks. Got to take some other calls. I'll tell the staff to postulate nerve gas. Clem Trainer? We'll find him."

The line went dead.

Jim jumped to his feet and walked in a nervous circle with his hands pressed to the top of his head. "Jesus Christ," he muttered, "Jesus H. Christ . . ." What the hell had happened? What was Karen doing when she . . . he had *told* her to be careful. . . . He reeled into the kitchen and drained half a cup of cold coffee, then opened a cupboard and took two swigs from a bottle of gin. Fortified, he went back to the phone and flipped through his address book.

Most of the numbers he had for Mountain Pacific Railroad in Reno and Sparks he knew would be useless—either no one would answer or no one would talk. MP, like other railroads, was not distinguished for its public relations, particularly in times of crisis. Stonewall everything, that was the policy. He tried the unlisted number for the Sparks control tower, hoping it hadn't changed in the several years since he last tried it.

The phone was answered halfway through the first ring. "Spence Kesson," a clipped voice said.

"Is this the Sparks tower?"

"Yep."

"Are you the yardmaster on duty?"

"Yep."

"I'm Jim Eagan. I had your job ten years ago. I'm with MP in the San Francisco office now and I'm trying to piece together what's going on up there."

"It's a goddamn madhouse, people running in and out."

"Did you know about the people who've been hurt?"

"Shit, I'm the one who found them! I could't raise Clay, Clay Corman, so I went down the stairs and practically stumbled over the woman. Then I look up and—"

"What woman?"

"Name's Sara Schuler, alive but bleeding like a stuck pig, draped over Track One. Then I see Clay in a pool of blood sprawled out on the platform opposite another guy, also dead."

"Clay Corman is dead?" When Jim was stationed in the Reno Division, the jovial policeman was one of his best friends.

"Yep. Shot. All three of them shot. The other guy looks foreign, an Arab or an Indian, don't have a name for him yet. Well, Christ almighty, this place is swarming with big shots, as you can imagine, and me with a job to do, I'm the dispatcher tonight too. Bet you never had anything like this to deal with."

Jim's mind raced. Sara Schuler, that was the woman who worked at Draegler, the one mentioned on Karen's tape. A shoot-out at the railroad yard, two people dead, one maybe an Arab, a gas leak in Truckee, probably near the tracks . . . Jim struggled to make it add up.

"Kesson, what time are you talking about? When did you find the bodies?"

"Half past eleven. I know the time because—"

"Did you have a train leaving about then? A freight?"

"A couple of minutes before, yeah."

"With a shipment from Draegler Chemical?"

"Yeah, come to think of it."

"Do you know about the gas leak in Truckee? All the casualties and so on?"

"I heard there was some sort of disaster, but, shit, I got my hands full at the moment. No time to listen to the radio. Gotta ring off—my supervisor's coming up the stairs."

"Put him on the phone. We got a problem, a very big problem."

CHAPTER 21

Beyond Saramento was a good fifty miles of relatively straight, level track, and it was here that Joe Dori hoped to make up lost time. Once the train crossed the Benicia Bridge at the Carquinuez Strait at the north end of San Francisco Bay there would be curves and one town after another to slow him down. He pulled the throttle to notch eight and smiled at the smooth, powerful response of Saber One. Automatically, the power in the two trailing locomotives was adjusted to match.

Every so often Joe reached out with his left hand and nudged a small lever that protruded from the control panel. It was the latest safety device dreamed up by desk jockeys back in Pennsylvania who seemed to live in constant fear that locomotive engineers would fall asleep on the job or have heart attacks. The lever had to be bumped at least once every thirty seconds or a reminder light would flash, followed a moment later by a warning horn. If a minute went by with no agitation, the brakes were automatically applied and the train brought to a stop. Another nuisance dreamed up by college graduates to irritate the workingman. The old "dead man's pedal" that you were supposed to fall off of if you died was too easy to disarm with a rock or a lunch bucket. You couldn't just hang something on the new lever because it had to be jiggled, not just pressed down. Fail-safe and idiot-proof, the designers probably thought. Young squirts in white shirts probably got promotions for thinking of it. They didn't know much about the resourcefulness of the men in the trenches.

The speedometer needle crept to sixty, then seventy. It was nineteen miles to Davis—if he couldn't hit the speed limit of seventy-nine miles an hour by there, then surely by Vacaville, sixteen miles farther on. Ninety or even a hundred miles an hour would be possible with three Saber locomotives instead of only one. Next year he'd have three, if the performance so far was any indication. The bugs usually found in a new piece of equipment were blessedly missing. Fuel economy looked great too.

Earlier, the wind had been in his face, now it was coming from behind at ten or twenty miles an hour. Hard to say how much a tail wind like that helped, but it sure didn't hurt.

He ran his eyes over the diagnostic display panel. Journal bearings, alternators, wheel-slip correctors, generator voltage, grid blowers, motor field current, air manifold pressure, everything was normal. He wished the display covered the trailing units as well, but that no doubt would come in the fullness of time.

Joe settled himself on his seat at the right side of the cab, feeling good. It was a beautiful moonlit night and there were miles and miles of straight track ahead. He was at the controls of the greatest piece of rolling machinery ever made by man, and he was surrounded by the sounds and vibrations of speed and power. Jet pilots? Race-car drivers? Shit, they didn't know what real power was. Three locomotives weighing more than a million pounds hurtling through the night at seventy-nine miles an hour chased by fifty loaded freight cars—now *that* was energy! *That* was power! After a lifetime as an engineer, Joe still was awed and thrilled by it.

The gauges and displays all read normal, true, but there was no instrument for evaluating his copilot. "Cracked!" such a meter might say, or "Goofy!" Tommy Talbot had gone down the three steps at the front of the cab a half hour ago and was still sitting on the toilet with the door open and his pants around his ankles. He was carrying on a cheerful, one-sided conversation about how psychic he was. Coincidences and hunches—call them premonitions if you want—peppered his life.

"Just last night," he said, waving his arms so widely that his hands hit the sides of the cubicle, "I had a dream that this trip to San Francisco would be so fantastic that we'd get airborne. Know what I mean? We'd get going so fast that we'd fly through the air like Mary Poppins or the Ghost Riders. People would look up and see us sailing across the moon and think we were Santa Claus and the reindeers. Donner and Blitzen. Sneezy and Dopey. Huey and Louie."

Joe blasted the horn in hopes of drowning him out or breaking his train of thought.

Talbot shifted to his early life. "I used to watch freights

go by as a kid. I was fascinated by the nose on the front of the engine. I thought it was where the controls were or the atomic power plant. The mysterious nerve center, the giant brain. Know what I mean? Well, holy shit Marie, I remember the first time I sneaked into a cab and opened the door to that secret compartment and found out it was the toilet! What a letdown! I guess I thought engineers were such gods they didn't need toilets."

That was sort of funny, Joe had to admit, and he chuckled briefly in spite of himself.

The loudspeaker hissed. "MP Oakland tower to MP seven six six one west. Can you read me?" The voice was weak. The dispatcher at Sacramento was supposed to monitor the train until it passed Fairfield, then Oakland would be in charge. It was the first time Joe had heard from Oakland so early.

"This is MP seven six six one west to MP Oakland tower. You're weak, but I can read you. What's on your mind, if any? Over." Joe knew that all calls to dispatchers were recorded and that he should keep his remarks stiff and humorless, but it wasn't his style and never had been. His alleged superiors had several times suggested that he forget the jokes, but had given up years ago trying to change him.

"MP Oakland tower to MP seven six six one west. Problem of some kind at Sacramento. Can't reach them by phone or radio. Power failure there, it looks like. Over."

"Really? Just went through there a few minutes ago and was talking to them. Over."

"MP Oakland tower to MP seven six six one west. So were we, but now they're off-line. For the moment, we'll take over. What's your location?"

"MP seven six six one west to Oakland tower. Fairfield ten minutes ahead. Just passed mile post five nine."

"This is MP Oakland tower to MP seven six six one

west. I've got eight two two nine east approaching on same track. Broken rail on eastbound track, so you take the Fairfield siding. Otherwise you'd have to stop on mainline and wait for eight two two nine east. Switch is set, you're all lined up. Take it easy until you see the caboose of eight two two nine clear, then I'll let you out on the west end. Over."

"Wait a minute, we're Green Line . . . we've got priority. Over."

"MP Oakland tower to MP seven six six one west. Our instructions are to get you to Oakland as fast as possible. You'll reach the siding first. Is this Joe Dori? Don't argue. Take the siding. Confirm. Over."

Joe sighed tiredly. "Okay, Oakland. Approaching distant signal now. Over and out."

Over the course of the next two miles Joe dropped the speed to fifteen miles an hour, so slow that when he struck his head out the side window the wind was on the back of his head instead of his face. He tried to raise Sacramento on his radio; Oakland was right, Sacramento was missing. That was another first. A dispatching center that couldn't be reached? If their main radio was out, why didn't they use their backup? A power failure was no explanation because they had emergency generators. Joe shook his head and gave a low whistle. Somebody in the Sacramento Division was in deep shit.

Saber One lurched to the right and entered the two-mile-long Fairfield siding, which brought an immediate response from the caboose.

"What's happening, Joe? Stopping for cigarettes?"

"Orders from headquarters. We've got to meet an eastbound. Hope this doesn't spoil the poker game."

"Christ, we could derail and these guys would play out the hand."

Joe looked to the rear and watched the train swing through the switch onto the siding. In the toilet Talbot was singing golden oldies with his own words. "I've grown accustomed to your face" became "I've grown accustomed to disgrace." "Hey," Joe shouted, "close the door or pipe down, would you? I'm an opera fan."

"A thousand pardons."

By the time the train reached the west end of the siding, the eastbound had passed. Joe checked with Oakland and received permission to proceed. When the train was back on the main line, he moved the throttle from notch three to notch eight. There was a slight change in the sound of the engines in the trailing units. Joe frowned. Acceleration wasn't what it should be. He called out to Talbot, "Are you almost done? I'm going back to check the trailers." He leaned to the left and looked down the stairs. His distinguished colleague was wiping his ass.

"Coming right up, boss."

No reason to wait for him, Joe thought. The safety lever could easily be disarmed. He had been toying with it for an hour, hanging various objects on it until he found one of just the right weight and bounciness. His watch, chain, and fob were too heavy; they pulled the lever down and held it down. His key ring, without the Swiss Army knife, was perfect. He hooked a flashlight on his belt and smiled at how easy it was to outsmart the experts. Nothing was idiot-proof.

He worked his way to the rear along the narrow outside walkway like a sailor on a heaving deck, steadying himself with one hand against the engine hood and the other on the handrail. The train was gaining speed, swaying and vibrating as it crossed a stretch of roadbed that was rougher than it should be. He made a note to report it to Maintenance of Way.

One thing he liked about a brand-new locomotive was that everything was freshly painted, including the handrail, and felt smooth and clean to the touch. That changed for the worse the moment he stepped across the junction between the first and second locomotives. Now everything felt like grease, grime, and corrosion. Both the second and third locomotives were veterans with years of service and looked like they had been through the tunnels of hell.

Picking his way carefully to keep his balance, Joe climbed inside Number Two cab. It took only a few minutes to see that everything was okay . . . though not perfect. A red light indicated that something was wrong with the sanders, but no action was needed because there were no grades steep enough in California's Central Valley to require sand on the rails and no chance of ice. He'd mention the malfunction to the mechanics at the end of the run.

In the cab of Number Three another warning light was on. Radiator water temperature was too high. The thermometer stood at close to 200 degrees—much hotter and it would boil. Water-pump failure? A leak in the line? A blockage of some sort? Any number of things could cause it. He'd have to go all the way to the rear of the third engine to check it out.

Halfway along the walkway he noticed the small patches of blue mist clinging to the steel surfaces but he paid little attention. The color was faint and fleeting and he had all he could do to keep from getting pitched over the railing. Christ sakes, if there was track work to be done, here was a good place to start.

He opened the control panel at the rear of Number Three and aimed the flashlight upward and played it on the air intake grill on the roof. The six-foot-diameter radiator fan was whirring normally, but as he suspected the grill above it was clogged by a mat of pine needles and leaves. A souvenir from the storm, Joe guessed, returning the beam to the control panel. He turned the fan off, then reversed its direction. Instead of drawing air into the radiator, the fan blew it upward, and as soon as it was up to speed the debris on the grill erupted and was whisked out of sight in the wind.

Joe reversed the fan again. "So much for that," he muttered, nodding in satisfaction. When he closed the panel door he noticed that it had turned blue. Frowning, he looked around and saw that the whole back end of the engine looked like it had been coated with glow-in-the-dark blue paint. It was even on his hands and wouldn't come off when he wiped them on his clothes. What the hell was it, static electricity? Some sort of fog? A reflection of the northern lights?

He turned and aimed his beam forward. The entire length of the locomotive was glowing faintly. At the cab a kind of struggle was going on between the glow and the wind: the glow was trying to advance, the wind was trying to beat it back.

Joe felt the flashlight slipping from his grasp. For some reason his fingers refused to tighten their grip. The flashlight bounced off the metal walkway and into the night. "Shit," he said, making a lunge for it. His motion was as slow as a hundred-year-old man's. There was something wrong with his hands and feet . . . in fact, his arms and his legs didn't feel right, either. They were stiffening up and seemed suddenly cold. Taking steps was like wading through molasses that was steadily thickening. Was he having a heart attack? He had never had any heart trouble, nobody in his family had, everybody was as strong as horses. . . . Jesus Christ, now he couldn't move his legs at all! He hated to admit it, but he needed help.

"Tommy!" he shouted hoarsely into the roar of the wheels and the engines. "Tommy!"

Everett Ordman, Ph.D., leaped to his feet, knocking his chair over. He threw his cards facedown on the table. "Fuck you guys," he said, not entirely in jest. "Deal me out."

"Come on, one more hand," Trainer said, refilling his glass with scotch.

"Nothing doing. I must be out two hundred bucks."

"Big deal," Vanneman said. "I spend that much on belt buckles."

Colonel Aref raked in the pot with caresses. "It is kind of you to show such hospitality to a visitor to your wonderful country."

"Piss off," Ordman said, stomping to the rear of the caboose and through the door. He stood on the back platform with his hands clamped on the railing talking to himself. "I should have my head examined," he muttered angrily to the receding tracks. "I didn't want to play. I played just to be a good sport, and now I'm out two hundred frigging bucks." He spit into the wind. The noise of the train surrounded him and gave him a welcome feeling of isolation from the other men.

He didn't even want to make this stupid trip, and came along only because Trainer practically got down on his knees and begged. "You're the scientist in charge," Trainer said, "so the Arab wants you along. And me, too, and Vanneman. He insists on it, or the deal is off. If Mannequin is safe to move, he says, why shouldn't we travel with it the same way we expect the Iraqi soldiers to?" Oh, all right, Ordman finally said, I'll do it, even though I'll lose a night's sleep and have to spend *hours* with Aref, the coldest, creepiest prick I ever met in my whole life. Don't say I never did anything for you, Clem.

Then the poker game, then the big pot, then Aref beating his two pair with three of a kind. It was enough to make a man embrace Islam. Worse, Ordman was now feeling faintly sick to his stomach, maybe from staring at the speeding tracks. If vomit rose in his throat, he'd run back inside and aim it at Aref. "Oh, sorry!" he would say. Now his neck was aching, too, and his hands and ankles. His back was already a wreck and could hardly be worse, not to mention his eyes. Was he now going to be burdened with arthritis or some goddamn thing as well?

There was something odd about the ground that was rushing away from the back of the train—it had a faintly blue cast. . . .

"Doc! Doc!"

It was Trainer, shouting at him from inside the car. Through the open door Ordman could see the general sitting at the table trying to stand up and moving his arms as if trying to swim through an invisible fluid. Vanneman was on his hands and knees on the floor. Aref was sitting stiffly with his arms protectively around the money he had won, staring fixedly and working his jaw. The conductor was twisting his shoulders back and forth and shouting, "What's wrong? What's happening?"

Ordman stepped inside the door and gasped when he saw that the walls and ceiling were tinted with blue. He took a step backward and looked over his shoulder at the tracks—the train was going fifty miles an hour at least and to jump at that speed in the darkness meant almost certain death. But to stay . . .

"Gas leak," Trainer managed to say, getting to his feet and then falling heavily across the table.

Aref pushed himself away and tipped over backward in his chair, landing beside Vanneman. The two men writhed on the floor like fish in slow motion, their bodies quickly becoming covered with a pale blue haze.

The conductor lurched toward a red emergency handle on the wall. "A gas leak? A gas leak? Got to stop the train—"

"No!" Ordman shouted. "Stop the train and we're dead for sure!" The old scientist, wiry for his age, sprang forward and knocked the conductor off his feet. He grabbed the bottles of scotch and bourbon from the card table and upended them, splashing liquid on his shoes. "Our only chance is to cut away!" He stood over Shieving, helping him up, asking him how to disconnect the caboose.

"The . . . the cutting lever. Horizontal bar . . . lift it . . . that will get the pin . . ." Shieving gestured with his eyes toward the front. The three other men were trying to talk, too, but failing.

Splashing alcohol on the floor ahead of his footsteps, Ordman threw the front door aside and climbed over the railing, emptying the bottles on the blue film that covered the coupling. In reflected light he could see the steel lever that had to be lifted to break the connection. The noise was deafening, and he tried not to look at the ground speeding by below his feet for fear of vertigo.

The conductor had managed to follow him out. "Got to turn . . . the angle cock to trap the air," he said, forcing the words. "Otherwise, the train will stop. . . ." He spotlighted the valve on the right side of the forward car with his flashlight, then lost his balance and fell to the floor, unable to coordinate his muscles. "Got to warn Joe," he whispered to the rushing wind.

Ordman's legs and arms were tightening fast, and his curved hands were already frozen tight. Climbing over the railing and kneeling on a small ledge, he managed to lean forward far enough to turn the angle cock to the left until it wouldn't turn anymore. He noticed then that there was a similar valve on the caboose. He didn't know anything about railroad technology, but from what the conductor had said he guessed that the braking system was set up to be fail-safe. Interrupt the air lines at any point and the brakes would be applied. He decided to isolate the air in the caboose lines as well, otherwise it might stop so suddenly, he wouldn't be able to hang on. After turning the caboose angle cock, he worked his way to the coupling knuckles between the cars. He hooked his fingers under the cutting bar and tried without success to raise it. His ability to move at all was draining away fast. He shifted his knee under his body for better leverage, and thrust himself upward in a last desperate effort to save himself. A blanket of gas surged over the top of the forward car and poured down on him like a waterfall.

There was the sound of steel scraping against steel and a deep *clunk* as the cars separated.

Ordman was completely immobilized. One arm and one leg were hooked through the struts of the railing, leaving him hanging like an insect in a laboratory display. He couldn't move any muscle so much as an inch. He could still see, and he watched as if looking through a tunnel at the widening gulf between the caboose and the last car of the train.

The caboose gradually slowed down until it was barely moving. It came to a stop after rolling for almost two miles. There was a gentle creak, almost a sigh, then nothing. Except for crickets in adjoining fields, the silence was complete.

Interesting, Ordman thought as blackness invaded his mind, at that speed and with such a low coefficient of friction, I thought it would roll farther.

It would have rolled farther on a level track, not on a 2 percent upgrade. The silence lasted only a few seconds. Ordman was unconscious when the caboose gradually began to move. Slowly but surely it rolled east, steadily picking up speed.

Sounds came first, and she couldn't make sense of them. Groaning, whispers, footsteps, squeaking carts of some sort being pushed across linoleum. Shopping carts? Luggage carriers?

Then the light. Wherever she was, it was bright. She grimaced in the effort of trying to figure out what was going on. The effort paid off, and her thoughts began to form a coherent pattern. It occurred to her that she could open her eyes, and she saw the white ceiling of a corridor.

She became aware of her body, which felt as if someone had tried to flatten it from head to toe with a rolling pin. She tested her arms and legs and fingers. They were sore. From what? Where was she? She turned her head to one side and was surprised that she could, her neck was so stiff. But just in the effort of moving her muscles, the stiffness and soreness diminished.

She was in a hospital corridor, still wearing the clothes she had on to go to the movie with the Yosts. There were people lying on the floor, most of them motionless. Next to her was a young man on one knee with a stethoscope around his neck tending to a gray-haired woman. He had her arm in his hands and was lifting and lowering it. "Does this hurt? Does this?"

"My God," Karen breathed, everything rushing back, "what time is it?" She raised herself to a sitting position, and it wasn't easy. She looked at her wristwatch. "Two o'clock? Two o'clock? You mean I've been here for *five hours?*"

She started to get up, ignoring twinges of pain in her legs, but was forced back to the floor by the kneeling man, who had taken hold of her upper arm and wouldn't let go. "Take it easy," he said, "just take it easy. I'm a doctor."

"And I'm a clarinetist! Let go of me! Let me up! There's been a terrible disaster!"

"We know," he said soothingly. "The best thing for you is to try to relax."

"No!" Karen tried to pull away, but his grip was too strong. She groped with her free hand and felt something metallic. She took hold of it and swung it at the hand that was restraining her.

The doctor sprang back, wiggling his fingers. "Orderly!" he shouted. To her he said, "You shouldn't have done that. . . ."

Karen tried again to stand up and this time succeeded.

"I'm sorry," she said quickly, "but I know what happened. I've been—all these people have been—hit with a type of nerve gas. It's called Mannequin and it's made by Draegler. You've heard of Draegler Chemical? There's a sabotaged train full of nerve gas headed for Oakland! I've got to get to a phone. . . ." Karen looked at her hand. She was holding a bedpan. She had hit a doctor with a bedpan.

The doctor sprang forward and grabbed her in a bear hug, pinning her arms to her sides and lifting her off the floor. Through clenched teeth he said, "I told you to take it easy." Again he shouted for an orderly.

A burly man in shirt sleeves answered the call, hurrying over an obstacle course of victims on the floor. Instead of helping the doctor with the struggling woman, he looked at her and said, "Would you by any chance be Karen Ellis?"

"Yes! Yes! I am! Tell this maniac to put me down!"

"Put her down, Darrell. Miss Ellis, I'm Ernie Crowley and I've just been on the phone to a Jim Eagan, who says that you might know something about—"

"Jim! I've got to talk to him!"

Walking was difficult, but got easier with every step. Karen leaned against the bulky Crowley as he guided her toward his office, telling him as much as she knew about the gas. Oxygen, lots of oxygen, is the best antidote.

"We give oxygen as a matter of course. . . ."

"Then give more."

Sitting at Crowley's desk and dialing Jim's number, Karen stretched her legs and arms and moved her shoulders and head back and forth. The soreness was ebbing and the strength was coming back. She knew she was going to be all right. She flashed a small smile of reassurance to Crowley, who was using his intercom to summon aides.

Karen heard a series of clicks as her call went through to Jim's Sausalito houseboat. She hoped he wasn't such a heavy sleeper that the ringing wouldn't wake him. After a pause, there was a series of buzzes.

The line was busy.

Tommy Talbot felt much better with his lower intestinal tract thoroughly evacuated. Move those fecal poisons out, that was the secret of radiant good health. Letting them ferment for even a minute longer than necessary played hell with a man's energy level, his complexion, and his whole outlook on life. So what if it meant sitting on the pot a little oftener and a little longer than other people? It was worth it.

He sat in the engineer's seat watching the rails stream toward him out of the night, and he sang a happy tune: "Some enchanted evening, you may meet a strangler . . ."

He glanced around. The instrument panel and computer display made him feel like a jet pilot. Maybe someday he *would* be a jet pilot. For now he'd concentrate on becoming a locomotive engineer like Joe Dori, who knew everything there was to know about it. Now you take the gadget Joe had hung on the safety lever—that was *clever.* You can learn a lot from these old farts. Where was he, anyway? He said he was going back to check the trailing units, but that was ten minutes ago.

Tommy looked through the window behind the seat. No sign of Joe. As the minutes and the miles went by, Tommy got more and more worried, and finally grabbed a flashlight and climbed down to the walkway. The wind was terrific and he had to keep a solid grip on the handrail to keep from getting blown away.

He checked the walkways on both sides of Saber One—no trace of the old man. Tommy hurried toward the rear and began to wonder what he would do if Joe had fallen off. Oh, God, don't even *think* of such a thing! At the back of the second locomotive he stopped and aimed his flashlight along the side of Unit Three . . . there he was! All the way at the back! He was on his knees, motionless and staring, as if he had died of fright.

"Joe! Joe! What's wrong?" There was no way the words could carry eighty feet over the roar of the engines and the wind. "Hang on, Joe! I'm coming . . . I'm coming . . ."

CHAPTER 22

Wayne Galway, Reno district supervisor for Mountain Pacific Railroad, was suspicious. "I can't tell you anything about seven six six one," he said. "It's Green Line."

Jim shouted his response: "I can tell *you* something about it—it's almost certainly carrying nerve gas that is leaking out all over the place."

Galway stayed calm. "Eagan, you said your name was? You are calling from where?"

"What difference does it make? I'm at home in Sausalito. Check your time logs and you'll see that when the train pulled out there was—"

"Calling from home in Sausalito in the middle of the night? How would you know so much about what's going on?"

"Three people got shot just as seven six six one left your station. When it passed through Truckee, fifty or a hundred people got gassed and are in hospitals right now, haven't you heard? The train has to be stopped as a precaution if nothing else. Where is it right now?"

"I told you its status. It can't be stopped unless there's an emergency."

"People getting gassed in their sleep and shot down on

an MP platform isn't an emergency? Tell Spence to get on the radio and—"

"You have no proof of a connection between—"

"Gas might be leaking from one of our trains! We don't need proof! Radio the engineer and tell him to stop in the boondocks till we know what the hell is going on. Are you there? Can you hear me?"

There was a whispered consultation, then a resigned sigh from Galway. "We'll radio the train and see if the crew has noticed anything."

"Thank you *so* much. I'll hold."

When Galway returned there was a slight tremor in his voice. He reported that engineer Joe Dori and conductor Bud Shieving weren't responding. "The train has passed through Sacramento, Kesson thinks. He's trying to reach Sacramento control now, but they aren't answering, either."

"Terrific! You keep trying. If you reach somebody, tell them to stop the train away from any town."

"I would need authorization before I could do that. Even talking to you at all is a violation of procedure. Proper procedure calls for a written—"

Jim hung up in exasperation and dialed the Oakland control tower. The dispatcher on duty was Frank Tajima, a man he had known for years.

"A gas that freezes people in position?" Tajima said, sure that Jim was kidding. "I think some of that has gotten loose at city hall. . . ."

"No joke, Frank. Oh, I wish to God it was." Thirty seconds later Tajima was willing to accept—at least until he learned otherwise—that seven six six one west was carrying nerve gas and that it was leaking. Reno couldn't reach the engineer or the Sacramento dispatcher, Jim told him. Maybe Oakland would have better luck.

Tajima confirmed that Sacramento was off-line for some reason, but told Jim that he had been talking to Joe Dori not ten minutes earlier. "I put him on the Fairfield siding to let an east-bound go by. He didn't mention anything unusual. Hang on, I'll get him on the horn again. . . ."

The effort failed.

"Frank, we've got to assume the worst. The track passes within twenty feet of the dispatcher's office in Sacramento. Could be that the gas has done them all in. When the train was on the siding, maybe it got the crew too. Do you suppose it's still there?"

"Only Sacramento would know for sure. My block display panel doesn't extend that far."

They quickly decided what had to be done next. Tajima would alert his supervisors, then call the Fairfield section foreman at home and ask him to drive out to the siding and see if seven six six one was still parked there. If it was, he was to push the disabling button on the side of the lead engine to keep it from moving. Tajima would keep trying to reach the crew by radio and would also alert the local police and the state's disaster office in Sacramento. Jim would wake the Benicia section foreman and tell him to go down to the tracks and make a visual inspection if the train went by and report his observations to Oakland. They both expressed the hope that they were getting excited over nothing.

The instant Jim hung up, the phone rang.

"Your line has been busy for twenty minutes." The voice was thin, but Jim recognized it instantly.

"Karen! Thank God! Are you all right? What happened?"

"I got a whiff of the gas, but I'm going to be okay. I'm improving by the minute. Jim, the gas is on its way. Sara and I tried to stop it, and what went wrong I don't know. I dropped her off at the station in Sparks and then tried to get ahead of the train and block it with my car. I just missed it in Truckee and was trying to phone you when my whole body tightened up and I couldn't even talk. I woke up in the hospital a few minutes ago."

Jim told her that Sara was one of three people shot at the train station. Two were dead, a railroad policeman and an unidentified man. Sara was in critical condition at a Sparks hospital.

Karen groaned at the news. The unidentified man, she guessed, was probably Jamal, who had been chasing Sara and her and who had helped sabotage the train.

"The train is *sabotaged*?"

"Yes, by two Iranians who don't want the gas to reach Iraq." She summarized what she had learned from Sara when they were in the car together. "The gas is in three silver tank cars labeled MILK. They are divided into compartments, five each, I think, and they are wired with bombs that go off by radio. Transmitters are hidden in towns along the way. It's all automatic."

"What towns? Holy mother of God . . ."

"Jamal and a man named Mahmed, they didn't want to wreck the train, they wanted to spread the gas across the state. A dose of our own medicine, something like that. Sara gave me a list of the towns . . ."

Jim scribbled furiously: Truckee, Auburn, Sacramento, Fairfield, Benicia, Richmond, Berkeley. The worst explosion would be in Oakland—one whole car would blow up if the train got that far.

"Don't worry," Jim said. "We'll stop it even if we have to send it off the tracks." He tried to sound reassuring, but in his mind doubts bloomed like thistles. If the train had a disabled crew, there were few places left where it could be safely derailed. Benicia was only seventeen miles past Fairfield, and from Benicia to Oakland, a distance of some twenty-five miles, there weren't many uninhabited areas—one town merged with another. Would it be right to derail a train with men on board who might still be alive? What if Karen had the wrong information? "Karen, how do you know all this? Why were you with Sara?"

"I'll tell you later. Listen carefully. The gas is tinted

blue, tell the emergency workers that. It has no smell. It goes through skin, so gas masks aren't enough."

"Is there an antidote or any way to stop it?"

"A little knocks you out for a few hours. More and you might die, unless you get oxygen. More oxygen than paramedics usually give. Got that?"

"Got it. . . . If you find out anything else, call me in Oakland—I'm heading for the control center." He gave her the number. "You stay put and do whatever the doctor says, okay? You've taken enough chances for one night. God, I can't tell you what a relief it is to hear your voice! I was so worried about you, I couldn't think straight. I love you even more than I thought!"

"The feeling is mutual, and I'll tell you more about that later too."

Jim went to work with an explosion of energy. He ran to the rear deck and leaped across the water to the powerboat in the next berth. He cast off the bow and stern lines, jumped into the cockpit, and slipped behind the steering wheel. "Hey, Alan!" he shouted, groping for the control box with his right hand, "I want a ride after all! How do you start this stinkpot?"

From below there was the sound of a squeaking bed and curses. "What the goddamn hell . . . Jim? Is that you? Are you out of your cotton-picking mind?"

Jim turned the keys and the twin engines came to life with a deep-throated, muffled roar. "Yes, I'm crazy! The moon is full and I want to go to Oakland!" He threw the transmission into reverse and the boat backed away from the dock.

Alan Loomis staggered up the stairs wearing only a towel and a look of confusion. "Jim, for the love of God, you want a ride *now*? Can't you see I'm busy?"

Jim managed to shift to forward just before the boat crashed into the houseboats on the other side of the inlet. The change in direction put the attorney face-first onto the deck. From below came an alarmed female voice: "What's happening? Is it an earthquake?"

Jim floored the accelerator. The boat rose and leveled off as it rocketed toward open water, pressing him into the back of the leather seat. In the night's stillness the noise of the oversized engines was thunderous.

"Is this some sort of practical joke?" Loomis gasped, crawling into the seat beside Jim. He had abandoned the towel and was naked, his skin a ghostly white. "You think this is funny? I'll get even with you for this, you goddamn tinhorn Casey Jones. . . ."

"No, I don't think it's funny. There's a crisis—a gas leak with people dead—and I've got to get to Oakland the fastest possible way. It's ten miles by water, twenty by road. You've got a phone on this tub, haven't you? Let me have it. . . ."

Loomis squinted at Eagan closely to make sure the moon hadn't turned him into a werewolf. "This is no joke?"

"Get me the phone. *Please.*"

"Tell him to go away, Alan," the woman called from the top of the stairs. "Can't you just tell him to go away?"

Jim dialed Tajima while Alan and Helga looked at him as if he was throwing some kind of fit.

When Tajima was on the line Jim had to shout to be heard over the engines. He told the dispatcher what he had learned from Karen: the gas was blue and anyone coming into contact with it should be given plenty of oxygen.

Tajima had news of his own. The train had shown up on the Oakland display screen, having tripped the block signal west of Fairfield. It had covered the six miles from the siding to the signal in roughly thirteen minutes. Assuming that it had come to a stop on the siding, it now had to be traveling at least fifty miles an hour. In a high-pitched, fast-paced voice, Tajima reported that while there was still no answer from the crew, Sacramento was back in action with emergency personnel. Just after the train passed the control tower there, the six men on the night shift were put out of action, the district dispatcher, the yardmaster, two brakemen, and two maintenance men.

"What about the Santa Rosa switch? Can you throw it remotely? If the train's out of control, let's send it north where there aren't so many people."

Tajima said the remote switches around Benicia were shorted out because ground squirrels had eaten the insulation on the buried wires. The best chance was the engine that Sacramento had sent in pursuit from a siding near the grain elevators at Dixon, eight miles east of Vacaville. If it could get up to, say, ninety miles an hour, ignoring the red block signals, it ought to be able to catch the runaway before the Benicia Bridge, latch onto the caboose, and activate the brakes. "That's assuming the runaway doesn't pick up speed on the downgrades. If it does, then—"

Jim interrupted. "Frank, the train has been sabotaged. When it goes through a town, remote-control bombs blast holes in the gas compartments."

"Lovely!"

"We may end up with another crew dead and another engine out of control. Tell them to stay away from the ass end of the runaway if it looks blue . . . that's the color of the gas."

"Not much chance of that, is there, at sixty miles an hour? The gas couldn't travel along twenty-five cars all the way to the caboose and still be strong enough to hurt anybody, could it?"

"The fact of the matter is that I have no fucking idea. I'm getting my information from . . . well, from somebody who hasn't been wrong yet. Tell those guys who are in pursuit, it's riskier than they think."

"That won't stop them. Any other ideas? Did you reach Kempinski in Benicia?"

"Yes. Soon as he gets a look, he'll call you."

"How about a helicopter? Think we could set a man on top?"

"At night? No way. Too many signal structures, power lines, overpasses. Whoever tried it might hit the engine and get roasted by air from the stack or fried on the grid. Farther back and he's in the nerve gas."

"How about asking the Army or the National Guard to shoot a coupling apart? That would break the air lines."

Jim didn't like that idea, either. "'It would take an hour to organize that and we've got minutes. Easier to derail the mother . . . provided we could do it in a remote spot."

"Let's wait for Kempinski's report. Anything else I can do? I've called Magnus." Leon Magnus was MP's vice president of Operations.

"Call me a cab. I'm in a powerboat off Alcatraz. I'll be pulling into the Outer Harbor Terminal in about ten minutes."

"Somebody will be there to meet you. Jesus Christ, Jim, I hope this whole frigging thing is a false alarm. I hope we're hallucinating."

"So do I."

A very sleepy railroad man named Eric Kempinski, wearing coveralls with no underwear and shoes with no socks, piled into his Chevy Blazer and headed for the tracks a half mile away. He rolled down the window and stuck his face into the cold night wind to help him wake up. What the hell time was it, anyway, two-thirty? Three? He had been up till midnight playing billiards at the Vallejo Elks Club and felt like a zombie. Maybe if he had beaten the Egyptian, he'd feel a little more chipper.

The man on the phone, Eagan he said his name was,

had sounded awful excited, and there was so much noise on the line it sounded like he was calling from the Sears Point Speedway. A train might be out of control, he said, going west God only knows how fast. Watch it go by and see what you can see. Crew in cab not responding. Crew in caboose not responding. Silver tank cars in the middle might be leaking toxic gas. Jesus, Mary, and Joseph, if a report like that couldn't wake him up, nothing could.

At the crossing it was cold and quiet. The moon was full and so bright he couldn't see a single star. No lights of any kind anywhere. There were a few farmhouses scattered around the vicinity, a mile this way and a mile that way, but they were dark and buttoned up, as they should be at this time of the night. Kempinski shivered and wished he had taken the time to throw on a jacket. Say what you want about California, it cools off nice at night no matter how hot it gets in the daytime. Makes for good sleeping. At three in the morning a man should be under the covers sawing wood instead of driving around in the dark thinking about billiard shots missed and billiard shots made. He cut the engine and listened hard, looking down the tracks to the east. Was there a faint hum? No, he guessed not. Wait! There was a sound in the distance, yes, no mistake, he could hear it plainly now. A train was coming. He could see the pinpoint of its headlight as it came over the hump at the Laffoon ranch, three miles distant. Moving at a good clip, too, it looked like.

He started his engine and turned onto the frontage road, which was hardly more than two ruts in the grass on the edge of a vast field of alfalfa shoots. The road ran for two miles in a straight line before dead-ending at an irrigation canal—plenty of distance for him to get up to the speed of the train and give it a once-over.

Adjusting his side mirror to keep the train's headlight in view, he accelerated to thirty miles an hour. He switched on the spotlight mounted on the cab roof and by twisting the knob above his head angled the beam upward and to the left into the space that would soon be occupied by the locomotive. In the mirror he could see that the train was gaining on him. He stepped up his speed to forty, then to fifty, then to fifty-five, which was as fast as he cared to go on an unpaved road. Before the train was upon him he saw the stab of its headlight sweeping from side to side, a machete slashing at the night.

With a growing roar that combined the hum of diesel engines, the steel-on-steel whine of wheels, and the rush of self-generated wind, the lead locomotive pulled alongside the Blazer, cutting off Kempinski's view of the moon and putting him in a shadow. One sound that was missing was that of a horn; there was no sign from the train that the engineer could see the Blazer's headlights, no sign of warning or recognition even when Kempinski sounded his own horn. Kempinski had seen thousands upon thousands of locomotives, and had even raced a few, but never one like this, never under these conditions. Silhouetted against the moon, it looked enormous, a great, black hulk that seemed somehow remote and evil. It *was* enormous, as big as any he had ever seen, a new model of some kind with a distinctive roar that proclaimed its tremendous power. It was more streamlined than conventional engines, and the windshields looked like eye slits in a primitive mask. Kempinski blasted his horn over and over without result. The train ignored him the way a charging black rhino might ignore a fly.

Kempinski managed to match the locomotive's speed exactly and risked a quick glance at his speedometer—fifty-nine miles an hour. Driving with one hand and twice almost losing control, he twisted the spotlight knob until he had the beam focused on the cab high above him. There was nobody at the engineer's side window. He pulled slightly ahead and dropped slightly behind in order to change his angle of view, but couldn't see any indication that the train was under human control. It was a wild beast, blind and mindless, racing toward the sleeping cities that lay ahead.

Struggling desperately to keep the speeding Blazer in line, he dropped farther back, playing the spotlight on the cab of the second engine, then the third. No sign of life. How in hell could that be? Had everybody jumped overboard? Had the engineer and his assistant killed each other or had heart attacks at the same time, the conductor in the caboose along with them? It seemed impossible, yet there before his eyes was a speeding freight train with nobody at the controls, nobody who could—wait, what's that? On the walkway at the rear of the third engine? He lowered the spotlight until the beam was centered on two men—one was on his hands and knees facing forward, one had his back to the wind and appeared to be trying to help the other to his feet, but they weren't moving—they were as rigid as statues in a museum. Kempinski sounded his horn, again without effect. The men were either dead or might as well be. They looked like they were posing for pictures. The man on his knees reminded him of . . . was that Joe Dori? Yes! There was no mistaking that shock of gray hair. . . .

"Joe!" Kempinski shouted into the teeth of the wind. "Joe!"

Kempinski tore his eyes away just in time to see the end of the road rushing toward him. He slammed on the brakes and skidded for two hundred feet. The Blazer climbed the curbing that lined the edge of the canal and came to a stop at a steep downward angle with its engine half underwater. Kempinski wasted no time feeling sorry for himself. The spotlight was still working, and he redirected it upward so the circle of light hit the sides of the railroad cars that were racing by above him. The two-way radio was working, too, and he heard Frank Tajima asking him to report his position. No time for Tajima—the train would soon be gone.

The door wouldn't open. Kempinski unbuckled his seat belt, squeezed through the window, and scrambled up the embankment until he was beside the tracks, squinting to keep the wind and flying grit out of his eyes. He wanted to see the caboose; maybe he could rouse the conductor with a shout and get him to stop the train.

Looking east, he could see the end of the train approaching, though there was no red side light that marked a caboose. When the last car rushed by, the rumble and the wind vanished, leaving only a rattle that receded with the train. There was no caboose! The train had no fucking caboose! There was just a boxcar swaying gently back and forth in the moonlight and getting smaller and smaller.

CHAPTER 23

"Sorry, there's no listing for a Draegler, Jeremy, on Ashford Avenue."

Karen was using a pay phone, holding one hand over her ear to shut out the commotion in the hospital corridor. "Does he live someplace else?"

"I have a Draegler Chemical Corporation on Sentinel Canyon Road."

"They don't answer. I want Jeremy Draegler."

"There is no Draegler, Jeremy, on Ashford."

"What about some other street?" Karen asked, her voice rising in impatience.

"No listing in the Reno area for a Jeremy Draegler, D as in Donald, R as in Ronald, A as in Arnold—"

"So he's unlisted. You've got to give me the number—this is an emergency, Operator. . . ."

"You are an emergency operator?"

"No! This is an emergency and you are the operator! Give me the man's phone number!"

"Sorry, it's unlisted."

"You mean he has no phone, doesn't live in Reno anymore, or has a number that's listed as unlisted?"

"I beg your pardon?"

Karen was shouting: "I've got to have Jeremy Draegler's phone number! If you can't give it to me, who can? Your supervisor?"

"You can talk to the night supervisor. I doubt if she will give you an unlisted number."

"Maybe she will if I can get it through her thick head that there's an emergency! What's her name? Put me through!"

"She's stepped away from her desk for a moment."

"Jesus!"

"She'll be back within the hour—"

"Within the *hour*?"

"I'll have her return your call. What is your number?"

Karen shouted that her number was unlisted and slammed the phone down. She held her hands to her temples and made her way toward the front desk, trying to decide what to do. She picked her way carefully, stepping over patients on the floor and staying out of the way of doctors, paramedics, nurses, and orderlies. Victims were still arriving, some under their own power, others on stretchers and gurneys. A few who were unconscious when Karen first saw them were now sitting up.

Draegler was the only person she could think of who might know how best to fight a major leak of Mannequin. He was a little otherworldly when he visited her with Trainer after Gil's death, as well as at the earlier office party at his home, but he wasn't completely detached, and if he didn't know how to combat the gas, he would surely be able to reach someone who did. He appeared to be a kindly old duffer, hardly the type who would make nerve gas or kill people who stood in his way, not at all like Trainer, who possibly had kept him in the dark. Trainer scared her; the old man she felt sure she could handle.

The hospital lobby was crowded with television, radio, and newspaper reporters as well as relatives and friends of victims. Dr. Crowley was there, clipboard in hand, leaning over a counter and conferring with the admissions nurse and supervising the triage area. Four security guards were keeping a lane open to the glass front doors, which were flecked with raindrops. Outside, Karen could see the roof lights of police cars, ambulances, and taxis. On the wall was a large clock: it was three-thirty in the morning.

Crowley asked her how she felt.

"A little stiff in the joints," she answered, stretching her arms and twisting her shoulders from side to side. "A slight headache. Like I drank too much after a day of skiing."

"Find a place to lie down. Don't exert yourself."

"Later. Right now there's something I have to do." She pushed open the glass door and walked outside. Crowley waved her away and turned his attention to the chaos around him.

Karen had her purse and keys, but not her car, which as far as she knew was still parked in Truckee next to Dwight's Depot Diner. She found an empty taxi and climbed in. "Ashford Avenue," she said, "and I'm in a hurry."

San Francisco Bay is ten miles wide and fifty miles long, and living within a ten-minute drive of it are more than two million people, almost all of whom are blissfully asleep at three hours before dawn. At the north end, south of Vallejo and the bridges crossing the Carquinez Strait, Mountain Pacific Railroad's tracks follow the eastern shore, passing such towns as Pinole, Richmond, El Cerrito, Albany, Berkeley, and Oakland. Connecting Oakland with San Francisco is the Bay Bridge, which is twice as long and almost as magnificent as the Golden Gate. Continuing south, the tracks pass San Leandro, San Lorenzo, Hayward, Fremont, Milpitas, and finally San Jose, but there was little chance that number seven six six one would get that far. Mountain Pacific's Oakland marshaling yard in the city's industrial and waterfront district was choked with standing cars.

Jim Eagan got the bad news from Frank Tajima when he arrived at the Oakland control center, soaking wet from his speedboat trip and breathless from sprinting up three flights of stairs. Half a dozen men were crowded into the small room, which was darkened to make it easier to read electronic monitors and displays. Entering behind Jim was the head of Operations for the Sierra Region, Leon Magnus, disheveled from being rousted out of bed, and on the job for the first time in his life without wearing a tie. Jim ignored him and elbowed his way to the dispatcher's console.

"There's a hundred-car string parked on the mainline," Tajima explained, gesturing toward a schematic of the yard. "By the time we get it divided and onto sidings, the runaway might be on us. The sidings are blocked too."

"What about twelve and thirteen?" Jim said, studying the map and pointing at the tracks that skirted the edge of the yard.

"The curves are too sharp to shunt it to the outside. At sixty miles an hour it'll derail."

"It's going that fast?"

"That's what Kempinski said. He saw it go by. He saw Joe Dori and his fireman on the walkway of Engine Three as stiff as boards. We've got to hope we can clear a path before it gets here or there's going to be a hell of a wreck. With a clear path we can let it run south till it's out of fuel."

"How much time have we got?"

"Thirty minutes at the outside."

Jim shook his head. "Passing it through is no good. The gas tankers are wired to explode in Richmond and Berkeley, with the big one right around here someplace. We've got to stop it before it gets to Benicia."

"Too late. It's past there already."

Magnus pushed forward. "Now see here, Eagan," he said, "what makes you think you can barge in here and take over?" He was plainly unhappy about an emergency that he seemed unwilling to acknowledge.

"Because I was the dispatcher here for five years and know every inch of track. Because I have information nobody else has."

"Crazy information, too, about bombs and sabotage and poison gas. Where are you getting all this?"

"I'll explain it in the morning. Would you please go back to your office, Mr. Magnus, and let us handle this?"

"You'll explain it, all right. There will be a lot of explaining in the morning."

"Yes, and you'll be doing a lot of it. Who gave this train Green Line status, which is supposed to be reserved for the military? Why were toxic chemicals not labeled? Why were favors done for Draegler Chemical? You and Wayne Galway in the Reno District better get your stories straight."

Sputtering, Magnus left the room threatening to have Jim arrested.

Jim waved his hand in disgust and turned back to Tajima. "Let's see if we can stop it before it gets to Pinole," he said. "There are stretches around there without a lot of population, the Hercules straightaway, for instance. Where's the pursuit engine that Sacramento sent? Get it on the radio and tell the engineer to hang back until the runaway is near the straightaway—that's where he should couple with the caboose and bring the whole thing to a stop. Once it's stopped, tell him to back off and—"

Tajima cut him off with a raised hand. "There's no caboose," he said, his voice weakening. "Kempinski was sure of it."

"Then it's been dropped off somewhere, because it was there when the train left Sparks. Bud Shieving's the conductor and there were four civilian passengers. I talked to Galway in Sparks no more than twenty minutes ago."

The two men stared at each other, then turned to the display screen for the Fairfield–Benicia section. One red segment was the runaway's block, another was the pursuing locomotive's. The block between them changed from yellow to red. "What the goddamn hell," Tajima whispered, "is that the caboose? Must be rolling backward! I told Harry to keep his eyes open, but . . . Christ . . ."

Tajima picked up his radio microphone. "This is Oakland tower to Special X. Harry! Harry Collins! Do you read? Watch for a caboose! May be rolling toward you in the next block! Over."

"If he sees it in time," Jim whispered, "he can pick it up and run with it in front. Tell him that. Tell him he's got to catch the runaway before Pinole—"

"Harry!" Tajima shouted. "Do you read? Harry! Goddammit, he's not answering!"

Gradually, Bud Shieving regained a measure of consciousness. It was dark. He could hear moans and crickets and a distant hum. There was a glow, ghostly, as if from a full moon. The moon *was* full, he remembered. . . . When they had come down from the mountains and the rain stopped, he stood on the rear platform and noticed that the moon was as full as it could be, a big yellow silver dollar in the sky, racing along behind the tips of the pine trees. He focused his eyes on something inches away. It was a playing card, the four of spades. Nearby were two more, one facedown. The faceup card was a queen, black, maybe the queen of—

Everything rushed back into his memory at once: the poker game, the blue gas, the bald man running to uncouple the caboose, the shouts, the confusion, the sensation of falling helplessly when his body was gripped by a powerful paralysis. He remembered telling the bald man how to turn the angle cock to maintain the air pressure and how to get the pin by lifting the cutting lever.

He opened and closed his hands. . . . They obeyed reluctantly and slowly and with considerable pain. The hum grew louder. With his cheek he could feel the floor quivering.

Concentrating and devoting all his strength to the task, Shieving managed to raise himself on one elbow. Darkness returned as clouds covered the moon, but he could make out two bodies on the floor: Trainer, the pompous ass from the chemical company, and the foreigner, whose name he couldn't remember. Trainer was grunting and trying to roll over. The foreigner was snoring. Ordman? Shieving slowly turned his head. The front door was open. He could see Ordman's white sleeve hooked over the railing.

Shieving turned his head to one side and saw that before losing consciousness he had managed to crawl halfway through the door from the front platform. It was the front, yes, he was sure of it, yet the caboose was rolling in the other direction. Had Ordman turned the valve on the caboose as well? He couldn't imagine why he would do that. Didn't he want the caboose to stop? They had cut away on an upgrade, that must be it, and for whatever reason the caboose was rolling backward. Pretty fast. At least twenty miles an hour.

The hum, what was that? What was the stabbing white light?

The conductor turned his head to the east. The back door was also open, the way Ordman had left it when he dashed inside and knocked him down and grabbed the bottles of booze from the card table. The door framed the blackness of night, at the center of which was the headlight of an approaching locomotive. The hum grew louder. The floor trembled as if in anticipation, making Shieving think of the tiny waves that formed in his milk when the el went by their apartment in Chicago. God, he hadn't thought of that in forty years.

The light was so bright, he could hardly keep his eyes on it, yet he couldn't look away. "Train coming," he tried to say, but the words that came from his constricted throat were mangled and he had no idea if the other men understood him or were in any shape to respond. "Jump!"

There was no way he could jump. In the ten seconds before the collision he managed only to get to one knee and make a single lurch toward the door. He lay still and watched the headlight streak toward him like a bullet. Why so fast? It was coming at seventy or eighty miles an hour, at least. Didn't the engineer see that the block signal was red? Didn't the dispatcher warn him that something was on the track? Don't they see us? Maybe the caboose had just now rolled from one block to the next, changing the signals before the engineer had time to hit the brakes; yes, that was probably it. He nodded, pleased that he had solved the puzzle.

The shining point of a sword was speeding toward his face, and he was helpless to get out of the way. The hum swiftly rose to thunder.

He could barely hear Trainer's hoarse whisper: "What is it? What is it?"

The words were obliterated by the sound of the horn, tremendously loud and rising in pitch. There was a squealing noise, too, as locked wheels slid on rails.

Yes, they see us now and are sounding the horn and applying the brakes. Two hundred tons of steel hurtling toward him at seventy miles an hour with only two hundred feet to stop. A hundred feet. Fifty feet. Why? What had he done wrong?

Without a blindfold, Shieving closed his eyes. He breathed, "Lord have mercy," and hoped that understanding would soon be his.

Blocking the driveway was an elaborate wrought-iron gate.

"This is it," Karen said to the driver. "Stop right here and wait for me. Block the driveway so nobody can leave."

"You kidding? I'm not getting involved in your family fights . . . unless I get combat pay."

"Just wait for me, then. Leave the meter running."

"Have no fear."

The house was set back from the street and was hidden behind a high hedge. Karen managed to squeeze through a space between the end of the hedge and one of the brick gate posts. Jogging up the curving approach road, she could see lights as the house came into view. A tall, thin man was loading suitcases into the trunk of a car and calling to a woman standing in the front door.

"What difference does it make?" he was saying. "We can buy whatever we need when we get there." Karen recognized the reedy voice.

"What difference? Honestly! How can I pack if I don't know if we're going to the Amazon or the North Pole?"

"Just throw something in a bag and let's go, for God's sakes! If I tell you, it won't be a surprise."

Mrs. Draegler was a regal seventy-year-old who stood in the doorway like the captain of a ship. "Well, I'm going to take a fur, just in case. This whole thing is madness. It's the middle of the night!" She turned and streamed into the house.

"Going somewhere?" Karen asked, coming up behind Jeremy Draegler.

He turned, startled, but quickly recovered. "Mrs. Trott? Did we wake you? Sorry. I'm taking Mildred on a surprise birthday trip and . . ." He closed the trunk and looked closely at Karen. "I thought you were Mrs. Trott from next door."

"You've heard about the gas leak and are bailing out, is that it?"

"Who are you? You look familiar." Draegler fumbled with the car keys, sidestepping warily to the driver's door.

Karen grabbed his wrist, which was as hard and thin as a broom handle. "I'm Karen Ellis. Gil Ellis's widow. You can't go anywhere right now, Mr. Draegler. Your gas is leaking from a train and we need your help."

The old man jerked his arm in an effort to free himself. "Have you lost your senses?"

Karen hung on. "You have to tell everything you know . . . now! There's been a disaster and it will be much worse unless—"

Draegler twisted violently. Karen was surprised at the strength and vigor of a man who seemed so frail. She managed to maintain her grip and prevent him from opening the door.

"Let go of me," Draegler hissed, "and get out of here or you are going to be extremely sorry. . . ."

"I'm going nowhere and neither are you until you get on the phone and tell the hospitals and the railroad what they are up against."

Draegler swung his free arm against the side of Karen's head; it was like getting hit with a hickory stick. When he swung again she managed to catch his other wrist with her free hand. They twisted and turned, mirroring each other's moves in a silent dance. In a burst of anger, the old man lashed out with his foot, aiming a wild kick between her legs. She blocked it by closing her knees, never letting go of his wrists.

"Kick me in the balls? Think about it. I can kick too." She let him have one in the shins with the point of her shoe and heard him cry in pain. Lunging forward, she backed him against the side of the car and tried to pin him there, but he was too strong for that. He slipped to one side and bent hand her back until he had an arm around her neck. The cloth of his sleeve filled her mouth like a gag. He was an old man and she was a young woman in excellent physical condition, but because she was not fully recovered from her encounter with Mannequin, they were evenly matched. In fact, he seemed to be the stronger of the two and was gradually getting the better of her.

Then Mildred Draegler was beside them, her arms full of furs and her eyebrows arched in astonishment. "May I ask what on earth you two are doing?"

What the old man was doing was trying to bang Karen's head against the car and what she was doing was resisting. The result was a nearly motionless test of strength.

"Jeremy! Who is this woman?"

"A . . . crazy . . . person . . ." he said between wheezy breaths.

"Shall I call the authorities?"

"Yes! No! Help me . . . knock her out . . ."

Karen sunk her teeth into the sinewy arm, and when Draegler's headlock loosened she surprised him by releasing his wrists and throwing her arms around him in a bear hug, pinning his arms to his sides and driving him against the car. Their faces were inches apart.

"Give up or I'll bite your nose off," Karen hissed.

"Mildred, help me!"

Mrs. Draegler carefully placed her furs on the roof of

the car and picked up her tote bag, wrapping the straps around her fist.

"There's been a gas leak," Karen said, fighting for breath and straining to keep the old man pinned. "Nerve gas made by Draegler Chemical is leaking from a train. People dead. People dying . . ."

"What? Nerve gas? Is that true, Jeremy? You explicitly assured me that you were not making nerve gas, that you would never make nerve gas no matter what that fool of a general wanted."

"Hit her!" Draegler gasped. "Hit her!"

"No," Karen cried, "hit him! He's trying to get out of the country! He'll be a fugitive . . . he has to tell what he knows about the gas. . . ."

Draegler's wife was swinging her tote bag menacingly. "I think she's right, Jeremy. Deciding to go on vacation in the middle of the night? That's just not done."

Karen felt an upsurge of energy from the old man as he threw his arms upward and broke her grip. Before she could react he had her by the hair and was swinging her head toward the car. She tried to extend a foot to brace herself, but tripped over the bony leg he had put in front of her. Momentarily helpless, she couldn't stop him from knocking her head into the car with stunning force; she felt her head being yanked back and brought forward again.

A dark blur sailed past her face as Mildred Draegler swung her tote bag and caught Jeremy full in the face. It knocked him onto the ground on his back. Karen pounced on one of his arms and Mildred pounced on the other.

"You lied to me, Jeremy," Mildred said, lowering her face to his. "Getting up in the middle of the night and dashing about like a maniac, I knew you were up to something."

"You . . . you believe this madwoman instead of me?"

"Yes, because what you say makes no sense and what she says explains everything."

"The gas is leaking," Karen said, catching her breath, "and now the train is out of control. It could crash . . ."

Draegler grimaced. "Out of control? I was told about the leak in Truckee, but not—are you sure?"

"The train has been sabotaged by Iranians. Several bombs on the gas cars have already gone off. If it gets to Oakland, a whole car will blow up. Is there any way to keep the gas from spreading? Is there an antidote? Is there anything at all that can be done? *Please!* There's hardly any time left. . . ."

They let him sit up. He shook his head and said, "I . . . I never should have . . . I *knew* something like this would . . . I *told* Trainer that we . . . If only I . . ." He drew his hands hard across his face and sighed profoundly.

Karen pressed him: "If a whole tank car of that damned gas blows up in the middle of a city, what should be done?"

"Only one thing I can think of, but I don't know if it's possible. . . ."

Karen listened hard to what he had to say, then ran inside the house looking for a phone.

CHAPTER 24

"Water?" Jim Eagan said into the telephone. "How much water? From fire hoses?"

Jim could hardly hear Karen's voice over the talking in the room. He held up a hand and strained to catch her words.

Behind him Leon Magnus and two uniformed railroad policemen pushed their way through the men crowding around the console in the Oakland Control Center. Jim ignored his request to hang up.

"Fire hoses won't be enough," Jim heard Karen say, "not if a whole car explodes. Draegler says you need a flood. In the lab they keep samples in tubs of water for safety. Water neutralizes it."

"For God's sakes, we're not in a lab—we've got a train barreling in here! We don't have a tub!"

"You've got the Bay. Put the train in the Bay."

"Are you nuts? Is that your idea?"

"Draegler's."

"Sure, it's not his train. Okay, look . . . keep the line open—some of our people will want to talk to him. Karen, go back to the hospital—you're going to kill yourself with all this running around."

Jim handed the phone to the man on his right and started to explain to the group what had to be done. Magnus cut him off.

"Wait a minute, Eagan," the supervisor said, "this is my show. I give the orders here, and if you don't like it, I'll arrest you for trespassing. You don't even work in this department. I'm clearing Track One so the runaway can pass through and go south until it's out of fuel, which should be somewhere around Watsonville."

"Leon," Jim shouted, shaking his fists in exasperation, "will you back off and let Frank and me handle this? A tank car is going to explode somewhere along this stretch of track. We *can't* let it pass through and spread nerve gas from here to hell and gone. . . ."

"You don't know it'll explode. How could you?"

Jim tried to explain without wasting too much time: "A woman named Karen Ellis—the widow of a guy who helped make the gas—she .. oh, shit—a friend of hers knows the guys who planted the bombs—that phone call was from Draegler's house in Reno—he *owns* the goddamned chemical plant—completely under water is the only way to—"

"We don't even have proof that the gas is *coming* from our train. . . ."

"Open your eyes, Leon! Hospitals in Truckee and Sacramento were swamped minutes after seven six six one passed through, and I'll bet the same thing is happening right now in Benicia. Compartments are going to be ruptured by bombs in Richmond and Berkeley, and I don't know where else, then a big blast in Oakland! We've got to send the train into the drink!"

"Like hell we do! We're not going to destroy three engines and fifty loaded cars because of wild guesses we have no way of checking."

"The choice is to take the chance of gassing thousands of people—"

"There may *be* no bombs! A leak, maybe, but bombs? You're hallucinating. You might be crazy—this Karen woman might be crazy—"

Jim was on his feet and shouting: "This isn't going to fizzle out in the artichoke fields of Watsonville! It's going to blow up in our faces right here in Oakland! You're in the soup, either way, Leon, because you approved Green Line for a private shipment. Quit hoping the whole thing is going to go away—"

"I'm not going to approve an act of destruction that will bankrupt the whole railroad! We're talking about twenty million dollars' worth of engines and rolling stock, not to mention the cargo!"

"Fuck the engines and the rolling stock and the cargo!"

Magnus sputtered and turned red and looked as if he was going to burst into tears. "Your plan won't work! There's no way to put the train in the Bay—"

"We'll *find* a way."

One of the other men shouted a question: "Kempinski saw Dori and Talbot on the side of Number Three. . . . What if they're alive?"

"We'll get them off," Jim said, not sure if it was possible.

"How in hell—"

The room erupted in argument as a dozen men shouted their opinions. On the display panel, lights showed that the runaway had left the Pinole block and entered the Richmond block. It would be in Oakland in fifteen minutes.

Tajima came up with the saving compromise. He told Magnus that the city of Oakland's police helicopter, which was equipped with a searchlight, was already over El Cerrito headed north. It could follow the train and hover above the tank cars. If there was an explosion in Richmond, Jim would try to rescue the crew and ditch the train. Without an explosion, Magnus would take over and the runaway would be allowed to head south through Oakland on the main line.

Jim nodded. "Fair enough. Leon?"

"Well . . . I . . ."

"Good! It's a deal!"

Within minutes of the agreement, every phone at the Oakland station was busy. Police and fire departments from Richmond in the north to San Jose in the south were warned of the crisis and the possibility of a catastrophe. Oakland and cities farther south were told to try to evacuate residents within two blocks of the tracks while fire departments hosed down adjacent streets to inhibit the spread of the gas. Hospital switchboard operators were urged to round up every possible medical worker; for advice on how best to treat Mannequin victims, doctors were referred to Reno General Hospital and Ernie Crowley, who in turn was given Jeremy Draegler's home number. Television and radio stations were asked to alert the public to the nature of the peril and to tell them to keep windows tightly closed and listen for further instructions. State and local disaster officials, well organized in the San Francisco Bay Area because of the constant threat of earthquakes, were notified and immediately headed for their offices; they would quickly set up an emergency communications network, prepare to bring in whatever outside supplies and equipment might be needed, and work with the Red Cross in setting up shelters for evacuees. Pacific Telephone was told to brace itself for an avalanche of calls and to keep certain phone lines and wavelengths clear.

Messages were coming into the control center as well. Rescue workers west of Fairfield reported that the runaway's caboose had been utterly demolished and scattered across several acres of farmland. One set of wheels on the locomotive that hit it had derailed on impact and torn up half a mile of track before coming to a stop. The crew in the cab was uninjured; the conductor and four unidentified passengers on the caboose were dead.

The pilot of the Oakland police helicopter radioed that he had picked up the train at Brookside Drive in north Richmond and was tracking it south at an estimated sixty-one miles an hour. After locating the silver tank cars and following them for half a mile, he saw a plume of blue gas or smoke appear. Impossible to be sure at night, he said, even with the help of the moon, but gas appeared to be spreading toward the residential district east of Rumrill Boulevard. On hearing that bit of news, Leon Magnus threw up his hands in despair and wished Jim luck.

A phone call from the director of St. Mary's Hospital in Benicia was relayed to Magnus in the control room. A train had passed through town a few minutes earlier "at tremendous speed," the doctor said. It was a miracle that it didn't derail crossing the bridge across the Carquinez Strait. Ambulances and cars were arriving at the hospital with victims of a mysterious paralysis. Did the railroad know anything about it?

In a voice filled with resignation, Magnus told the caller what he knew, then walked tiredly to his office on the floor below and sat down at his desk. He remained there quietly for the rest of the night in shock, unable to participate in managing the crisis.

South of Hoffman Boulevard a switch engine pushing a dozen oil-tank cars toward the Chevron refinery at Point Richmond slowed to a stop in the middle of a highway overpass project. Luther Jackson wondered why. Jackson, a black civil engineer in charge of a night construction crew, had waved the train through a minute before and could see no reason for it to stop and disrupt his whole operation. Was the engineer one of the railroad men he knew who was deliberately trying to aggravate him. "Hey!" he shouted upward at the cab. "What's going on?" The driver of the train—Jackson refused to think of an equipment operator as an "engineer"—was facing away from him and seemed not to hear. "Hey!" he shouted again, louder.

The door to the cab flew open and a second man came running out as if being chased by a dog. He tore down the side walkway to the rear, and when he got there he reached down and yanked the lever that released the engine from the cars it had been pushing.

Jackson poked his head between the cars. "What's the deal?" he said. "You gonna move this piece of shit, or what?"

"Emergency," he gasped. "There's a runaway coming down the main line. . . ."

"A runaway? You mean a runaway *train*?"

The man ran back toward the cab. Jackson ran alongside on the ground shouting at him. "Hey, don't leave these cars here . . . I got ten men trying to do a job!"

Workers behind him were laying down their tools, and

several were lighting cigarettes. "It's okay, boss," one called. "Those cars are just fine where they are."

The trainman stopped and looked down at Jackson. "Could we borrow one of your men?"

"Aw, man," Jackson pleaded, "don't leave these cars parked here! Shit!"

"We can save two lives! We need a big, strong guy willing to take a chance. Right now! Got to leave right now!"

One of the workmen came out of the shadows. "I'll volunteer. What needs to be done?"

Jackson waved him back. "Get real, Marco. No wimps allowed. That eliminates all you turkeys." To the trainman he said, "Will I do, bubba? I'm six four, two-twenty, and the strongest sumbitch in Contra Costa County."

"Climb on and let's go!"

Mike Shamos, the engineer, and Bob Baskin, the fireman, explained the situation to Jackson as they sped southwest toward the junction with the main line. "It's crazy," Jackson said when he heard the plan. "It's bare-ass fucking crazy! It's a job for Rambo or Robocop or some superdude like that."

"This is the only road engine in the vicinity," Shamos said. "A switcher wouldn't be fast enough. It's us or nobody."

Luther Jackson looked from Shamos to Baskin and back to Shamos. They didn't seem to be joking. "You want me to reach across and snatch somebody from another train? At sixty miles an hour? The wind will tear my pants off!"

"The air will be partly carried along between the engines and the wind won't be so bad . . . at least that's what Eagan thinks."

"Who's Eagan, an astro-fucking-physicist? It's just as

likely there'll be a venturi effect with increased air velocities."

"And what are you, a civil-fucking-engineer?"

"As a matter of fact, yes."

Shamos turned his palms up. "If it looks too dangerous, don't do it. One of us will."

Jackson chuckled. "Are you kidding? What chance would either of you guys have with those little stubby arms? Leave this to Luther."

Once the engine had negotiated the right-hand curve at Potrero Avenue and was headed south on the left-hand track—usually reserved for northbound traffic—Shamos pushed the throttle to notch eight and radioed his position to the Oakland tower.

Eagan's voice came back: "The runaway is about a mile north and closing fast. Shamos? If you can't get the job done by Emeryville, give it up. That gives you about six minutes."

With no load to pull, the engine responded quickly to maximum power, and in less than a minute had reached forty miles an hour. Shamos was at the controls at the right side of the cab; Baskin and Jackson were wedged into the space behind his chair with their heads out the window looking toward the rear.

"I see it," Baskin shouted, "here it comes!"

A slight curve in the track had obscured the runaway—now, as the track straightened out, a headlight was plainly visible, suspended and trembling above the south-bound track and casting its beam relentlessly from side to side. Closer and closer the headlight drew, gaining at the rate of one car length every several seconds, finally becoming too bright for comfort.

Luther Jackson watched in silent awe as Saber One drew alongside and moved slowly ahead. The aerodynamic design of the front housing and cab and the way the high, paired windshields looked like squinting eyes in a frowning face gave the engine a surreal look, as if a stylized child's toy had come alive and grown full size in a nightmare. There must have been storms in the mountains, Jackson thought, for the front and sides of the runaway were streaked and spattered with mud. It made him think of a wild animal that had been wounded and maddened in a fight and now was running at full speed, intent on destruction and revenge.

Jackson had never seen a bigger, more powerful, more dangerous, more evil-looking locomotive in his life, and he wished he weren't seeing it now. To hear about a runaway train is one thing, but it's quite another to be beside it with the roar of its diesels in your ears, feeling the wind in your face and the vibration in your bones. It was frightening to be so close to something so enormous and out of control. It was out of control all right—the men had a direct view into the cab, and it was plainly empty. Jackson glanced at Shamos and saw him swallow hard.

"I don't see anybody," Jackson shouted, barely loud enough to be heard above the fury of the engines and the wind. "You said two guys were on the walkway."

"On the other side," Shamos shouted over his shoulder. "You'll have to step across and go around the back of the housing."

"Sheeeesh! This gets worse! Hey, once I'm over there, why don't I just shut the engines off and pull the brake?"

"Because nerve gas is leaking a few cars back . . . the train has to be put in the Bay!"

Jackson stared at the fireman and said, "Nerve gas? I thought you were my friend."

Saber One moved grandly ahead, followed by the two trailing locomotives. Half a dozen boxcars went by before the speeds equalized and the rescue locomotive began to gain. By the time Shamos had positioned his engine alongside Unit Three and matched its speed exactly, the desperate race was two minutes old. Four minutes were left.

* * *

At the rear of the walkway, Luther Jackson swung his long legs over the railing and held on to it with his hands behind him. Baskin had a firm grip on the back of his belt to help him fight the wind. Jackson tried to judge the distance to the railing of the other engine, which was swaying and bouncing dangerously.

"Mother*fucker!* Must be ten feet over there!"

"It's less than three feet . . . come on, you can make it. You must have played basketball—this is easy compared to basketball."

"Never played. Too clumsy. I can't even eat a piece of watermelon without having it squirt out of my hands."

Baskin was aghast. "What?"

"Just kidding."

Jackson reached out with one arm and managed to catch hold of the opposite railing. "Let go my belt—I be fine."

Baskin released him. Jackson had his feet on one engine and his hands on the other. He was committed—now he had to go across. He didn't know if the wind was greater or less than the speed of the trains, but he did know it was raking his clothes like claws. Saber One, as if sensing an invader, pulled slightly ahead, stretching Jackson's body at an angle. He took a deep breath and leaped over the gap, immediately vaulting the railing. He ran along the walkway and disappeared around the rear of the engine. In thirty seconds he was back, dragging a gray-haired man in a plaid shirt behind him. "They're both alive," he shouted to Baskin. "Lots of groaning and moaning." He lifted the paralyzed Joe Dori up like a sack of potatoes, got both his hands underneath him, and thrust him across the gap into Baskin's cradled arms as if he were bench-pressing a barbell.

"Catch," he said.

A minute later Shamos was on the radio to Oakland. "We've got them," he reported excitedly, "and they're alive and kicking!" As he spoke the Pacific Plaza tower went by on his right. Ahead were the Bay Bridge approach overpasses.

The response came from Tajima because Eagan had left for the waterfront in a helicopter. "Don't slow down," Tajima told him. "One of the tanker compartments blew up in Berkeley and a lot of gas is coming from the middle of the train. Keep ahead of it. When the runaway peels off for the docks, then hit the brakes. An ambulance is waiting."

CHAPTER 25

The runaway roared into the Oakland marshaling yards like a storm striking a seacoast, its engines sending out a wall of thunder and its wheels a high-pitched scream. It careened across switches that urged it toward the right, toward the waterfront, rocking back and forth dangerously with every change of direction as it threaded its way through the labyrinth of branching tracks. Into corridors between standing cars plunged Saber One, disappearing momentarily before bursting into view again like a snake leaping from a hole with its fangs flashing and its impossibly long body streaming behind.

From the control room atop the Sixteenth Street station, Frank Tajima and the men around him watched in numb silence as the juggernaut hurtled past. The sight made Tajima's breath stop and his toes curl in his shoes. The train was an apparition, something from a wild dream, bizarre, astounding, and his mind wanted to reject the reality of it. At sixty miles an hour, the sixty-foot-long cars streaked by at the rate of one every second and a half, three times faster than he had ever seen anything move in the yard. The siding tracks and switches weren't designed for such speed, and the resulting vibration shook the station and rattled windows, doors, ashtrays, cups, pencils—anything that wasn't nailed down.

When the last car passed and the tornado's roar dropped to a whisper, Saber One was already entering the right-hand curve that would bring it parallel to Seventh Street, between the Oakland Army Base and the Naval Supply Depot, and it was less than ninety seconds from the docks. The men looked at each other as if they had seen—and felt and heard—a ghost.

Tajima's skin was crawling all over his body when he picked up the two-way radio. His voice caught in his throat when he said, "Jim . . . it's . . . it's coming . . . it's made the curve and you should . . . you should just get out of the way. . . ."

A fire in an oil drum flickered in an empty lot, warming a shadowy group of derelicts. They looked up dully as the tandem tractor-trailer rig rolled by as if to make sure it wasn't a giant paddy wagon intended for them. Big John Teerink, not feeling totally secure in the cab of his truck, made sure the windows were closed and the doors locked. The whole industrial district west of the Nimitz Freeway made him nervous even in the daytime; at four in the morning it positively gave him the creeps. It was an area of warehouses, factories, railroad sidings, chain-link fences topped by barbed wire, abandoned cars, junkyards; a few blocks away, standing like a row of long-legged insects or invaders from Mars, were the gantry cranes at the Outer Harbor Terminal, his destination. The moon had been bright earlier, now it was nowhere in sight. A stiff breeze coming off the Bay was drawing a sheet of fog across the East Bay lowlands. Streetlights in the dreary side streets were hardly more than pinpoints. An odd sense of dread came over him, and it almost made him smile. Tourists always thought of the San Francisco area as glamorous. They should see this part. It would make their blood run cold.

Teerink downshifted as he approached the railroad crossing at Seventh Street, carefully maneuvering around a pothole. He had a full load of red wine from the Napa Valley headed for, of all places, France, and he wanted to be sure it got to the dock without the sediment stirred up. He was a wine lover himself, and he always carried it as gently as nitroglycerine. There was a pile of fluttering newspapers on the street, and he steered around that as well; might be broken glass underneath. A flat tire in this neighborhood was not something devoutly to be wished. If he got that unlucky, he would pull over, shut everything off, and sleep in the cab till dawn. He might have to do it anyway if there weren't any longshoremen on duty to help him unload. He hadn't intended to arrive on the graveyard shift.

Leaning forward against his safety belt, he turned up the volume on the radio to catch the words of a song he hadn't heard in years: "Always Late." "You're always late," he sang defiantly to the surrounding gloom in unison with the late, great Lefty Frizzell, "with your kisses. Why, oh, why do you always treat me this way?" He was in second low gear and almost to the railroad tracks. Trains didn't run at four in the morning so there was no reason to stop . . . he would just ease across the rails ever so gently. "How long do you thank"—he gave "think" Frizzell's hillbilly pronunciation—"I can wait, when you know you're always late?"

The kisses were late, and so was Big John's load of fine

Napa Valley wine, half a day late thanks to six different kinds of mechanical breakdowns in Vallejo. Well, better Vallejo than the Oakland waterfront. His old rig was wearing out. Maybe when he was unloaded he should just drive it into the Bay and forget about it. Tell the insurance company the brakes failed.

With the windows closed and the cab filled with the sound of the radio and his own voice, he was insulated from outside noise. He saw the stabbing beam of light coming from his right just as his cab straddled the rails.

Motherofgod, is that a train? It must be! It is! Coming around the curve like a swinging hammer!

He was frozen in a panic of indecision. . . . Should he throw it in reverse, step on the gas, or jump out? He stepped on the gas and stared at the slashing headlight rocketing toward him. The truck lurched forward, whining in protest and straining against the weight of its two loaded semitrailers. Comparing the speed of the train with the distance remaining, Teerink guessed that the rear trailer would just barely clear the tracks in time. He threw himself against the steering wheel in an effort to push the truck to greater speed and watched the locomotive's headlight sweep back and forth from the front of his rig to the back as if probing for a good spot to hit.

In the side mirror Teerink could see his back bumper and the last set of tires bouncing across the rails. "Come on . . . come on . . ." he prayed as the thunder grew in his ears— No! Too late! He braced himself for the impact, and when it came he was wrenched violently to his right, then upward. His head struck the roof of the cab, then he was driven down hard into the seat.

It was over with startling suddenness. He was sitting behind the wheel staring ahead. His feet were off the pedals and the engine was dead. The headlights were on, boring two tunnels through a wall of swiftly moving fog. He moved his torso and his arms. Nothing was broken.

Behind him he could hear the rumble of the passing railroad cars and a delicate splashing sound. Could that be diesel fuel? He switched off the lights and the ignition to be safe, waited a few seconds for his nerves to settle, then unhooked his belt and opened the door.

His relief at being alive was quickly replaced by anger. The train had clipped the back of his second trailer, tearing it free of its hitch, turning it at right angles to the street and tipping it over. The rear doors were ripped off and cases of wine were scattered across the pavement—*bottles* of wine were scattered across the pavement, some of them still rolling. In the glow of a streetlight, the road glistened with wine so red it looked like blood.

For more than a minute the train raced by, and when it was gone, leaving in its wake a vortex of swirling dust and paper, Big John was shaking his fists and shouting into the night, "Goddamned railroads! Why no signal? Why no horn? Why so goddamned fast in the middle of the night! Jesus Christ! You goddamned crazy sons of bitches! Who's going to pay for this? It's always the truckers who pay! Never the goddamned crazy railroads!"

Wait a minute, he said to himself, calming down. The insurance company can pay. This could be a blessing in disguise.

From nearby shadows came the figure of a man, a derelict. Teerink watched him move slowly to the curbing under the streetlight, where he stood unsteadily, surveying the debris. His shabby overcoat offered little protection against the cold wind. Poor bastard, Teerink thought, having to sleep outside on a night like this . . . and a train hitting a truck practically in his lap. Must have scared the living shit out of him.

The man leaned down carefully—he looked old—and picked up a bottle in each hand. He held the labels in the light, studied them, and turned his face upward.

"Thank you, Jesus," he said.

* * *

The tracks at the end of the line disappeared under the steel hangar door of a warehouse on Pier Nine, which Jim Eagan chose because it was the only one the runaway could reach without sharp curves that might derail it. The warehouse rested on pilings driven into the mud of the Bay bottom and was flanked by concrete decks wide enough for the gantry cranes that loaded and unloaded oceangoing ships. The rear wall, the one facing San Francisco, stood above water forty feet deep. A mile to the north across the water were the cantilevered spans of the San Francisco–Oakland Bay Bridge.

When Jim got off the helicopter he was met by a security guard and three longshoremen.

"Why isn't it open?" he shouted, running toward them and pointing at the hangar door.

"Waiting for the guy with the key," the guard said. "This isn't my regular—"

"No time to wait!"

He led them to the south side of the warehouse and shook the knob of a locked office door. "Shoot the lock off," he said to the guard, "we've only got a few minutes. . . ."

The guard, a thin young man in glasses and an ill-fitting uniform, hesitated. "Oh, Lord, I couldn't do that. . . ."

"Do it! If we don't get the big door open before the train gets here, there's going to be nerve gas all over the place! Shoot! Shoot!"

The guard gulped, aimed his .45-caliber revolver as if he had never held it in his hand before, closed his eyes, and fired.

Tied to the pier at the left and riding high in the water was a Liberian freighter, its curved bow towering above the warehouse roof. At the sound of gunfire two merchant seamen on night watch appeared at the railing. Jim looked up and shouted at them.

"Hey! You speak English? We need help! Runaway train coming!"

Inside, somebody found the lights and the switch for the hangar door, which rumbled upward while alarm bells jangled. The railroad track ran down a central aisle between storage bins and stacks of containers and was blocked in several places by forklifts, a pickup truck, a stack of lumber, and several huge spools of cable.

"Clear the track!" Jim shouted, jumping aboard one of the forklifts and starting its engine. "Clear it all the way to the back!"

The rear wall was hidden behind piles of cardboard cartons, apparently part of a shipment of Japanese television sets, videotape recorders, and home computers. No time to move them, Jim thought, but they shouldn't offer too much resistance. He fiddled with the controls until he found out how to activate the forks, then went to work moving six concrete blocks that served as a switch-engine bumper at the end of the rails. He abandoned the job when he got the message from Tajima that the runaway had made the Seventh Street curve.

"That's it!" he shouted. "Everybody out!"

The other men had managed to clear everything off the track except the pickup truck, which was locked. The men joined forces and tipped the truck on its side, clear of the tracks. Outside, through breaks in the blowing veils of fog, Jim could see the approaching headlight of the runaway. He joined the others in running for his life.

The rear wall of the warehouse exploded as if struck by a gigantic fist. Saber One burst into the air like the point of a javelin, carried over the water partly by its own momentum and partly by the force of the two pursuing locomotives. With great sections of wall clinging to them, they dropped ponderously to the water, Engine Two turning slightly sideways and Engine Three cartwheeling upward. They vanished behind an enormous upwelling of water and under the stream of boxcars, hopper cars, tankers, and flatcars that poured out of the rear of the warehouse like an anchor chain spilling off the deck of a ship. Cars sank swiftly beneath the water, but not swiftly enough to get out of the way of those immediately behind, which climbed over the top of the sinking pile or were deflected, spinning, to the side, where they hit the surface like the heels of hands, sending up tongues of water hundreds of feet high.

It took forty seconds of cars shooting into the Bay before the silver Mannequin tankers flashed into view. They streaked off the end of the dock like artillery shells and crashed into a massive, rolling tangle of debris, flipped upward over the top as if trying to escape the cars chasing them, and rolled into the water like crumpled balls of foil. A cloud of blue gas boiled upward.

Still the cars came, following each other in a single-file stampede into the front of the warehouse and through the rear wall, which was soon totally blasted away. The din was terrific, a mind-numbing series of deep booms and explosions sliced with the shrieks of steel, wood, and concrete being torn apart and crushed.

In the final seconds the heap of twisted rail cars formed a mass that grew toward the pier as each succeeding car crashed into it. The last dozen cars had no escape, smashing into each other inside the warehouse and leaping left and right like fish trying to shake the hook. The walls and roof of the building from one end to the other erupted outward and upward in a furious and ongoing explosion that could be heard for fifteen miles.

For long minutes bits of metal and wood rained on loading docks, warehouse roofs, and streets while the mountain of railroad cars shifted and groaned and creaked as it sank lower in the water. Minutes later waves ten feet high rolling outward in concentric circles delivered a series of destructive blows to adjoining piers and vessels lying at anchor. Dry docks were flooded and containers were swept off staging areas. Sheets of salt water slid up low-lying streets, pushing parked cars into clusters. Marinas at Jack London Square, Emeryville, and Berkeley were swamped and hundreds of sailboats and yachts capsized.

Jim Eagan was overtaken by a swiftly moving river while running east on Seventh Street. The water rose to his waist before subsiding, and he had to wrap his arms around a telephone pole to keep from being carried away.

The blue cloud, inhibited from spreading through the air by the fog, collapsed into a blanket over the wreckage and was repeatedly battered by great splashes of salt water. Thinned as it spread over the surface of the Bay, it was absorbed as quickly as ink in a blotter.

Eventually the waves were a memory and the pile of broken railroad cars was still. Only the keening of sirens broke the silence of the predawn night.

CHAPTER 26

A week after the catastrophe the San Francisco *Chronicle* ran a summary of fact and opinion. In Sparks and Reno, where rain fell just as the train began its fateful journey, seventeen people suffered temporary paralysis, one a railroad worker named Pete Undiks, the rest overnight campers in an RV park close to the tracks. Truckee: nine dead, forty-two still hospitalized with nerve and muscle damage, seventy treated and released. Auburn: no casualties, thanks to heavy rain. Sacramento: thirty-one dead, two hundred and eighty injured. Fairfield: four killed when the caboose was struck by the locomotive; eighteen in the town treated and released. Vacaville and Martinez: no casualties; reason—failure of detonating transmitters. Benicia, Richmond, and Berkeley: seven dead and seventy injured, thirty seriously. Oakland: five dead from gas inhalation, nineteen temporarily paralyzed; three longshoremen killed when hit by debris during final pile-up. An undetermined number of deaths and injuries resulted from automobile accidents in areas where leaking gas drifted across Interstate 80.

Sara Schuler was still in the hospital and expected to remain there another week; co-workers at Draegler Chemical Corporation pledged to pay all of her medical expenses. Joe Dori and Tommy Talbot were fully recovered; Luther Jackson, their rescuer and a former power forward for San Jose State, was a hit on *The Morning Program, The Noon News, Afternoon* magazine, *The Evening News, The Tonight Show,* and *Late Night.*

The California Persian Cultural League, fearing backlash against Iranians of every persuasion, announced plans to erect a statue of Alek Mirkafai, martyr, at a yet unnamed location.

Jeremy Draegler, the side of his head swathed in bandages, gave a press conference on the steps of his mansion flanked by his wife and his attorney. He begged forgiveness for his sins, stupidity, and shortsightedness, and promised that in the coming investigations and legal actions he would be totally open and forthcoming. His wife led the applause while a reporter heard his attorney say, "Like hell you will."

The President of the United States announced formation of a commission to investigate the role of independent contractors in supplying chemicals to warring nations.

The state attorney general of Nevada promised a full investigation of a possible conspiracy among officials of the Sutro County sheriff's office, Draegler Chemical Corporation, and Mountain Pacific Railroad to violate laws governing the shipment of toxic materials. The sheriff, in response, announced the impoundment of the wrecked Draegler limousine as the first step in a probe into the death of Gilbert Ellis. Congressman Ron Dellums and Senator Alan Cranston, both of California, denounced the Pentagon for, on the one hand, failing to stop an operation it must have been aware of and, on the other hand, not being aware of it.

Jesse Jackson called on the Administration to stop making binary chemical weapons and to divert the money saved into tent cities for the homeless. He offered to chair a meeting of world heads of state to deal with the growing menace of chemical and biological warfare. William Buckley urged the American people to focus blame where blame belonged, on two involuted sociopaths, and to reject inchoate geopolitical etiologies. The mayor of Oakland said that never again would trains enter his city, later explaining through aides that he meant "dangerous" trains.

Mountain Pacific Railroad's only comment on the disaster was that the world's largest floating crane was on its way from Alaska to help with the job of removing the pile of railroad cars from Oakland's Outer Harbor, an operation that was expected to take six months and cost millions of dollars. The railroad's legal department denied that a Mountain Pacific train hit John Teerink's wine truck, or any wine truck.

Jack Anderson reported that his undercover agents at *Time* had learned that the magazine would name James Eagan and Karen Ellis Man of the Year.

The Anderson item gave Jim and Karen a much-needed laugh. Karen wondered if the magazine knew they were of opposite sexes.

Jim folded the newspaper and tossed it aside. "You know, we could probably make a fortune on the lecture circuit."

"No amount of money would get me to do that. I'm tired of being stared at and giving autographs and talking into microphones and cameras. My God, how many times have we been interviewed this week, a hundred? Two hundred?"

They were relaxing on the deck of Jim's sailboat on Richardson Bay between Sausalito and Belvedere. The sails were furled and the anchor was down. It was a sparkling weekend afternoon, the kind that drew hundreds of boats onto the Bay and made it hard to imagine that anything unpleasant ever happened in the world. Mount Tamalpais looked especially comforting, like an earth mother with her arms spread protectively. The beauty of the scene was spoiled only by the putt-putt of a motorboat headed their way from the Sausalito marina.

"I'll bet this is bad news," Jim said, nodding toward the man in the approaching skiff. "A process server. A financial planner. Somebody to tell us we're illegally parked."

"You know what we should do, Jim? Go away for a while. I'm worn out. Let's leave for the Caribbean right now. Why wait?"

"Wait a minute! A few days ago you said you wanted to stick around."

"I changed my mind. Women have been doing it for centuries. The thought of more interviews is more than I can bear. I'm ready for some peace and quiet and solitude. One more trip to Sparks to visit Sara, then let's go."

"We'll need a few days to get ready. We need to stock up on beef jerky, lemons, salt pork, radar scanning equipment, and whatever the hell else grizzled mariners stock up on when they venture forth to battle the sea. God, I should have majored in English lit. Wait a minute, I *did*!"

"Grizzled? Speak for yourself. Frazzled, in my case. If

we have to give depositions or something, lawyers can come to us in various exotic ports of call." She bounced up and down happily. "When can we leave? I'm getting excited!"

The motorboat pulled alongside. It was a small outboard and a man in his early sixties was sitting in the stern with his hand on the tiller. "Oops!" he said. "Didn't mean to bump you. I rented this tub and didn't get any instructions. Are you Ellis and Eagan?"

"Afraid so," Jim said.

"You're hard people to find! Thought you lived on the houseboat in Berth Nine." He was dressed in a khaki safari outfit that looked fresh off a Banana Republic rack. His Greek fisherman's hat was so covered with flies and hooks that it would have been suitable for Carmen Miranda.

"We do, but we got tired of being pestered by reporters."

"The price of fame." Waves were making it hard for him to stay alongside.

"You're the first one to find us out here. I admire your energy."

The man laughed. "I'm not a reporter."

"You don't look like a fisherman, either, despite your hat. Not much fly fishing done here on the Bay."

"My hat? Oh, my hat. I was on the way north to fish for cutthroat and was passing through town and thought I'd make your acquaintance. Here's my card. . . ." He rose half to his feet and handed a business card to Jim; it wasn't easy and the effort almost capsized his bobbing boat. "K. K. Sprague is the name."

Jim read the card and handed it to Karen.

K & K Sprague Associates Ltd.
Word Brokers
The Agency That Time Forgot
New York   New Paltz

"You're a literary agent?"

"You got it. Are you adequately represented? Have you thought about putting your experiences on paper?"

"Not really. Things have been pretty hectic. We're getting ready to leave on a little cruise."

"Perfect time to write a joint account of everything that happened. Alternate chapters if you want. Could be dynamite. Refuse to give any more interviews. What you've got to say is worth money and you should stop giving it away."

"Makes sense," Karen whispered in Jim's ear. "I like the idea."

"I wrote you a long letter," K. K. Sprague said, taking another chance on standing up and handing something to Jim. "Here it is. It outlines what I think the book should contain and how it could be merchandised. A word about the agency, our client list, how we operate, and so forth. You'll have to meet my wife—we only take clients we can both stand. That's why we call it the agency that time forgot."

Karen leaned over the side. "You have a nice honest face, Mr. Sprague, and we'll think about it."

"Do that. Then phone and we'll hammer something out. A detailed proposal describing the book that we could auction to half a dozen big boys, that's the way to go on this one."

"Did you know your boat has a leak?" Karen pointed at several inches of water surrounding Sprague's shoes. "I think you're sinking. Do you need a bucket?"

"It's not a leak. I shipped a little water when I climbed on board, that's all. For God's sakes, don't approach the publishers yourselves—that's amateur night at the Bijou and you'll get your pockets picked. Have a nice cruise." He gave the motor some throttle and headed back toward shore. He turned and shouted a final thought: "When you throw in first and second serial rights, foreign, film, paperback, and the clubs, this could be a huge, huge property. . . ."

When he was gone Karen smiled. "Write a book! One more thing to do together. I'll bet we could come up with a good one."

"No doubt about it. We could work on it when we weren't playing music. I've been nursing a romantic vision of playing duets as we sail under the Golden Gate Bridge, you on your clarinet, me on my Casio keyboard."

"I've been dreaming along those lines too. I've already picked the piece we should start with. Mozart's 'A Little Nightmusic.' "

Jim chuckled. "Perfect."

"I have the music, too, a reduction made for two instruments by the Cambridge Buskers. It's downstairs in my bag."

"We don't say 'downstairs' here on the briny. We say 'below.' "

"Aye, aye, sir," she said, running the tips of her fingers lightly across the back of his hand.

He put an arm around her shoulders and held her close. "I like the idea of playing duets with you. I think we should start practicing."

Karen looked at him with mock surprise. "You mean now? You want to make music now?"

"In a manner of speaking."

"Well, Captain, in that case I think we should go below."

He let her pull him to his feet. "Aye, aye, sir," he said, saluting.

ACKNOWLEDGMENTS

For providing technical information and reviewing the manuscript, I wish to think Stephen Adams of General Electric's Transportation Systems Division, Erie, Pennsylvania; V. W. Goodwill, Assistant Manager of Southern Pacific's Motive Power Division in San Francisco, California; Michael Hardisty, Assistant Yardmaster for Southern Pacific in Sparks, Nevada; and Ken Ready of Ready Outboard Shop, Sausalito, California.

Thanks also to Cynthia Nelms, Clay Shafie, Jean Conger, Russell Byrne, and Lynn Newell.

ABOUT THE AUTHOR

Robert Byrne, a former civil engineer and magazine editor, is the author of fourteen books, including six novels. He lives in Mill Valley, California.